Winter

By C.B. Cole

Deer Hawk Publishing

WINTER is published by:
Deer Hawk Publishing, an imprint of Deer Hawk Enterprises
www.deerhawkpublications.com

Copyright © 2011 by C.B. Cole
www.cbcole.com

Cover design by:
Ray Polizzi

Layout by:
Aurelia Sands

Library of Congress Control Number:
2011944993

Printed in the United States of America

To my family.

Chapter One

The crowd pumped electric now that they were finally here. The wait for the amphitheater to fill had been eternal. Bodies pushed roughly up against them from behind, the heat of them intense and smothering as they jockeyed for position, but she and Tor could go no further forward, one of the so-called benefits of being in the front row, she guessed.

Winter wasn't at all excited to be here, not excited about the band, not excited to go backstage and mingle with the stars. In fact, she didn't like their crappy music *at all*. If she thought about it, and you can believe she'd certainly thought about it tonight, there was not one song of theirs that she knew enough to even hum along.

Tor, God bless him, tried to play some of--in his opinion--their finer works in the car on the way over, but she just didn't get his attraction to them.

Or anyone's attraction to them, for that matter.

But she was here now. Unfortunately. And leaving again, after all the effort she and Tor expended navigating through traffic, and parking and jostling through the crowd to get here, seemed all the more exhausting, especially since her boyfriend was so darned happy to be here.

Winter sighed.

At least the entertainment value the crowd provided was enough to keep her from totally going apoplectic. For Winter, people-watching was an admittedly guilty pleasure and an art she liked to think she perfected over her eighteen years. Her lonely youth, spent on the outside of the popular kids' cliques, eating lunch on the bleachers with Tor, miserable eighteen years was not entirely wasted.

So, given her experience and qualifications, it would have been hard not to *excel* at it.

Once again, it seemed she was hanging about the edge of it all, never really understanding what all the people around her were so damned excited about. Everyone around her teetered bravely on the edge of giddy exhilaration, ready to tip headlong into hysteria at any moment, and Winter desperately wished she could share their enthusiasm, just this once.

She never did though.

She never had.

Winter never felt like she was on the same page as the rest of humanity. Hell, half the time she doubted they were reading the same book--and that, in and of itself, was a terribly depressing thought to have at eighteen years old. She always told herself she would grow out of it, but it hadn't happened yet. Because of that, she couldn't help thinking that senior year was going to suck.

Shake out of it, Win. You are reading too much into this. You should be having fun. It's not a pity party.

Besides, it was too late to do anything about it now.

C. B. Cole

Tor asked her to come, and since he was the one to thoughtfully provide the tickets, the passes and the ride to the concert, she thought it best if she gave up her current demonstration on how to fail at being a normal kid and go with him. Winter didn't even consider saying no when he asked, and that was her fault, she supposed, for not thinking things through properly. Now, she would just have to survive it.

Not that she would've said no anyway, since it *was* Tor asking, but she still should have given it a bit more thought. Winter pushed out a martyred sigh. She had to admit, whether or not she liked the music tonight, she certainly loved the feel of an excited crowd. There was something dangerous about being part of something so big, so wild. It was like the thin strands of constraint that held the mob within the bounds of sanity could snap without warning, spilling madness into the world. It was intoxicating to be surrounded by that many people focused on a common purpose. And a concert was one of the few places she felt that incredibly tenuous electricity of a motivated mass of people.

So there was that at least. The rest of it seemed incredibly bleak.

Behind her, a woman gave an excited whoop, and screamed *"Let's get on with it!"*

Indeed, she thought. Indeed.

Winter curiously turned around to see who made such a noise and spied a half naked female perched on the shoulders of a very large man. The duo was terrifying, wild, drunk and sweaty. Instead of being disgusted, Winter suddenly wished she could get that excited about anything at all.

*****

Tor watched her watch everyone else and thought Winter looked pretty miserable right now. Actually, that was probably the understatement of the year. Winter *was* miserable, all the time.

Even more so now, since her eighteenth birthday last month. She was changing before his eyes and he had no idea why.

The only time Tor thought she was actually happy about anything anymore, was when they were together. Or, whenever she was with her step-brother-uncle-friend-whatever-he-was, Bren.

Ugh. Tor shuddered. He didn't even want to *think* about that familial malfunction tonight. It was a waste of time and of the precious, mental energy that he was saving up for the concert. He spent way too many hours trying to sort that mystery out and it wasn't something he was going to waste more of his time on now, on the greatest evening of his life.

Winter was standing motionless, staring randomly out into the sea of people, her face unmoving, her eyes focused on something far in the distance. Tor poked her in the shoulder and she swayed a bit, like she was in a trance.

"Babe, seriously, you're doing it again," he teased when he finally noticed that she was staring into space instead of anything at all. Winter looked back at him blankly, blinking until she finally focused her eyes on him.

"Doing what?"

4

"You know, that *thing*? Where you act like you aren't a functioning member of the human race? Snap out of it! This is a concert, Win, not meditation hour. You are supposed to have fun, remember?"

"So sorry!" she said, bowing low in apology. "How could I have forgotten?"

Winter made a face, then punched him lightly in the shoulder for teasing her. She plastered on a very fake smile, complete with visible teeth, for his benefit. That was all the invitation he needed. Tor grabbed her and pulled her close, planted a sloppy, wet kiss on her face, then laughed as she wiped the slobber from her chin.

"Gross, Tor!" she screeched girlishly.

He continued to laugh to himself, and put an arm around her. She leaned into him with a sigh.

At least she was trying. She *was* changing though, and every so often, Tor thought it was only a matter of time until he lost her for good; but not tonight. Tonight she was still his.

"God I love you, Win, even if you act like an alien half the time." He kissed the top of her head gently.

"I love you too."

***

Winter did love him too, that was part of the freaking problem. She would definitely *not* be here right now if she didn't adore him like she did, but she was here and she could do little to change it now.

She peered up at the darkened stage, watching the furious movements going on behind the scenes. There was a mob of roadies, dressed all in black, working at the back of the stage, setting up for the main event; the reason they, and everyone else, were all here. The overworked men, gleaming with the sweat of exertion that she could see all the way from her vantage point, were dragging up instruments and set pieces, while simultaneously dismantling the remains of the previous band's stage. It looked like a well-oiled and complicated process and she wondered how many times the crew had done that same thing this summer. Probably too many to remember. In a job like that, Winter couldn't help but think that the days would blur into a depressing sameness that would drive her insane.

Their chore seemed so tedious. If she was in their position, she would resent cleaning up after bands that hardly mattered. The opening acts that had entertained the arriving crowd were both just all right in Winter's opinion. She would know, as Tor insisted they arrive right as the gates were opening so that they wouldn't miss a minute. The first groups to hit the stage were the kind of acts that were struggling with their mediocrity, striving for fame but not finding it, and were glad that a band as huge as *InHuman* even bothered to notice them. Winter thought those poor, determined, fame hungry souls probably performed every night like they were entertaining 50,000 people, even though she noticed the crowd was barely half full during their performances. She had to admire their determination though. It must be soul crushing to know that people weren't there to see them.

Shaking herself out of the thought and making a concerted effort to pull herself from the confines of

6

her head, Winter realized that she was standing there again, motionless in the vast sea of restless people just staring into nothingness. This was getting ridiculous. Thankfully, Tor didn't notice yet.

She needed to focus. He was right. It was weird.

She probably wouldn't have cared, but for him, she would try. Winter had long ago made her peace with her never-to-be-cool status, so she didn't notice her social handicap too much unless she was out with Tor in the "Real World" when they went out and she left the safety of the bubble she created for herself, either back home or in her own head. She was always painfully aware of the differences between her and everyone else, so why even try to act like she was just like them? They all knew she wasn't.

Suddenly, there was a man up on stage, deep in the shadowed recesses, dressed in the most God-awful black ensemble that Winter found herself hoping he was in the band and didn't actually make a daily habit of wearing outfits that looked like Gothic vomit on purpose. The man was tall, and dark skinned. He blended in with the shadows by the side of the stage so perfectly that if she hadn't seen the glimmer of the light reflected off his eyes, she probably wouldn't have noticed him at all.

It was strange that she would have noticed that. Most people's eyes didn't shine like that as far as Winter could recall, but they *flashed*, almost as if they had a weird reflective quality, like a cat's. He was partially hidden by the thick curtain, and she saw him eying her as if she was a new type of animal he had yet to see before. He tapped his fingers to his lips pensively while continuing to stare at her. Then, he smiled.

Oh my God.

"Tor," she whispered, the words lost in the surf roar of the crowd. She tugged at his hand and turned her eyes away for a moment to get his attention. Tor turned toward her and blanched at her panicked expression.

"What's up, Babe?" Tor asked, looking confused.

"Look. Up there, by the curtain," Winter gestured with a nod, not wanting to draw attention by outright pointing at that wild man up on the stage.

"What?" Tor squinted through the lights to the dark stage. Winter shielded her eyes from the glare. He was gone.

"There was... a man," Winter mumbled, wishing she never said anything. "Never mind."

"Probably one of the road crew," Tor smiled down at her, "I know, it's so exciting! It's getting close!" He picked her up and squeezed her tight before setting her back on her feet. Winter decided not to tell him what she thought she saw. It's not that Tor wouldn't believe her if she tried to describe it, but he always found a way to explain mysteries away. Tor wasn't the guy she went to when she swore that she had seen something strange.

For those things, she went to Bren.

Bren was special. He always believed her, no matter how wild her stories, even when she was small. Bren was the exact opposite of Tor in many ways. She and Bren could sit for hours together, and never say a word. It was almost a game with them, to see who could go the longest without saying a thing and the loser would invariably be required to treat the other to ice cream. Winter hated to be the loser and she loved ice cream. Tor would have never considered spending five silent hours with Winter.

Bren always told her never to worry about what others thought of her. He said she was different because she was made special and that only boring people talked all the time because they were afraid of the things people would think in the awkward silences left unfilled. He said those who couldn't keep their thoughts inside their heads for even one second just ruined it for everyone else. Bren always knew just what to say to make her feel better.

It seemed that Bren, while maybe not possessing a lot of *charm*, always understood her in ways that no one else could. Sometimes, when she was little, Winter wondered if they were both from the same strange planet. It made more sense somehow, that they were two alien beings trapped in this world. It was nice to be connected to him some way, even if it was just an imaginary one.

One glaring difference between her and Bren was that people *did* listen when Bren spoke, and actually cared what he had to say. It was probably because he had money--lots of it--and Winter supposed that people cared about whatever he *said* because of that fact alone. She had always craved his attention, but that was even before she realized he was loaded. Winter needed Bren and that was just a fact.

They weren't related, but they were family all the same.

There was a time in the not-so-distant past that she may have had a massive crush on him, but she refused to own up to it, and there was no way she could *ever* tell Tor she felt that way about Bren, ever. It would hurt him to find that he didn't hold that revered best friend position in her heart and if he knew the rest...well, of course, he would only start in on the "evils of Bren" again. It wasn't a fight worth having for the thousandth time.

As if he knew she was thinking of Bren, Tor elbowed her hard in the ribs and mouthed *"Be normal!"* to her with wide and googly eyes for effect, and then louder, with dramatic emphasis, "People are starting to stare at you again, Winter. Is it time for your medication?" he said with a wicked smile.

He shuffled closer to her, holding his arms out zombie-style until they found her shoulders and he pulled her into him. "You're such a freak!"

"So are you," she told him. "And they aren't staring at me, you moron. Or if they are, it's because they're just blinded by my ethereal beauty." Winter made an unladylike face at him. "Actually," she said confidently, "They're probably in shock and can't believe I'm wearing anything that doesn't contain metal studs as an integral fashion piece." She made a big show out of looking at her outfit, then looking around to prove her point. The piercings of the rest of the concert goers glittered like stars under the bright lights in agreement.

It was true, there were pierced and laced and safety pinned clothes everywhere she turned, even on Tor. He sighed at her and shook his head. "It's a rock concert Win, not high tea."

Winter frowned down at her own clothes. She never dressed like those other girls out there, done up from top to bottom. She despised it. It wasn't her style. She didn't wear skinny jeans or anything else that came from Hot Topic. The best she could muster in the spirit of this grand evening was a slightly ripped, ancient Rocky Horror Picture Show tee that Bren gave her a million years ago, and even then her outfit didn't even come close to the dress code the rest of the crowd adopted, and she was hard-pressed to even find *that* to wear.

Thankfully, Tor told her she looked beautiful no matter what she wore when she voiced her concerns. He was, at this very moment, ignoring her again in favor of sharing his favorite rock play lists with a pock faced geek boy excitedly gesticulating on his right.

"It's getting really close, Babe," she whispered in her best sultry voice in his ear, hoping to draw his attention back. He didn't turn, but shuddered, then grabbed her palm and kissed it before doing a little celebration dance in place. Winter giggled.

It was true. It was almost 9:30. People filled in totally behind them now, with very few empty seats remaining. She hadn't even noticed until just then, but the entire amphitheater was full and the lawn behind them was overflowing with bodies. She stood on her toes to see over the crowd. The lines at the bars and concession stands at the highest points on the steep hill were overly long and Winter shuddered when she thought about how traumatic the line to the ladies bathroom would be, full of drunken lovelies dressed in their finest rocker get-ups. The ultimate goal of most of the girls her age here tonight would be to attract the attention of a band member at best, or another boy at worst.

It was a little sad.

She looked to her boyfriend for confirmation, but Tor had turned his attention back to his new friend and they were talking loudly about all things rock. Winter sighed indulgently at his enthusiasm, even if he was leaving her stranded and bored to tears, and turned around again, satisfying herself with surveying the rippling sea of bodies behind her, unable to help but notice that there miles and miles of differences between her and them.

One thing was obvious: Black was the color of the evening. Yep, definitely black. Even Tor wore head to toe black, covered liberally in silver clothes pins and other things that would never let him get through security at the airport. Winter thought he was possibly taking the theme too far and even told him so when he picked her up, that he looked more like Pinhead from Hellraiser than a teenaged concert goer. Tor had merely rolled his eyes.

Far be it from her to criticize the art of personal expression, he said, for she certainly wasn't qualified.

Whatever.

Of course, he usually never dressed that way, only on special occasions such as this. Tor was a torn

12

jeans and paint splattered button up kind of guy, but he was also an 'embrace the theatric side of life' kind of guy too, so Winter wasn't surprised that he leapt at the chance to go all out. The black did wonders for his red hair and green eyes without making him look too thin or pale, that was for sure. Tor was a handsome guy, in a nontraditional way. Winter noticed more than one girl this evening watching him and she wasn't a bit surprised. She smiled at the back of his head fondly and brushed her hand over his mop of hair, causing him to reach up and catch her hand in his own.

Winter drew her hand back and cast a wistful glance at the throng of people behind her. She felt their eyes on her, watching her as she presided over their carnival of insanity that was playing out as an opening act just for her. She committed the raucous image to memory, knowing it would probably be the last time she could truly watch them before the lights went out, then she faced the darkened stage and leaned her head against Tor's broad back, hearing his deep voice rumble in his chest as he talked on and on.

Chapter Two

Tor was trying to shake his new "friend". Winter needed him. If something didn't happen soon, she looked like she might fall asleep.

"Really Win, you're gonna love 'em," he told her again, once he was free from that never-ending conversation with the kid beside him. "Don't give up on it yet." He dropped a kiss on the top of her jet-black hair. "Just give them a chance," Tor reassured for the millionth time.

It was probably getting old, but he desperately wanted her to have a good time tonight. He kissed her hair again and stroked some of the inky strands back from her slightly sweaty face. It was still hot for late September. Winter just rolled her eyes at him.

"So you've said."

"Charity said that at their last show, they pulled up a member of the audience when they sang *Wasted*! Can you believe it? And we're in the front freakin' row! That could be us tonight! And it's their final show of the year. It's going to be spectacular!" Tor rolled out every syllable of *spectacular* for her benefit.

He felt like she needed additional confirmation of how much she was underestimating their evening. She just smiled at him vacantly and nodded.

God, what is wrong with her lately? he thought in exasperation. She was always distant, aloof, but that was nothing new, just one of the things he came to love about her over the years. Lately, though, it seemed like she was in a whole other world. It was as if she turned eighteen and tuned completely out of her life, folding in on herself like a flower that closed itself against the night.

As far as he was concerned, he was *beyond* excited, even if she wasn't. There probably weren't enough words in the English language to describe how he felt. Tor had been trying to win these tickets from the radio station all week and yesterday, just in time, he did just that. It was fate, that's what it was.

When he asked Winter to come, she agreed. Of course, he thought, she didn't want to tell him no either. They were like that for each other, eager to keep one another happy. She was good at keeping him happy.

So here she was, in the front row of a concert she had no desire to see, listening to a band she cared nothing about, all because she loved him more than she loved anyone else.

Not that there *was* anyone else.

Tor had some satisfaction in knowing he had always been the only one for her. Winter had her Aunt Ramona, Bren of course (the bane of his existence), and then Tor. No one else had a chance. That's what he told himself.

He said it aloud this time.

"No one else ever had a chance," he chanted his mantra softly. The noise of the surrounding madhouse was enough that she didn't hear him, which was good.

15

Tor hoped no one else would ever have a chance either, but when Winter got that faraway look, or disappeared on her weird adventures with Bren, sometimes, he thought that wasn't exactly the truth.

He wasn't going to worry about it now: The house lights had gone down.

***

Finally, to the roar of the waiting crowd, the band strolled out onto the stage confidently, theatrically. Comically. It was about damn time.

Disgusting, she thought.

The four band members were all dressed similarly. They wore all black, *again with the black*, but the styles and materials were different. Each band member's costume had some sort of identifying characteristic to punctuate the black ensemble, an epaulette or sash, but there wasn't much in the way of individuality other than that. Winter thought it might be an attempt at unity and a way to separate themselves from one another as well, but on the whole, it was pretty unoriginal, as far as she was concerned.

Seriously, she had seen Coldplay this year and they practically did the same thing. Winter judged each of the band member's physical appearance just as harshly, thinking none of them had star quality, or were much to look at for that matter.

Is there anything worthwhile about these guys?

Then, the lead singer finally appeared, deigning to grace the stage to a well-timed pyrotechnic fanfare, with his own attire that was reminiscent of Victorian England on acid. He riled the crowd with a sweep of his arms, prowling the stage as he approached the

16

microphone and when he grabbed it, with one long look that she was sure he had practiced in the mirror many times, the crowd went wild, screaming and jumping, Tor included.

The singer's face filled the big, flat screens on the either side of the stage, and she got a close up shot of him smiling wickedly at the crowd.

He's awfully confident. Not bad looking either.

He was tall and lean with dark hair, dark eyes, dark everything. His short hair was artfully spiked into some wild creation and his eyes, well, they had to be contacts, to be that precise, glittering black, but he wasn't the guy she had seen before. She was sure of that.

His face, Winter decided, was handsome, rugged and oddly perfect. His skin was a gorgeous shade of alabaster that she thought had to be European. Irish perhaps?

At least he *brought the looks*, Winter thought sarcastically. Someone had to. The others were swarthy men whose only appeal might be that they were in a band.

The rock star surveyed his kingdom for the night, and the crowd swelled expectantly beneath his gaze.

"We're *InHuman*!" he shouted and the mass of bodies before him exploded in sound and motion. The guitar player, knowing his cue, swung his arm wildly and the instrument screamed to life in his hands. The drums beat a mad tempo behind them both. They reminded Winter of a book she read once about the drums of war that different cultures used to intimidate the people they were attacking. She certainly felt assaulted at the moment.

Lead Hottie, as she decided to call him, kicked in the air in a very Steven Tyler kind of way, before launching into his first song. As he strolled by the guitar player again, a flash of recognition slammed into her.

"Hey!" Winter shouted, tugging on Tor's arm. "That's the guy I saw earlier!" She pointed to the lead guitarist. Tor bobbed his head to the music and nodded noncommittally. She couldn't tell if he didn't believe her or possibly just couldn't hear her.

"Cool! What was he doing?" Tor shouted back, obviously catching her meaning. His lips were so close to her ear she could feel his breath. He glanced at the guitarist briefly, and then returned his attention to the main attraction.

"Oh, uh nothing, just watching the crowd, I guess." she shouted back.

"Sorry I missed him then." Tor said, or something like that. Everything came out jumbled in the noise of the crowd and the blaring music. Winter watched him carefully through narrowed eyes. Tor was barely paying attention to her; he was mesmerized by the show. She watched his eyes as he followed the lead singer's every movement as the song wound up. Suddenly, she wished she never said anything about it at all.

Tor joyfully sang right along with the singer, matching word for word, pausing in all the same places, even getting the screams right too. Everyone sang along, everyone but Winter. She remained as unmoved and stoic as before. All through the high energy first song, she just stared, despondent and miserable.

"You're not even *trying,* Babe," Tor chastised loudly after a few minutes, taking a momentary break from his sing-a-long to remember she was there. Winter shrugged apathetically and stared up at the stage, praying for some kind of inspiration to find her here on the sticky concrete, or, at the very least, a freak lightning storm that would bring this sideshow to an end. Anything would be better than suffering through this drivel, trapped below the lead singer's devilishly handsome gaze.

"Please, Win?" he wheedled again. "For me?"

"Oh, all right. But only for you." She gave him a basilisk glare that she hoped made him aware of the amount of effort it was taking her to live through this, and made a mocking hip wiggle in his direction. "Happy yet?"

"Not hardly," he told her seriously and continued to stare at her until she got the point.

Finally defeated, she grabbed Tor's hand and tried a little shimmy to the music. It was too ridiculous to be a serious dance move, but she never bothered to learn any. She pulled him close and moved in a way she thought might be sexy, letting Tor dance behind her and wrap his arms around her waist.

Winter hoped that if she could just fall in sync with the crowd and find a way to be like the rest of the people actually the night, that she might discover a way to like the band. Maybe that was the key–dancing. But her boyfriend, for all his boundless enthusiasm, could not find the rhythm either, and they failed to be compatible when it came to dancing. It was an utter failure and they abandoned the endeavor almost immediately.

At least we're compatible in other ways, Winter thought miserably.

Dropping his hands away, she resorted to moving her head from side to side, bobbing slightly, just watching the show unfold. She felt utterly pathetic. There had to be something that could captivate her, surely?

Winter decided to try focusing on the charismatic lead singer rather than his noise. She noticed appreciatively the way he commanded the crowd before him. He was good at that. He was dynamic, engaging. He could even kind of sing.

God, he's good looking though, she thought.

But not interesting enough, so Winter collapsed back into her seat, defeated.

***

Performing was always the best part. He could do without weaving the words into a melody. There were plenty of others to do that for him, and he was capable enough of delivering the song in a steady and clear voice. Not that it would have mattered whether he sang, croaked or squawked. The crowd was his from the moment they set foot in the amphitheater. He owned them. He could cast the music into a spell that moved the most disinclined person to dance their cares away. He put everything he could into his performances.

He had to.

They needed the crowed whipped into frenzy. It was his job, it's what they did. The band fed off every scream, every reaction the crowd hurled their way.

Shade was working hard tonight, too. After a particularly up tempo jam session on one of their more popular songs, he launched himself around the stage, dancing and leaping wildly, whatever it took to rile the crowd. They were putty in his powerful hands. Tirelessly, he went on with the show just like he had every night this summer. Singing, encouraging them, taunting them if that's what it took to get a reaction; whatever they needed from him, he provided.

That was why during this particularly intricate guitar solo, he even climbed the scaffolding on the side of the stage so he could survey his worshipers from the speakers hoisted high above. The crowd was an undulating sea of bodies below, waiting for his next command. Their eyes followed him worshipfully.

Except for hers.

A girl in the front row, seat 12A in fact. She wasn't even *looking* at him. Shade knew exactly what seat she was in because she was actually *sitting* in it rather than dancing in the possessed way the others were. She sat there, unaffected, unmoved.

It kind of pissed him off.

Sometimes, not paying attention wasn't that big of a big deal. It didn't matter if they weren't looking, he told himself. If she was arguing with her boyfriend, or too drunk to stand up, that would be okay, but from where he was situated, it didn't appear she was doing any of those things. She was just sitting there, not moving, just looking around and appearing to try very hard not to fall asleep.

Maybe there's something wrong with her, Shade thought hopefully.

He waited up there, perched on his vantage point, for as long as he possibly could while the guitar wailed below. He tried willing her to look up, but of course, she never did. She *would* be the kind of person that he couldn't work his magic on.

The guitar solo was drawing to a close and he couldn't afford to waste any more time worrying over it. Shade swung down and landed catlike and ready, not inconveniently, right in front of the girl. He looked up slowly, preparing his most sultry rock star gaze for her, just in time to see the raunchy woman next to her soak her with her beverage, and the strange girl walk away.

***

She wriggled down in the sticky plastic seat, trying to simultaneously get comfortable and make herself as small as possible so that Tor wouldn't notice her treason. Winter decided it was technically an acceptable place to take a break. Lead Hottie wasn't even singing right now. Instead, the guitarist launched into a squealing and ear-shattering solo so others around her paused in their revelry as well. Although, *their* pauses didn't involve sitting, mostly it just meant that the bulk of the screaming subsided for a moment.

Winter turned around and knelt in her seat, hoping the band didn't catch sight of her and think it was rude to watch the crowd again. Their gazes were still fixed, slightly vacant and rapt on the stage or one of the myriad projection screens behind her. No one even noticed she was facing the wrong way. They were captivated by whatever the singer was doing now.

She felt strange all of a sudden, almost ashamed for looking away from the stage. Winter had the most peculiar feeling, like some undecipherable message was being pounded into her brain. A new wave of sweat broke out across her shoulders, sending a shiver through her. She had a need: The urge to move, to turn around, possessed her.

That's just nuts, she thought.

Winter tried to fight the compulsion, tried to tell herself it was her imagination but the need grew inside her until it threatened to consume her if she didn't comply. Throwing all her better judgment aside, she let herself succumb to the crazy notion. Winter threw her arms up in exasperation.

"What!" she cried at no one in particular.

"What yourself!" slurred the rocker chick beside her, glaring at Winter over her giant alcoholic beverage. "I didn't even touch you!" the drunken woman screeched, lurching unsteadily toward her, looking ready to fight.

Winter just knew the woman was going to hit her. She screwed her eyes shut and braced herself for it, but what happened next wasn't exactly what she expected. The collision was not of hand to face as Winter assumed, but merely the woman stumbling directly into her. The shower of beer that covered Winter was met with curses by both women.

"Damn it!" Winter howled.

"My beer," wailed the sot.

"Screw your beer!"

"Hey!" Tor whirled around to see what she was yelling about. He tried to bury a smile as Winter glared alternately between him and her dripping shirt.

"It's not funny, Tor!" she told him in a lull between one hellish song and the next. "Bren gave me this!" Tor's eyes narrowed at her sudden explosion over the state of her wardrobe. Winter grimaced. "It was special," she said softly, and pointed to the wet stain down the front of her shirt, "Now, it's just disgusting."

"Right," he rolled his eyes and turned back to the stage. "The horror. Well, you better deal with it, I guess. I would hate for something to happen to a crappy shirt *Bren* gave you. I'm sure you won't be too upset to miss the show."

Winter thought it best not to say anything else for the moment. No need to make the situation worse. She took her hand and wiped off the excess liquid from her bare arm, shaking her dripping digits angrily back on the intoxicated woman for revenge. The idiot was so drunk she didn't even have the decency to notice.

"I hope you spend the rest of the night puking," Winter hissed at the drunk. *Well, there went any hope of me enjoying the evening.* She heaved a great sigh and leaned over to get Tor's attention.

Chapter Three

Tor let her tug on his shirt three times before he faced her. He wanted to be mad, but it was harder than one might think to stay angry with Winter.

"Tor, I'm going to the bathroom. I think I am going to puke if I don't get the beer out."

He nodded, since it was madness to try to shout over the music now that the band had launched into another song. She pursed her lips in dismay and he knew she thought he was still mad about the whole "Bren's gift is special" thing. He was, a bit, just not as much as he was letting her believe.

Tor knew it shouldn't bother him, that she was upset about her shirt getting messed up. He would probably want to clean up too if the same thing happened to him. It did bother him, though, because she used the magic word that pushed his buttons every time.

Bren.

She started to walk away, but he caught her hand, "Just be careful," he cautioned, mouthing the words.

He pulled her back and gave her a peck on the lips and a smack on the butt, and sent her on her way. She smiled triumphantly, knowing him well enough to figure out he'd forgiven her already.

Winter squeezed her way through the crowd, sliding between the press of bodies and the stage. It was a dangerous matter, Tor thought. The mob was so crazed, so entranced by the performance that they nearly crushed her several times.

Tor watched Winter walk away. He hated that she was going to miss so much of the show, but who was he fooling? She didn't want to be here anyway. That she came at all was a tremendous testament to their mutual affection.

Some of the guys checked her out as she passed, and he felt no small amount of pride that she was his girlfriend. She was beautiful. She had the blackest hair he'd ever seen. It complemented her creamy, pale skin. And her eyes, they were so blue, like the color of a glacier. He could get lost in them if he let himself. She seemed so small and fragile at times.

Like now.

Her dark head disappeared in the throng of people. Tor knew Winter just barely reached 5 feet 2 inches, but at times, like when she was angry, he swore she was more like a tiger than a little house cat.

Tor loved her more every day. There was something about her that he *needed*, though he never had the courage to admit that he craved her attention like a drug. She would have only laughed. He doubted she needed him the way he needed her by half, but she needed him enough, more than she needed anyone else, so that was something. He could probably count the number of days that he'd gone without seeing her over their whole lives together on one hand. It was impossible for him to imagine a day without Winter.

She was *so* good to him. When she looked at him sometimes, he swore it felt like the sun shone only for him.

Winter was there with him through the worst of it; when his parents died and left him with his crazy older brother, Sean, when he was ten. She stayed with him, even when Sean found religion and joined the army six years later. She and her Aunt Ramona helped him keep his sanity and his home. Winter was always the one to pick him up off the floor when he was sure his rage and depression would consume him. She was the antidote, the thing that kept all his pieces whole. Without her, he would shatter. She was every good thing he knew in this world. Tor was sure if something were to split them up, which he couldn't even bring himself to imagine, he'd lose it all.

He watched her continue to fight her way through the crowd, catching brief glimpses of her when she had to tiptoe to get by, and simultaneously fought his compulsion to run to her side and protect her. He let her be, and when he completely lost sight of her, he turned his attention back to the stage.

That was the real reason he was here after all.

The lights flashed wildly and the drum beat pulsed through him in the most hypnotic way. *InHuman* were fantastic; that was the only way he could describe them. They were dynamic and entertaining and *dark*. Tor thought about it on the drive to the amphitheater, while trying to give Winter a crash course in their music, about how influential they were for him. She asked him to play his favorite song for her and he realized he couldn't, that he loved them all.

27

Their music made him happy.

Sometimes, it even made him want to be naughty, to do wicked things, but he never told anyone that.

Their album was his favorite soundtrack to do his work to. When he wrote with their words in his ears, his thoughts came out clearer and more precise on the page. He could paint things that were more *real*. He felt full of passion and creativity and lust. They made him feel like no other band in the world could make him feel. Alive.

Tor looked up in awe at the singer that inspired him so much and wondered--as he was sure everyone in the audience did at some point--if they had anything at all in common. Shade passed by him, inches away, belting out his powerful words and Tor realized they were truly miles apart.

Of course, we don't have anything in common. How could we? Tor was a mere mortal compared to this rock god.

Tor shook the silly groupie thoughts out of his head and let the music take him into a frenzied dance that swept over the entire audience. He had to laugh at himself for thinking that Shade, the lead singer of *InHuman*, could love anything he could love.

***

When Winter was finally free of the crushing throng of people, she exited out to the pavilion area. Thankfully, it was vacant, everyone having long since moved to the amphitheater for the show. The lights blinked angrily behind her and she felt the thump of the bass, even though she was behind the grassy bulkhead that rose up high behind her and sloped back down gently to form the lawn on the other side. The breeze was much better here and she lowered herself down to the last of the concrete steps to rest for a few minutes, letting her head clear. It was like a fog had settled in her brain. She felt strange, like there was some message, some imaginary pull she couldn't quite decipher.

The relative silence on this side of the grassy embankment was a welcome change. She stared out into nothing for a long while, letting her head clear, until the breeze reminded her of the damp shirt she wore.

She didn't want to go back to her seats. Not at all.

But, she couldn't stay on the steps forever. Tor would be just as likely to come looking for her if she was gone too long, and she wanted him to enjoy the show even if she didn't. Winter lifted herself back up wearily, using the metal railing as an aid, and searched the concessions area for the ladies' room.

Thankfully, the bathroom line was manageable since the show was on and she didn't have to wait. The horrible smell engulfed her as soon as she entered the bathroom and she fought to move quickly through the narrow hallway that funneled the line into the concrete cave that held the toilet stalls. Even though the concert had barely begun, the bathroom was in total disarray. It looked like a herd of stampeding rhinos had come and gone. There was toilet paper everywhere but in the stalls, and the floor was wet for reasons Winter didn't even want to consider. Using the constant *drip, drip,*

drip of the faucet to steer her away from the filth and toward the sinks, she pinched her nose and walked as fast as she could.

The soap dispenser was already out, of course, but the hot water still worked. That would have to be good enough. Winter decided that the bathroom was empty enough that she felt comfortable taking off her shirt and standing in her bra to rinse it out in the sink. For all she knew, anyone that might see her would probably think that was the outfit she wore tonight anyway. Tor would have probably liked it if she dressed like those stupid girls out there. Well, she wasn't like them and never would be.

She scrubbed the shirt angrily.

Why does he have to get so mad about Bren all the time?

Winter ground her teeth together as she struggled to keep her temper. Suddenly, she realized she was *angry*. She was angry about the spilled beer, angry about being at the stupid concert, angry that Tor always gave her such a hard time when she talked about Bren. Her irritation surged and coursed through her.

Why can't he ever just be supportive or understanding?

Bren had never done a single thing to Tor, not that she could remember, and he certainly did *everything* for her. He was practically family anyway. Winter had known him since she was a baby. They had grown up together in a way.

Tor was probably just pissed that Bren was rich, well-traveled, and handsome to boot. Her anger swelled again at the thought of Tor and his inferiority complex.

Maybe Bren was right, maybe Tor isn't the right guy for me. Winter dropped the shirt into the sink with a thwack. She couldn't even believe she was thinking like that. This was ridiculous. Winter slopped the wet shirt around in the sink, swishing out the beer smell. She felt hot tears welling up in her eyes and she beat her fist angrily on the basin channeling some of her fury.

Then, realizing that she was on the verge of a breakdown, she fought to steady her breathing.

Oh my God. Why, am I so pissed? With a heavy sigh, she decided her problem, and everyone else's for that matter, was this crap music grating on her nerves. She took a few deep breaths before continuing her cleaning. It got easier. Winter focused on her task, letting the repetition of the work bring her back to herself.

When her shirt was cleaned to her liking and the stale, overpriced, beer smell mostly washed from it, Winter wrung it out as best she could and put it back. It was a little larger now, stretched out after its vigorous scrubbing, so she knotted it to one side to keep it from hanging halfway to her knees.

While still in front of the mirror, she checked her appearance and ran her fingers through her thick, black bangs, straightening them out. She liked them to fall straight across her forehead, but her hair had other plans. Her mascara, thankfully, still held through the evening and its sweltering heat. Winter couldn't help but notice the way the black of her lashes highlighted her blue irises. Her eyes had always been her favorite part. She winked at herself and left.

As she ventured back out, she heard the unwelcome retch of someone getting sick in a stall at the end of the row, and hoped it was the woman who doused her with her drink.

Screaming erupted from the crowd and she knew that they finished yet another song; that was three she'd missed. Tor would definitely be wondering where she was.

Or maybe not.

He was really enjoying himself after all, or at least had been when she left. Winter realized as she headed up the concrete stairs again, taking them two at a time, so that she might be even less excited now than she was before the concert began.

Heading back wasn't quite the adventure this time. There had been so few people there on the stairs that Winter had no one to dodge around or groups to push through. All of that changed though as she came back down the lawn. She avoided the main group of concert goers by curving around its edges, staying as far away from the middle as possible, and she surprisingly had few problems getting by. It was easier now that the bars had closed. There were no more people loitering on the sides except for the smokers, and they were easy enough to avoid.

As Winter wended her way down the hill and rounded the special divider, vigorously policed by underpaid event workers, they all stood together in a scrum, immediately blocking her way. Winter felt like she was trying out for American Gladiators, and prepared herself to run the gauntlet, but when she held up her flimsy pass card that hung from a special lanyard around her neck, the one that signaled her front row status, the security eased.

"She's with the band!" the lead security guy called to the rest and they moved back to their positions.

"I'm not *with* the band," she clarified quickly and loudly, noticing the hungry looks some of the people around her gave her. Winter grasped her pass like a talisman. She and Tor would get to go backstage later because of that special little card, so after security grudgingly let her pass she dropped it down the front of her almost dry shirt, so it wouldn't get lost. Or stolen, judging by the looks she was getting.

Tor was beyond thrilled at the prospect of getting to venture back to the band's inner sanctum, but Winter could care less. The music failed to move her, her evening was mostly spent on laundry duty in the bathroom and she sincerely doubted she would reconsider it all in the presence of the parties guilty of creating this musical junk in the first place. If she didn't love Tor as much as she did, Winter swore she would have left by now.

At least it was doubtful the night could get any worse.

Chapter Four

Winter made it back. Finally. He could just barely see her bobbing and weaving through the crowd. There were probably only two or three more songs left before the encore, but Tor had a feeling she planned it that way. He was still screaming and dancing of course, just as enthusiastically as he was when she left, but he had to admit he rested a bit easier knowing she was nearby. Thankfully, that drunken woman had moved on. She looked a little sick anyway. Not that Winter was the kind to *want* to get in a fight, but she had never taken repeated abuse of any kind sitting down either. It was a joke between them, the appearance of her volatile temper at the strangest times.

From where Tor stood, it looked like Winter was having to fight harder to get back to him this time, if that was possible. People were inches apart, bumping into each other accidentally, or purposely. There was a thick knot of men and women around them now that wasn't there before, people who rushed the stage sometime after she left, and it was hard for anyone to have any measure of personal space anymore.

Not that you should expect any at a concert anyway, Tor thought.

As she got closer, Winter reached out desperately to Tor, her eyes wide and pleading for a lifeline. He grabbed her and pulled her through the fray. He slid her small hand safely into his and did not let go. He didn't want to lose her to this madness.

She looked different somehow. Harried, yes, that was definitely part of it, but there was something else, too. She was sexier somehow. Only Winter could leave soaked in beer and come back hotter than she left. Actually taking his eyes off the stage for a minute, Tor studied her intently, spinning her in a little circle while trying to determine the cause.

"What?" she said self-consciously after her second pirouette. She tried to snuggle closer to him to take his attention off her.

"Hmm, I'm not sure. Oh wait, I see now." He reached out and fingered the knot she had made into the black fabric of her tee. "Nice shirt, Win! I actually might like it now," Tor said appreciatively. "Quite the improvement if you ask me. It shows off your tattoos!" he shouted at her. What he really wanted to say was that the damp cloth hung just perfectly against her skin, illustrating every curve and line.

But he didn't.

"Oh, uh, thanks?" Winter looked down at her flat belly, the points of the yellow stars on her hipbones poking over the top of her low-slung jeans. She slid her hand across her stomach self-consciously, covering her secret ink. "I almost forgot about those," she said with a wink and a smile.

"I never do," Tor replied.

***

She was too worried about showing skin and Tor's reaction to her exposed flesh that she jumped when the crowd roared again. The band finished what she hoped was their last song.

Please, please, please.

No such luck.

InHuman kicked into yet another high-energy ode to criminal behavior that sent the sea of people behind her into a frothing rage.

The music was still on the low end of tolerable. The band was decent at best, but nothing about the evening, other than the unexpected total hotness of the lead singer, would be classified as life changing. That was just how Winter preferred her musical encounters. She wanted a tortured singer-songwriter type, armed with profound lyrics and an acoustic guitar, not this electric, self-indulgent crap. She wanted feeling. She wanted soul.

She caught sight of Lead Hottie again. She wanted him too.

Just then, a particularly vigorous dancer plowed into her, almost knocking her off her feet, and Tor grabbed her just in time. Winter moved to stand safely in front of him, using his body as a shield. He wrapped his arms around her protectively and started singing the words of the song into her ear. They were atrocious.

Oh Tor. He did try so hard to keep her happy. She reached back and patted his face affectionately.

Tor had been her best friend, well, other than Bren, for as long as she could remember. They did everything together. He was everything she ever needed in a companion and when their relationship evolved into the next level, no one was surprised.

36

Well, except Bren and Aunt Ramona, and surprised probably wasn't the best choice of words for their feelings.

Winter always got the impression they thought she was too good for him. Bren always said cryptic things about it like, they were "from two different worlds" and stuff like that. Tor always thought it was because Bren was jealous, so she just never told him about his comments anymore. Now that she thought about it, it probably explained some of Tor's problem with Bren.

Winter knew that Bren didn't *hate* Tor; he only wanted what was best for her. Besides, Aunt Ramona had helped Tor by co-signing on the loan so that he could keep his house. She would not have done all that if they hated him, that much was for sure. Winter leaned back against him, soaking up his warmth and letting him rock her gently to the music. Tor kissed the top of her head again, and Winter smiled to herself.

See? They were fine together; nothing was going to mess that up.

With him supporting her weight and protecting her from the surrounding mob, Winter was free to finally take in the spectacle playing out in front of her without fear of wearing another beverage or being trampled by the crowd around them.

After watching a few moments, she noticed the members of the band each had a chance to periodically showcase their musical proficiencies. It was kind of pretentious. Behind them, wild, evil-looking creatures--backup dancers, she supposed, with very good makeup--slithered up and down an extensive network of ropes and wires so thin you could barely see them. They danced and swayed with the rhythm in a wild dance. Some even looked like they flew around above the band like demented moths attracted to the light and sound below. Crazy looking beasts stalked around the edges of the stage, sometimes growling or swiping at each other and even simulating more violent or even sexual acts. Winter thought that they were a strange concept to add, but the actors were extremely convincing and the makeup and costumes were...wow. She supposed that if a band had that kind of star power, and the budget to support them, they could put whatever they darn well wanted into their act. It actually surprised her that *InHuman* could be that creative.

"Those backup dancers are wild!" she shouted back to Tor excitedly.

"What?!"

"The dancers," she gestured up to the stage, "They are very good, don't you think? Kinda weird though." Tor squinted up into the lights uncertainly.

"You mean the backup band?" he asked.

"No, the *dancers*," Winter shouted impatiently, frustrated with their communication breakdown. "Can't you...oh, never mind."

Tor was so into Lead Hottie's performance that he probably didn't even know what a backup dancer was. He merely patted her shoulder and kept on singing.

Winter shook his hand off with a shrug, not feeling very friendly, mostly irritated.

The glare of the lights momentarily abated as Lead Hottie prowled by. Winter couldn't help but notice how ethereal he seemed with the glow of the stage behind him. He was tall and thin, sinewy and feral.

Gorgeous, she thought. *Mesmerizing.*

She could think of a hundred other descriptives.

Winter watched him move. He practically slithered, gyrating across the stage and back. He moved like nobody she'd ever seen, and he still sang and danced around as enthusiastically now as he did on the very first song. That was pretty impressive, especially considering the amount of energy he was expending.

"What's *his* name?" she shouted and gestured to the lead singer's position on the stage. She didn't look back at Tor to ask him, but luckily he knew who she was talking about.

"He calls himself Shade. It's kinda catchy, huh?" He kissed her on her ear, probably pleased she finally decided to show an interest, but this time, Winter didn't smile at his affection.

"Not really," she mumbled, doubtful he heard her.

In fact, she thought it was a completely idiotic name, but at the same time–*finally*--she was intrigued. After spending what felt like hours wasting her life standing here, not even pretending to enjoy the show, she realized all this time she was missing something big. Winter was caught in the spell Shade was weaving on the rest of the willing crowd and she didn't even care. She couldn't take her eyes off the stage, off the man. No one could. Winter couldn't even hear the music anymore. It felt like she was underwater, hearing only muffled thumps or distorted noises that had the strength to find her in the murky depths. It was like she was drowning and no one could save her. But she could *see*. Shade was all she could see. Everything else fell away.

Then, she was ripped from it all. The music stopped. There were no more words to lull her. The wild man on stage paused dramatically at some pre-rehearsed point in the song. Winter watched him as he peered out, breathing hard and shielding his eyes from the bright lights of the stage, looking for something unknowable to the rest of them. Shade grinned into the audience, then fixed his animal gaze on the front row. He made a big show out of surveying them all disdainfully, judging them. His eyes, so black and larger than life on the big projectors, held everyone captive.

His scornful appraisal stopped with her. He froze. Their eyes locked. Winter saw him and Shade saw her. She knew it.

Shade looked right at her for a long moment, and she knew, without a doubt, she knew even with all the lights and distractions, that he saw her too. She could feel it like a crackle and snap of electricity passed between them.

Oh my God, what was that?

He gave her an assessing look, judging every bit of her, and Winter held her breath. That strange feeling of being watched returned, crashing over her, weighing her down. She felt a thousand other pairs of eyes on her as well. Winter shivered.

Maybe I'm just paranoid, she told herself. There were obviously that many eyes behind her. They were at a freaking rock concert. Winter was captivated all the same, frozen by his stare. Then, he blew her a delicate kiss and turned his dark eyes away.

"Oh my God, Win! He saw you! He was totally checking you out! I have the hottest girlfriend here." Tor was going to pieces behind her, all congratulatory kisses and bursting with the irrational pride that his girlfriend had caught Shade's attention. "Maybe you can get me an autograph backstage," he mused hopefully.

"Yeah, maybe."

Winter heard Tor but stayed rooted to her spot, finally remembering to breathe after a moment, but remained transfixed all through the rest of the song. She never took her eyes off of Shade after that, even after he moved on down stage. She just couldn't. Only when the song was over did he release her from his spell so she was able to look away. The hollowness that followed, after he set her free, gnawed hungrily at her insides.

She had to see him, be closer to him.

She was such an idiot, no better than anyone else.

Winter whispered to Tor that she was ready to go backstage.

***

One hour and thirty-eight minutes. That's precisely how long it took him to get her to finally meet his eyes. When she did, he still didn't affect her the same way as the others. But he did get her attention, just not in the way he had wanted. She stared. That was all.

That girl in seat 12A was different. He could tell that much even through the blinding stage lights and violent screams for his attention.

She saw him. There was a sizzle between them, something intangible, but present.

More than that, he thought she might have actually *seen* him. Not the rock star, not the performer but *him*. That might be a problem. Humans weren't supposed to see him. It just wasn't possible. Unless...

He looked back to the band, giving them the signal this would be their last song, but when he turned back, the girl in 12A was gone, fighting her way through the crowd, clinging tightly to a thin, redheaded boy.

His first thought was, *She's leaving.*

His second thought was that he hated the redheaded boy for no good reason.

Dugan, his lead guitarist, gave him a strange look, shaking his head. Shade shrugged apologetically in response. He learned that, after all these years, he wasn't good at letting things slip through his fingers.

There was something there. He knew it. That moment they shared had to be worth exploring.

Dugan just rolled his eyes.

Maybe she is the One? The prophecy? he thought at his friend. Dugan leaned his head back, pretending to study the ceiling. He shrugged.

Whatever you think, Dugan answered noncommittally, the words reverberating inside Shade's skull, *But, you are right, this feels different somehow.*

That it did.

She was probably not different at all, possibly just damaged. Shade saw that more and more with humans lately, but it was worth finding out.

While singing the lyrics he had sung a thousand times this summer, Shade immediately began thinking of scenarios he could engineer so he could meet her again, rejecting the ones that seemed stalkerish, or too planned. He had to think fast, she was getting away.

Out of the corner of his eye, he caught a glimpse of her again. She stopped moving and was being held up by security. They were arguing at the backstage entrance.

Yes! he thought, *There may still be time.* Maybe they would keep her busy long enough he could catch up with them when the song was over. *Who says we have to do an encore?* He needed to know why: Why she didn't care, why he didn't affect her.

It could be something mental, he supposed.

Then 12A reached into her shirt and Shade caught the reflection of the light as it glanced off the plastic covering of the backstage pass.

Perfect.

He could solve this little girl's mystery and move on with his life before morning.

Chapter Five

Unfortunately, they weren't the only ones who decided to head backstage early. There was already a crowd by the entrance to the hallway that would lead to the band's dressing rooms, even though *InHuman* had not yet finished their encore. The group was something else too. If Winter thought the crowd as a whole were strange, the people backstage were far and above weird. Tor and Winter were the only ones who, in her opinion, came anywhere close to being normal.

It occurred to her that her opinion on the matter was fairly liberal at that.

The men and women who congregated back there, dripping in black and caked in over-the-top makeup, made her uncomfortable. They all oozed a desperate desire that Winter didn't believe could be attractive to anyone at all, let alone the men on that stage.

So she rested there, watching, waiting, with her back against a cinderblock wall that had received at least ten coats of the high gloss white paint that covered every inch of the pavilion. She hoped it was dry enough not to stick to her clothes. It certainly smelled fresh. Winter felt the sticky thickness of it where she touched the wall.

Tor, for his part, did not seem to notice the overpowering new paint smell and struck up a conversation with one of the relatively few men in attendance. His new friend was a total freak show, worse than that kid before. It annoyed her that he could be so lost in a shared excitement over something that clearly held no interest to her.

Where is his sense of loyalty?

Winter barely had time to fume over it. Something was happening. A cold rush of air pushed passed her, gusting down the long hallway. Then, the crowd outside erupted into a final fury of noise.

"It must be over," she whispered to Tor. The smile on his face looked like it would split him in two.

"Don't forget about that autograph," he winked at her. Winter felt a hot blush race across her cheeks as she remembered that strange moment her eyes locked with Shade's. She hoped she didn't make a total fool of herself. She pressed herself against the wall, making herself as small as possible to stay out of the way of the band.

Without warning, a pair of double doors not far from where she had taken up position exploded in on her with a bang. It startled her enough that she managed to jump clear just in time to avoid being smashed by them; only to find that out of the way of the doors, was now in the way of Shade. She floundered to move out of his path without falling flat on her face.

Crap. What a way to meet.

She felt strong hands supporting her, holding her just above the elbows.

"Watch it now. We wouldn't want a little thing like you to get hurt." Then he was there, practically on top of her. The front man was closer than she could have thought possible. He smiled a dazzling, unsettling smile at her, exposing perfect, white teeth. Never stopping his forward motion, he kept his hands on her to steady her, scooping her up and moving her along with him. It was a very graceful move. She stumbled momentarily and his hands were everywhere at once, keeping her upright.

"Thanks," she managed, but he said nothing. His arm slid around her waist as they walked. Winter couldn't help but notice how warm he was. She hoped she didn't still smell like stale beer. After a few paces, she found her feet and her balance, but Shade never let her go. Casting a look over her shoulder for Tor, she subtly struggled to free herself, not wanting to offend him by rejecting his assistance, but he held tight. They moved away from the entrance where she and Tor had patiently waited caught up in the sea of people.

"Wait, um..." she tried to think of a polite way to ask him to wait for her boyfriend, but couldn't.

"Yes, my dear?" Shade purred.

"I think I lost my friend," Winter squeaked. Boy*friend, Win,* she reminded herself.

She risked another glance back. He was still there, following doggedly. Tor's face, bouncing periodically over the shoulders of the rush of people that followed behind her was a mixture of awe that his girlfriend was being escorted by a rock star, and panic that he might get left behind. Winter heard him making excuses and scrambling to keep up, like a puppy desperately trailing the others. She thought she heard him shouting for them to wait, but her escort didn't hear him. Winter got the feeling that maybe Shade *pretended* not to hear him.

The hall stretched forever. Shade was leading Winter at such a fast pace she had to run every few steps to keep up. If it weren't for his iron grip on her, she probably would have fallen or at least lagged way behind. Forgetting the proximity of her ears to his mouth, he began shouting things at the very scary looking members of his road crew. Winter hadn't met many roadies or crew members of rock shows, but she was willing to guess that they weren't all quite as sinister looking as *InHuman*'s crew. He was shouting at them in words she'd never heard before. Winter wasn't sure of the language he was using, but it was definitely not English. Racking her brain, she tried to remember if Tor ever mentioned where they hailed from, but her thoughts were interrupted by the awkward scrambling and dodging of men both she and Shade had to perform to keep from being knocked out of the way.

Everything was a whirl of motion around them and Winter's head was spinning. Though the concert had been over for only minutes, pieces of the stage were already being broken down and carried past her,. Heavy speakers rolled down the narrow hallway and cables sat coiled in preparation. *That was fast.*

"Did you enjoy it?" Shade asked, taking her by surprise.

"Huh?" she asked intelligently. The tall man next to her was watching her in a predatory way, his intense interest in her own opinion inexplicable. His grip on her arm loosened slightly, but his hand still rested firmly around her upper arm. The flat of his palm burned on her bare skin below the hem of her short sleeve.

"I wanted to know if you enjoyed the performance." Shade nimbly jumped over a coil of cable, never taking his eyes off her. Winter found it interesting that he used those words. It had been *quite* the performance.

Winter, pursed her lips in thought and risked a peek up at him. He was more handsome up close than she imagined. His dark hair fell perfectly across his face and she wondered if he styled it or it just did that on its own. Considering his obvious lack of make-up, she doubted he would sit still for someone to do his hair for him. Winter shook herself out of it and managed to bury all of her stupid star blindness long enough to answer him.

"Um, yeah," she said agreeably, "It was very...dynamic," was the only polite thing she could think to say about the show. "The backup dancers were...wow." Winter could never tell him to his face that she thought he was ridiculous, with his stupid name and dramatic performance. It would insult the man who was clearly the creative force behind this thing she disliked. Winter would never admit to him that the only thing interesting about his vanity show, unfortunately, *was* him.

"I don't believe you." He said teasingly, after giving her the strangest look, but Winter wondered if he wasn't being a little serious. Maybe he *had* noticed her sitting down. A wave of panic swept through her. "Were you not entertained even a little?" he continued, then laughed in a way that made her sure he didn't find any humor in the situation. Shade was clearly used to receiving more praise than she mustered.

Oops.

"Yes, yes, of course," she stammered. "It was very, um...eye-catching."

***

She was lying to him, he could tell. In his life, he'd met plenty of liars. 12A was getting more interesting already. They breezed through another hallway, then burst through another set of heavy double doors, bypassing the dressing rooms completely. That boy she came with was so far behind them now that he thankfully couldn't see or hear him anymore.

The boy was quite annoying with his pleas not to be left behind.

Shade knew that boy would be upset with the girl for leaving him, but there was nothing she could do about it. He certainly wasn't going to stop to wait for him. Why would he?

Then again, she hadn't asked him to stop and wait either.

Interesting.

Shade wanted to keep her moving. If they stopped even for a second, she might have time to ask that very question. He noticed with some delight, that she kept stealing glances at him. She probably was awestruck by her new and unlikely escort, he told himself.

It happens to them all, he thought proudly. Then again, she didn't look very awestruck. Mostly, she looked just confused.

He muscled through another heavy set of doors. Seconds later, they were out in the alley. The asphalt radiated its latent summer heat back at them, but the welcome breeze was filled with the coolness that night would bring. Shade loved the wind. It ruffled the girl's hair about her face.

12A was quiet.

That was something new. Most of them babbled on and on, and on. He thought about the look Dugan gave him on the stage and his words of warning. Shade hoped he wasn't wrong about this. He hoped Dugan was right.

She could be the One. He looked at her again. *Maybe.*

***

She could breathe again. Thankfully, they were no longer in that tiny, oppressive hallway. There wasn't enough air back there. Winter drew in a steadying breath and made a mental note of the coming rain.

Rain, she thought, always had a distinct smell that announced its arrival. Most weather did, though. She would probably never see a drop of it. Summer storms, even those that came this late in the season, never lasted long. It would be gone by morning.

Winter closed her eyes and counted to ten, imagining that when she opened them again, she would be waking up. Tor would be standing over her, worried, and she would find herself sprawled out, back on that concrete floor, coming around after being knocked senseless by the massive doors instead of here in Shade's company. That would be more likely than her current scenario.

When she reopened them, she saw five massive and very expensive looking busses looming in front of her, humming like contented animals. The band members streamed by them silently, without so much as a word to their lead singer, each retiring to their own bus, ghosting away into the night. Only one remained, half hidden in shadows.

"Dugan," Shade nodded in acknowledgement. The dark man stepped forward and Winter backed away unconsciously. It was him, the man who watched her from the wings. She stepped back until she bumped into Shade behind her. He draped his arm over one shoulder in a possessive and sensual way.

"Have a good night," the guitarist said, his lips twisting into a wicked smile. Shade's hands went to her shoulders protectively; his fingers digging into her flesh, and Winter wondered if she was right to be afraid. Then Dugan walked away, climbing into his own bus that admitted him with a hiss. Winter let out the breath she was holding and Shade dropped his hands from her shoulders, letting his palm slide fire down her arm. He put his hand in hers and she turned to face him.

Is he really going to stand there just holding my hand? Winter thought incredulously.

This was wrong. She shouldn't be here with him. Winter started to protest, started to ask him about

Tor, but Shade pulled her toward the bus door, and Winter was strangely not stopping him.

I should be stopping him, right?

"Wait," Winter said firmly and shook free of his grasp, "I...I am here with someone." she stammered in protest, digging in her heels in case he tried to pull her again. "This is wrong. I mean, what are we doing anyway? No one is even behind us anymore." She looked around one more time for Tor. He was nowhere to be seen. There was no one.

Shade stared at her like she had three heads. Winter was certain he never had a female complain about being alone with him.

She continued with her argument. "We should be with the others, right? Everyone is here to see you. Why do you even want to be with me?" she added, her voice trailing off. She thought she knew the answer to that question already. He gave her a long look, and suddenly, Winter felt very small and very young. She shouldn't be here.

"Interesting," was all he said, cocking his head as he examined her, then he leaned forward so that they were eye to eye. Shade, cast in the shadows of the dark alley, came even closer, keeping his face very near Winter's. He was invading her space, flooding her senses. He was all she could see, hear, and smell. *God, he smells good.* Normally, she would be scrambling to back away if someone crowded her like that, but she wasn't. She stood her ground.

Then he moved so close that his nose barely grazed her earlobe. She heard him swallow as he

52

prepared to speak and then he parted his lips. "Do you want to leave?" he whispered.

Winter could barely breathe. This was her chance to get back to Tor. She opened her mouth to say yes, but the word didn't come. Instead, nothing came. She wasn't thinking that she put herself in a very dangerous situation or that she should be trying to find Tor. Winter was only concerned now about what Shade thought of her.

If Bren knew about the poor decisions she was making right now, God, he would probably come unglued. She shuddered at the lecture he would give her later. Winter knew she going to get one too because Bren was sure to find out about this. He would find out because Tor was just the type to tell on her, just to get a rise out of him. It was inevitable.

And then there's Shade. God, he's gorgeous.

He clearly wanted something from Winter. She just didn't think she should want to give it.

That was a problem.

Because she had yet to say she wanted to leave.

Not once.

"Do you not want to be alone with me?" he whispered in that same ear, his words thrilling her. "They all want to be alone with me, you know. That's why they are all here." He made a sweeping gesture back toward the amphitheater, then took a lock of her black hair and twisted it in his fingers carefully. "Are you trying to be the exception to this rule, my lovely girl?"

Shade lifted his other hand to brush a few errant strands of her hair away from her face and

Winter thought she might die if he didn't touch her soon. She shivered as his fingers grazed her skin and had to try harder than normal to tell herself it was because of the breeze.

Her mind was at war with itself, simultaneously wanting him and wanting to get away from him.

"I...I," she stammered awkwardly, trying to think of something to say that wouldn't be rude or embarrassing, but at the same time, refuse him. Nothing was immediately coming to mind.

Crap.

While she racked her brain, a car turned in at the end of the alley, briefly illuminating his face.

Oh God. That wasn't helping her resolve. Shade was like a dark angel in the shadows of the alley.

Winter tried to steady her breathing so that he wouldn't know she was losing it. He was too beautiful for her to even think straight. His dark, spiky hair, as black as night, as black as her own, fell down over his eyes, blocking her view of them. He moved a hand to brush it out of the way, but she surprised herself, and surprised him even more, by beating him to it. Winter needed to see his incredible eyes again, the ones that held her so decidedly earlier. They were the key to her attraction, she thought.

Winter felt like there was something strange about them. They were so dark, so beautiful, glittering all on their own like stars in the night sky. Yet more than that somehow. She pushed his thick hair away and almost melted when their eyes met again. Once they weren't blocked by the inky blackness of his hair, she

54

C. B. Cole

saw an impossible light shimmering behind his eyes, promising secrets only she could unlock.

And those eyes were fixed intently on her.

Waiting.

Winter fought for a reason. There surely had to be a good reason, why she couldn't be alone with him, the famous Shade, on his tour bus here in this dark alley, but she couldn't remember one.

Improbably, she conceded by taking a step forward, admitting her defeat. She at least had enough restraint to keep from saying the words "*no, I'm not the exception*" aloud. That would have been more than she could have lived with.

"That's a good girl," he said and took her hand again. The doors hissed as they opened and let them in.

Chapter Six

Shade led the fragile-looking girl into his sanctuary as he had with so many others. But then, of course, Shade was not *really* his name; it was just the name he wore because he must in *this* world.

He hated it, actually, but it was necessary. There was no need for his real name to be floating around out there. Who knew what could happen? Letting a human have that kind of power over him was foolish.

She didn't want to be there, unlike the rest of them, and that was intriguing. And unlike the rest of them, he didn't move her the way he moved them. She wasn't awed, not inspired and he wanted to know why. Dugan said she was different.

Mysteries were meant to be solved, he told himself.

He wanted her to respond to him.

How is it that I, Kieran, King of the Dark Court, the most powerful Dark fae in all of Faerie can't hold sway over this pathetic, barely interesting creature?

There was, of course, the slight chance she could be the One, though, and that was why she was here now. That little moment they shared while he was on stage was promising and even now, there was a glimmer of hope, but it was unlikely and frankly, he was tired of searching. It would be too easy it seemed, to find her this way, too easy for her to walk into one of his shows and plop down in the front row. In his experience, things just never happened that way. His optimism from earlier was waning.

Dugan was probably right about the other bit as well, like always. Kieran's fascination with the weak and delicate human girls never made sense to his friend. Hell, it never made any sense to him either. But she had to be out there, as one of them. That was the only way she could have been hidden this long.

"What is your name?" he asked slowly, like he was talking to a child, indicating with his hands that she should continue with their conversation. He didn't bother to look at her when he asked her. Right now, she was just a toy, a fascination. He was not going to give her the satisfaction of having him rapt over her every word, if that was the game she was playing, though it seemed unlikely that she planned everything out just that way.

This little girl, 12A, was merely an annoyance, a puzzle, he told himself, and once he figured out what was wrong with her he would send her back to her boyfriend to continue her life as broken and worthless as all the others that came before her.

Kieran began taking parts of his stage persona off, dropping his jacket directly on the floor, then his thick, studded belt on top of it. He didn't undress any more than that. She didn't deserve a strip tease. He didn't reward those who irritated him, and if she was the One, well, he guessed she would see him naked soon enough, he thought with a wry smile. Realizing that she had yet to reply, he turned to glare at her and waited for her answer.

Long seconds later, it came.

"Winter." she pouted out the words, obviously unhappy over her decision to stay with him. She had taken a seat at the little kitchen table, and was looking dejected.

What an unusual name for this pale little beauty. It was strangely complimentary of her too. Interesting.

Kieran examined her more closely this time, now that he had the proper light to do it. He was curious about this shy girl. The bus had a yellowish artificial light that was nowhere sufficient enough to perform an in-depth review, but it was better than the darkness they came from. At least he could see her face better than in the alley.

So yes, it was still possible, that she could be *her*. Supposedly, the One was still out there and admittedly, this girl, Winter, had that something about her.

Something.

There were no obvious signs to confirm or contradict his theory, which would have made his search infinitely easier, but that was always the problem, wasn't it?

Kieran did a brief self-inventory.

He didn't feel any unnatural pull toward her, other than wanting to interrogate her about her apathy. He always thought that when the time came for him to meet the One, it would feel like a lightning strike or something would resonate deep within him, but he did not feel anything close to that with this small, quiet girl. Kieran studied her clinically and she shifted uncomfortably under his stare, dropping her chin into her hands. There were no outward signs that screamed otherworldliness. No glow. No vibration that made him think of home. Nothing.

No, this was probably just another let down. Kieran braced himself for the disappointment that was surely coming.

Winter was pretty though; prettier than he had initially given her credit for. She had dark hair, just like his, but her eyes were blue, an intense light blue, the color of the sky on a cold, cloudless day. They were so blue that they may have been gray at one point, or maybe they would be one day soon. Her skin was pale, but not sickly. It was vibrant and alive, like there was a luster beneath it just dying to get out. She was not tall, but she was thin in a healthy way and it didn't make her seem overly tiny, just small.

Kieran realized that her differences from the other girls that were usually in attendance at his shows were infinite. Those women were tired and used. They always smelled of smoke and beer, but not her. Not Winter, she smelled sweet, like wildflowers.

He kept coming back to her eyes. There was an unknowable secret she held just behind those eyes. She was teasing him. Daring him to solve her mysteries. He needed to really look in them. He needed her to really *see* him.

Maybe there's more to her than just her apathy? he thought. In his personal experience, humans were mostly uninteresting, and that this one held his interest this way, was appalling on some level.

Moving like a cat, Kieran joined her at the little table, sliding silently beside her on the bench seat, and placed his hand on her face, stroking it from temple to cheek.

"Look at me won't you?" He used his softest, most comforting voice. For some reason, he did not want to scare this fragile girl.

Winter did look, turning the full force of her gaze on him. There was no reluctance this time, no regret or hesitation, but pure anticipation in her eyes.

He sucked in a breath. He felt like he had been punched in the gut. His head swam, making him dizzy even though he sat. Kieran felt every boundary that she tried to maintain between them fall into a pile of emotional rubble. There were no secrets between them now.

And *zap*.

The impossible light that he merely suspected before, could have only hoped she contained, suddenly escaped, breaking free from those blue, blue eyes and burned right through him.

Here I am, they told him, *you finally found me*.

Winter held him there, pinned like a moth to his seat and he wondered if she knew what she was doing to him. It was slightly uncomfortable and he didn't want to, but he managed to look away after a few seconds. His barely acknowledged suspicions were confirmed in that all-too-brief gaze.

This girl in front of him, Winter, *was* different. He knew.

He knew without a doubt in that moment that she was the One. She told him so in a way that left no doubt. He knew so certainly that he couldn't believe it had taken long hours of reflection in order to reject the others he had considered. If only he could've known it would be so blatant, so simple to see. He tried not to panic and fought to keep breathing normally.

Stupid. Stupid. Stupid.

Kieran berated himself for being so proud. If he hadn't taken it as such a personal affront that she didn't like his music, he probably would have known already. It was right there on her face this whole time. He could see it clear as night. There may not have been some magical pull or visible pyrotechnics, but there was a definite signal.

But I would have figured it out anyway, Kieran told himself, *As if she could have hidden what she was from me much longer.*

He tried to justify it, deciding that he felt *something* when they arrived in this generic town, felt the signature energy of someone powerful. He thought it might have just been the closeness of more of his kind, but perhaps it was her, alerting him to her presence.

Not knowing what else to do, Kieran reached out to pull her close to him, wrapping his arms around her protectively and tugging her into an embrace. Her soft hair brushed his cheek and he lowered his chin so that it rested on her small shoulder. He was afraid to let her go.

"I have finally found you," he whispered. She did not fight him. Winter let him hold her willingly, without a word of protest.

"I didn't know you were looking," she whispered back.

"All your life," he replied softly.

She sighed into him and, for the first time in centuries, Kieran felt peace. There, with the fabric of her thin shirt brushing softy against his skin, he breathed her in memorizing her scent and...

And smelled something else entirely: Something that was distinctly not Winter. He pushed away and gripped her arms hard, pushing her against the little window behind her. She squeaked in surprise. Kieran stifled an inhuman growl as best he could. He was so shocked that he couldn't bring himself to hold her at more than arm's length.

"Wh...what did I do?" she cried. "Please don't hurt me." Tears welled up in her blue eyes. Kieran knew he shouldn't be so cruel, but he knew that *other* smell; knew the person who wore it all his life.

So he had figured it out too; figured it out much sooner than Kieran had it would seem, and kept her from him. That scoundrel had known all along. It was so obvious. Of course, his brother would have never told Kieran if he found her.

Why would he?

Kieran slammed his fist down on the flimsy table, all the while holding her away and Winter jumped. Someone would die for this deception.

Later.

62

"Don't hurt me, please," was all she said. "Just let me go." Her eyes were wide with fear and Kieran saw how his fingers dug deep into the flesh of her upper arm. He realized that she was trembling, like a frightened rabbit. Kieran sat up, releasing her immediately, and straightened himself in the seat to give her some room. Winter breathed a sigh of relief and he cursed himself for scaring her.

Her fear, while a beautiful emotion in others, didn't need to taint this creature. Those shaming tears reminded him that his focus should be on her now, always on her now.

Forever.

He tried to give her what he hoped was an apologetic smile, feeling his face twist in an unnatural way. Kieran had never smiled before, so he hoped he got it right. Her eyes glinted with the fresh promise of tears and he thought he should say something to reassure her.

An apology?

Kieran opened his mouth to speak, but something in her eyes caught him and pulled him back down, all the way down into her soul. It was delightfully dark.

She is going to be dangerous, he thought gleefully.

"I'm sorry, Winter," he told her and she nodded. "I have something I need to show you. Will you see it?" She blanched and he squeezed her hand. "You have to trust me. Do you think you can?"

"I can only try."

He nodded. What he would do now would be the ultimate test, but he already knew she would pass it. If she didn't, it would kill her and it wouldn't matter anyway.

He dropped his eyes, and then his glamour. Kieran pulled on his real self, imagining it coming to him from all directions to settle on him lightly like a cloud of ash. He waited patiently, eyes closed, for her shock and horror. For her screams. All the others had screamed before they died.

He waited for his hopes to be dashed, as they had been repeatedly.

Winter did not make a sound.

Confused, Kieran looked up, worried that she perished right away without a word. Winter was watching him with a renewed curiosity, looking very much like she would like to touch him, and then, much to his surprise, especially now that he was his true self; she grabbed him roughly and kissed him.

This was going to be easier than he hoped.

***

How can he ask me to trust him when he's been so odd?

But then, just then, there was a change, something about him that was so irresistible she could barely stop herself from touching his face. He seemed more attractive, more delicious, more necessary, more everything than anyone she had ever known. Winter felt the softness of the night all around her, smelled the damp earth outside, the promise of rain fulfilled. She imagined the frozen ground of the coming winter, dead and cracking before it snowed, crunching hard below her feet and the steel gray of the clouds that threatened with icy whiteness. Somehow, he put those images in her mind, and spoke to her without words, told her she belonged to him.

She had to do it; she was compelled to do it.

Winter never once thought that it was wrong to kiss someone other than Tor. She just had the need.

His lips needed hers.

His mind found ways to reach her the way his words and music had not. Finally, a connection. There was no going back.

The things inside his mind were not beautiful. They were awful, horrible; darkness and fog and all things that should scare even the bravest of men. When their lips touched, she remembered the mournful wail of the screech owl in the woods behind her house, heard the baying of hounds on the hunt. Fingernails grated on chalkboards and children cried for their mothers because of this man. Trapped there in the horror of his careful touch, Winter felt like she no longer had any choice.

She was his.

He told her so.

Shade had become more beautiful, more delectable than any other person, man or woman. He claimed her and she relented to his conquering caress. Then Winter reached out, lacing both arms around his neck to pull him in close and kissed him hard. The feel of his soft lips further ignited her want for him. She lusted for him. Winter was half-crazed with it. She attempted to take off his shirt in a hasty, desperate way, ripping at the edges to touch his skin beneath it.

Winter was disgusted with herself, but unable to stop. Tor was so far from her mind she couldn't even remember what happened to him, nor did she care. Shade helped her with his shirt, undoing the buttons that her shaking fingers couldn't manage, and then gently held her hands in his own to stop her when she tried for more. She paused to look at him questioningly, and he smiled sadly.

"Stop, Winter," he whispered, almost begging her to keep her virtue.

She felt sick.

Oh God. She was a fool. He was rejecting her.

Winter wondered if he thought her as desperate as she felt, wondered if, by stopping her, he was letting her down gently. The thought of him not wanting her was painful, but not entirely surprising. He probably had a thousand women throw themselves at him just this way. She felt a hot tear slide down her cheek. Winter moved to brush it away, but he was already there, kissing it gone. He pressed her trembling fingers to his lips and then moved them lower and held them tight to his chest, over his heart as he helped her stand.

She wobbled a little and stubbornly refused to look at him as he led her back to his most private place on the bus.

Her last thoughts before they entered the room should have been, *"This is a mistake."*

Chapter Seven

Her touch on his skin was unbearably perfect. When her pale fingers brushed over his bare chest, they sent volts of electricity through him.

So there was lightning after all, he mused.

He allowed himself to kiss her back, and let her take his shirt off, but Kieran did not feel right letting her go any further even though it was clear she wanted to. And it was more than apparent to him that he wanted her to too. When he stopped her, the exquisite look of rejection was almost enough to make him let her continue to do whatever she had in mind, but he did not want to be greedy. There would be time enough for that. Kieran decided that he would berate himself later for missing out on her, for not noticing her for what she was minutes, hours, days earlier.

He was with her now and he should enjoy this small victory. He would have to give her back to the real world eventually. The gauntlet was thrown. Now, he must woo her and win her heart.

But not just yet.

Kieran was already dreading what he was going to do his queen. She would be angry and distrustful of him if she ever found out about it, but it would be necessary tonight. He needed just a little more time. Maybe she would never find out. Still, he couldn't risk Winter knowing about his Court, not yet. He would take her back there again soon enough, when she could remember it.

Just not tonight. Not without her choice being made properly. Tonight was going to have to be a secret even from her. He wanted her to love him, respect him, and not only fear him. His Court, though, would terrify her.

Though her fear would be exquisite, he thought joyously.

He was going to manipulate his queen for his own selfish reasons. He was going to tamper with her memory just because he couldn't wait to see her in the Dark Court where she belonged.

Kieran took her hand in his own, gently helping her to her feet and then led his perfect beauty, the first one to really see him for what he was, back to his home.

Winter was not afraid of him and took his hand willingly, not even flinching though he wore his true countenance.

And that is how he knew for sure she was the One.

The One, whose eyes held that perfect fire of duality that he needed his queen to have. She had been hidden from him, waiting for him to set her free. Winter was born special. Born to be the only way to break the balance that persisted between the Light and Dark Courts, rendering them both powerless for ages. It was foretold. She was perfect with that cool midnight darkness inside her that sang to him and the fragile whiteness of her other half that cowered before him.

She was perfect.

And he finally found her.

Once they were safely behind the flimsy door of his bedroom on the bus, he willed it shut with the flick of his fingers and mentally turned the lock as a precaution. Winter looked straight ahead and then back at him imploringly, her eyes wide with wonder and disbelief and he felt his heart take flight. The Dark King lifted her carefully into his arms and carried her down the stone hall that stretched out in front of them. The careful arches of the dark granite particular to the wing that held his personal rooms echoed with his footsteps. He was home now; his bedroom in the bus was merely a gateway back to the Dark Court. A cleverly crafted disguise made touring with the band and ruling his subjects possible at the same time.

His Dark fey tripped out of his way at the sight of him, surprised by his sudden reappearance. A collection of bogies ran together comically, falling over themselves to clear a path as he growled his warning at them.

"The queen," they whispered in unison. "The queen."

"Shut up, idiots," Kieran hissed and kicked out at the mob, managing to make contact with one of them. His heavy boot made a sickening *crunch* as it connected with its shoulder. He heard the squeals the rest of them made as they fought over who would be responsible for getting their companion back up on its feet again. The king's wrath was a thing to fear.

Winter twisted back to see what the commotion was about, peering warily over his shoulder to see.

Kieran did not stop her. She wouldn't remember any of it anyway. She looked back at him after the chattering mob disappeared from view and her mouth was pursed in the strangest way. He laughed at her, he couldn't help it and she frowned, her forehead wrinkling delicately.

She's too proud to ask about what she just saw, he thought. *She probably thinks she's going crazy.*

Just a few steps more and they would be to his room. The king quickened his step, shifting her slightly in his arms so that he didn't jostle her overmuch. At the very last second, he thought he caught a glimpse of Dugan at the end of the hall, but Kieran didn't bother acknowledging him. One of the benefits of being king was the he didn't have to.

Hastily, he kicked open the door to his own chamber so he wouldn't have to put her down. He crossed the chamber in record time and laid her out like a doll on his magnificent bed then stepped back to enjoy the view of her there.

"Door," he whispered to himself and heard it close and lock at his command.

Winter, not noticing his trick, beckoned to him, her thin pale fingers gesturing to him to join her there.

"Can we sit? I won't climb all over you, I promise," she told him.

Honestly, he would have preferred she say something to the opposite effect. "Not just yet, my lovely," he told her. That beautiful, wounded expression that she had worn on the bus, returned.

***

70

She wondered what she did wrong. Again. Or maybe she should be wondering what he slipped her? Winter was sure that she saw some creatures out in the hall that were definitely not human. It was enough to make her question her grip on her sanity.

And speaking of that hallway, how on earth is a 150 foot stone hallway attached to a tour bus anyway? Then, he just tosses me unceremoniously on this big bed, only to leave me without a touch? she thought, fuming silently. He was making a fool of her. She had thrown herself at him and he denied her.

Twice.

Now, he was having a laugh at her expense. She shouldn't be here. She should be back with Tor.

Winter wished that she continued her trend of not enjoying herself, then she could have made Tor take her home after the show instead of going backstage. She could be back at the house, watching a movie on the couch with Bren or snuggled tight in her bed with a book, not stuck in this compromising situation with one of the most famous men in the world.

She'd stupidly tried to make a move on him, which failed miserably and now, she was here, alone, on his bed.

Maybe she was doing it wrong? Winter had never actually kissed anyone other than Tor before. *That was probably it,* she thought to herself. She was a kissing failure. All these years, Tor was too nice to tell her she sucked at making out.

Whatever it was, Winter knew she had done something unforgiveable to drive him away in his own

71

room. She was *too* desperate for him and now, he was punishing her, making her feel like the foolish little girl she was.

He wasn't even facing her anymore.

Winter didn't want to admit it to herself, but her body missed the warmth of him already. She shouldn't feel that way. When he carried her in his arms, she silently thrilled at the danger and unexpected lust she felt just from being close to him. And now, it felt like in his absence, the sun suddenly set behind a mountain, leaving her in the coldness of the shadows.

***

Kieran walked away from her, no matter how much he really wanted to be beside her, and poured himself a glass of wine from the cabinet a few paces away. He raised his drink at her, using it to ask her a question rather than use more words. *Would you like a drink?* He wasn't sure what to say to her anyway.

Winter shook her head dejectedly. It was killing him for her to look so sad.

He almost thought she was angry with him. It certainly looked that way at times. They had barely spoken a word since their kiss. If he didn't know better, he would think she was pouting. It was kind of sexy.

Winter reclined back on her elbows and then crossed her legs in front of her, trying to get more comfortable, still looking hurt over the intentional distance he put between them. She gave him a wan smile.

"You're sure you won't sit?" she asked sweetly.

"Maybe soon." His eyes swept over her and he started counting in his head to one hundred so that he wouldn't look desperate at her invitation. He was making great strides, but by thirty he was faltering. At sixty-seven, as if to taunt him, that knotted old shirt she wore, the one that carried his brother's scent, lifted slightly higher so that he caught sight of yellow stars on her hipbones.

He stared at them, his lips trembling with the need to press against her skin. Kieran tired of counting at seventy-five.

Fuck it.

He tried, damn he tried, but he couldn't stay away from her anymore. Whether it was the sight of the secret ink that was carved into her pale skin, or the thought of his brother having her near him, hidden all this time, the Dark King wasn't sure but something made his need for her unbearable.

He dropped the glass, not caring that it shattered on the floor and crossed the distance between them in two great steps, his left arm hurriedly encircling her waist and pulling her tattooed hip toward his mouth.

With his free right hand he swept his palm over her frightened eyes and whispered, "Sleep." She fell back, unconscious immediately, limp in his arms. He could have done everything he desired at that point, but he did not. Kieran would never harm his queen, nor enjoy her charms unless they were wed.

It was the one pure thing he would have in his life. He gently placed a kiss on each of the small, perfect stars and then laid her gently back on the bed unravaged.

The Dark King sat there beside her for a long time, watching her breathe slowly.

In and out.

In and out.

Not daring to touch her. Finally, when he was sure all of his self-control was used up, he called for Dugan. The captain of his guard was there in an instant, slithering in from the shadows.

"My lord?" The questioning words oozed out of him in a very pleased manner, willing to participate in Kieran's every twisted plan, but when he saw the queen, he froze. His eyes fixed on her and flashed expectantly. Kieran stifled a growl and Dugan cleared his throat apologetically. Still, he never once looked at the King, but stared in a wondrous way at the dark beauty on the bed, like he had seen her before.

He should've recognized the girl by now from the concert, he told himself trying to calm his boiling blood. Kieran gestured to Winter, and wondered if Dugan could tell, just by looking, what she meant for not just him, but the rest of the Court as well.

"You were right," he told him. "She was very different. Go. Find her boy, wherever he is," he added dismissively. "Make sure no harm has come to him or fix it if it has. Get him home and give him some sort of memory of tonight. It has to be a good reason why he would need to leave with her early. When you are done, come back and deliver our future queen to her home as well." He stroked her hair affectionately. Winter was beautiful even in sleep.

74

Dugan, who never altered his expression for any reason, looked incredulous after hearing him address her so. He helped his king search for so long, and now it was all over.

As an afterthought Kieran added sarcastically, "I think we may already know where she lives." The Dark King reached out tenderly and smoothed the leg of her jeans that wrinkled as she slept.

"Do we?" Dugan asked.

"Someone has been keeping her from us, Dugan. I am sure the answer won't surprise you." Kieran didn't look up. His longing for Winter was unbearable, not in a sexual way, or rather not *only* in a sexual way, but Kieran was sure they could be happy together in other ways as well. He was glad Dugan came when he did, or things may have turned out differently. Kieran was not exactly known for his self-control. Still, he wasn't ready to let her go just yet.

Until she makes the choice, though, I can't be hers. He promised himself that one, small thing.

Dugan was still watching Winter sleep. His face shone in awe and Kieran tried very hard not to let it bother him. The discovery of the queen was a good thing for all of them, as long as they could keep her safe until she could ascend to power. They would be fine as long as his brother did not win her first. The battle for her affections may have begun for Kieran only tonight, but for his challenger, the king of the Light Court, it had probably been fought for some time now.

Kieran cursed his brother under his breath.

He noticed that Dugan was still there, just staring.

"You can leave us now, Dugan." Kieran said bitingly, dismissing his captain. He wanted a little more time alone with his future queen.

And she would be his.

The Dark King curled around her, his hands brushing back her dark hair, and stared, just to watch the wonder of her sleeping, until Dugan came back to take her home.

Chapter Eight

Winter woke with a smile on her face, in her own bed, and in her own room. The golden rays of late morning poured in through the window and bathed her in the most exquisite warmth. She twisted and stretched, taking the covers with her wherever she moved. Absently, she twirled one of her bed-frazzled locks slowly around her fingers.

I just had the most fantastic dream!

Then she bolted upright, fear clouding her pleasant awakening, forcing it away with the cold dawn of realization. Winter remembered the concert alright, but how did she even get home? And where was Tor? The last thing she remembered was being in the bus with Shade.

Oh God, did he drug me? Did he...?

Panic gripped her.

Winter did a quick appraisal of her body, but found no marks, no evidence that anything untoward happened. That much was a relief. Still, last night remained a mystery. A fantastic mystery.

And Tor? What happened to him?

She hoped he made it home all right, and then selfishly added a silent prayer that he had not broken up with her either. If he was angry that she went with Shade--and he really should be--it was doubtful that they were still a couple. If Tor had any idea of what happened, or might have happened as it was purely speculative at the moment, and he still loved her, she didn't deserve him.

Winter reached over to the bedside table, fumbling. Her phone was in the same place she always left it thankfully. There were no missed calls. That was either a very good sign, or a very bad one. She pressed and held down the #2 button until it began calling. Tor answered on the third ring.

"Tor!" she practically screamed in to the phone, "You're home."

There was a faint rustling on the other end of the line.

"Of course, I am. And I *was* still sleeping, Win. It's not even 10 yet. On a Saturday," he added with dismay. It was true, she roused him from his sleep; his voice was thick with it.

"Oh, sorry, Babe," was all she could manage. None of the other options, or questions she wanted to ask, seemed worth mentioning now.

Winter was unsure just how to proceed without damning herself completely. If he wasn't angry with her, she didn't want to start either of their days out by giving him the opportunity to change that. Luckily, he changed the subject before she was forced to speak.

"How are you feeling, Babe? You were so sick last night. Your fever was through the roof! We barely got to hang out at all backstage." Tor sounded genuinely worried, and more than a little disappointed at his version of the course of events.

"Better, I guess, but I don't...really remember much. My head hurts." Winter said truthfully. She tried to sound agreeable and pitiful simultaneously.

"Well, it should. You went down like a sack of potatoes in front of the whole band, Win. Shade looked totally disgusted and made me leave with you. If I didn't love you so much, man, I would have been totally embarrassed." She could hear the pretend scorn in his words. "But, they made their limo bring you home, so I guess that was something."

She worried the frayed edge of her green quilt, "Yes, that is something." She tried to sound interested, but in truth, Winter was miles away; miles farther than her Aunt downstairs mopping the kitchen floor, miles farther from Tor in his bed. None of that seemed familiar. She had a sinking feeling that Tor's night and hers were very different.

"Winter, you still there?" Worry returned to his voice.

"Yes. Yeah...I'm here. I think I...need to get some rest, Tor. Still feeling a little off, I guess. I love you," she said optimistically.

"I love you too."

***

She still sounded bad. Tor doubted Winter slept much last night. She sure didn't sound as if she had.

Last night was an adventure, though. That was the only way Tor could describe it. Between having front row seats to the biggest show of the year, then getting to hang backstage with the band, albeit briefly, man, there wasn't much better in life than that.

And of course, there was Winter's run in with Shade. The lead singer saved her from not only being crushed by a heavy metal fire door, but also personally escorted her to the green room. Tor was a little disappointed she didn't try to get an autograph out of it for him. Thankfully, she didn't do that weird aloof thing that she was perfecting lately and she certainly *tried* to enter into meaningful conversations with the band from what he could remember.

Tor rolled over and pressed his palm against the pane of glass in the window just above his bed.

When he picked her up last night before the show, he offered to let her spend the night after the concert at his house, hoping in the back of his mind that it could have been a special night in its own way, but no. Winter wanted to go home, and when the guitarist who was sitting on the couch in the green room next to him heard him ask her again if she wouldn't just like to stay with him, Tor could have sworn that he *growled* at him.

No, it was probably just the noise of the wheeled speakers being rolled down the narrow hall, Tor told himself dismissively at the time.

Of course, shortly thereafter, she decided to faint, for the first time he could ever remember. Well, if anything good could be said about the evening after its abrupt end, it would be that thankfully Bren wasn't waiting up for them. Winter didn't mention he was going to be in town, but she wouldn't have dared broach that subject with him either.

And Tor swore he saw his expensive car in the drive last night.

***

She hit the END button more times than necessary, but it was a habit. Winter flipped the phone open and closed.

Open and closed.

Wondering where her memory of the night before went. She honestly didn't remember her evening going the way Tor described. None of those surely memorable moments rang a bell, and Winter was pretty certain that if she passed out cold in front of the super-hot lead singer, she would have the wounded pride to prove it. Nothing about the evening reeked of that kind of embarrassment.

Open. Closed.

Open. Closed.

Open...

And then on the third flip, she noticed a text message in her inbox. Her fingers shook as she pressed the necessary keys to retrieve it.

HOPE THIS MORNING FINDS YOU WELL AND REFRESHED MY BEAUTIFUL WINTER

She didn't recognize the sender, but that didn't matter. Winter knew, of course she knew, it was from *him*. That only confirmed her suspicions about Tor's account of the evening being wrong. She pressed and held down the key to call back the sender. It rang once before he picked up.

"Are you well, my pretty Winter?" His voice came out like spun silk, dark and luxurious, even over the phone. Waves of lust crashed down on her, just as uncontrollable as they were the night before. She may not remember everything, but she did remember that part. She also remembered her wanton attack on him, trying to rip his clothes off like a deranged super-groupie. Winter felt a hot blush sprint over her cheeks, and just like the night before, she was ashamed.

"Y...yes. Um. How did you know it was me calling you? I don't remember giving you my number," she accused halfheartedly. "I don't remember anything actually," she added.

It was all she could say.

Winter was trapped, her throat tight with his memory, his voice, and his presence as if he was here with her even now.

Her bed felt wrong.

It should be bigger.

It should be his. She had the feeling she didn't spend the whole night tucked in safe at home as Tor would have her believe.

Winter sighed contentedly at the idea, which too, was all wrong. She tried to tell herself she loved Tor and didn't know a thing about this man, that she should use this opportunity to say goodbye and forget all about him.

"Shall I come for you? We could do anything you want," his quiet voice, tinged with a smile, brought her back to their strange conversation. The one she couldn't believe she was having.

He was in bed too; she knew it without him telling her. She heard the soft rustle of fabric over the phone line, the slide of a body over sheets. It sounded wonderful. Winter wished she was there with him. The longing for him she felt was surprising, and unbearable.

"Yes," she whispered, not believing the words she was saying. And then the line was dead.

Great.

Chapter Nine

Kieran wondered if she would call him back, if she would realize who the message was from. He had to admit he was pleasantly surprised that she responded so quickly. Their meeting last night had been all too brief for his liking, briefer even for her, since she was unconscious for a lot of it, but he was confident that he had made a necessary connection with her.

And now he was reassured.

After Dugan took her home, he crawled up into his big bed and wrapped the covers she had slept on, around himself, surrounded by the magical scent she left behind. She smelled exquisite; her beautiful, wild smell was trapped in his nose, wiggling its way into his brain and sleep had come so sweetly last night that even in slumber he dreamed of his queen. He was sure he could fall asleep with her in his lungs every night if she was his.

The Dark King lounged about only a few minutes more before rising and preparing himself to meet her.

Kieran actually felt some giddiness, some nervousness at seeing Winter again, wondering if the magic they shared would disappear when faced with the brilliant light of day. He wanted nothing more than to go to her as just himself, as a king to meet his queen, but it was not yet time for that. She may have seen him truly last night, but it was too dangerous to reveal himself again in the human world. Kieran regretfully pulled on his most subtle rock star glamour, toning it down lest she have a protective human guardian who would be frightened by him. He couldn't believe that any of the White Fae would be there, watching over her. Still, he left enough of his hardened persona showing, the one she would expect, and softened his rougher edges enough not to scare her.

But she wasn't scared before, was she?

He didn't bother with any meal or news of the Court that would have normally started his day. Kieran was singularly focused on the goal at hand. He needed to woo the future queen, and he would need to make it impressive.

Today was going to be a revealing day.

He needed to know about her, where she had been all this time. Most importantly, he wanted to find out how long his brother had been hiding her.

A light tapping at the door preceded Dugan's entrance. It was his own fault that he allowed it. He had been without a companion for so long that his captain no longer waited for him to grant permission to enter. Kieran eyed him fiercely.

That would all change when he no longer slept alone.

***

Winter jumped up immediately after the phone call, no longer feeling poorly, but alive. Shade was coming here, to see her. She eyed her space, her sanctuary, warily.

84

Her room was a wreck, unmade bed and piles of clothes were everywhere, but she wasn't worried about him coming up there. Winter was more worried about the prospect of finding anything that was presentable, and at the same time, clean to wear. Her concert dirty hair was a stinky, smoke laced mess, though she doubted the smell would bother him.

He should be used to it.

Winter, on the other hand, was not. She showered quickly and thoroughly, and then dashed to her closet, flinging open the door and peering inside with trepidation. Somehow, the basic staples of her wardrobe were not feeling adequate for her king.

Why did I just think that?

"Winter, dear!" Her strange reverie shattered.

She turned, clutching her damp towel to her chest, to see her Aunt Ramona, her slight shape, graceful and lean, in the doorway behind her.

When Winter was a kid, she thought her aunt was the most beautiful woman she had ever seen. Even now, there were very few women that Winter ever met who could rival the delicate beauty her aunt possessed. She always looked exactly the same, young and pretty, for as long as Winter could remember.

Beautiful or not, she still had a temper, just like Winter and at this time she was blissfully unaware of her new ink and Winter would like nothing more than to keep it that way.

No, today isn't the day to tell her. The prospect of discussing her decisions behind getting a tattoo with Aunt Ramona was less than appealing.

Probably more so than usual, since Bren arrived back in town last night. The two of them could deliver a tandem scolding that would have shamed even the most defiant teen.

"You have a visitor, Sweetie. Did you remember Bren was here?" She smiled happily at Winter. Whenever Bren was in town, she was always in a good mood. She seemed lighter, both emotionally and however improbably, in her physical appearance as well.

"Yes, of course I did, but..."

But.

Aunt Ramona gave her a stern look that told her that any reason for not going down for a visit with him would be viewed as unacceptable and Winter thought better of mentioning that she was going out.

"I'll be right down," she told her, then Aunt Ramona was gone.

Winter was nervous.

She was excited.

Peering into the frightening depths of her closet, she searched frantically for the perfect thing. She wanted, *needed*, something worthy, something sexy. Eventually, she settled on a long black skirt, with Chaco's and a pale, ice blue tank top.

Winter skipped down the stairs, with a heart light as air. She thought she could juggle her visit with Bren effectively enough that whenever Shade did arrive, it would not be World War Three if she left. She entered the sitting room to find Bren frowning worriedly in a deep conversation with Aunt Ramona.

Her Aunt was sitting beside him, her hand on his knee in a comforting way.

He looked like he was scolding her.

Winter pressed her back against the wall of the stairwell and ducked out of sight before either of them noticed. She wanted to hear what they were saying.

He was angry with Aunt Ramona, she could tell.

Chapter Ten

"What do you mean she came in *unconscious* last night? Who brought her?" he was distraught and knew it showed. Why didn't his sister call for him if there was a problem? He specifically left instructions that she was to do just that if he was not here when something happened. Bren cared for Winter more than anything. It would have been easy for Ramona to find him.

Even though they already carefully engineered a predetermined arrival for him last night anyway, it would not have been difficult to appear at just a moment's notice.

"Tor brought her home, from the concert," she said brusquely, not lingering on a subject she knew he already despised. "Besides, what could you have done, Bren, that I could not? Would you have tucked her in and watched her sleep, like I did? Of course, you would have, there would have been no difference. I have raised her with some success over the last 18 years, you know." Her tone could have carved ice.

She was right, of course she was. She had done just that, and amazingly too. Ramona had been totally unprepared for the task he had laid at her feet, but she accepted it with alacrity and performed it with the surprising grace and skill which she did everything.

Bren patted her hand. "Of, course. You're right, Mo. You always are. It's just, you know how I worry.

It is getting closer. I can feel it every day. I can barely stand to be here at all anymore, at least not without potentially doing something I would regret." he winced at the weakness he displayed in front of her. Ramona, unfazed, rubbed his knee reassuringly.

"It will be fine, Bren. You have done a good job. She is a good girl. All we can do now is wait. She will make the right choice, don't worry."

It sounded good, what Ramona was saying, but he did still worry. Winter was so fragile. It would be easy for anyone with a cruel and unforgiving heart to hurt her.

Bren couldn't help but wonder if she would ever be safe from it all, the way he always hoped for her to be, but unfortunately, it was no longer up to him. He did everything he could do get her safely to adulthood, and now it was out of his hands.

There was a loud and awkwardly deliberate noise on the stairs as Winter poked her lovely head around the wall.

The look on her face told him she heard every word.

***

Bren looked up, surprised as she came down the final stair with an audible *thump* and the two whisperers pulled away. Aunt Ramona managed to find a smile for her only niece, but Bren still looked worried.

They were talking about her, and she didn't care if they knew she overheard them. She was, as they said, technically an adult and what she did now was not much of their concern.

But it was still touching.

"What's going on here?" Winter demanded, then playfully added a smile. Whether or not they were being secretive, they had her best interests at heart, so she couldn't bring herself to be angry. Bren and Aunt Ramona were dutifully shocked at her scolding. She thought they were mostly relieved that she wasn't going to call them out over their secretive discussion.

"Bren, leave that lady alone." Winter teased.

Bren smiled just for Winter. He had been around, floating in and out of her life, for as long as she could remember. Though he was not much older than her, not even five years separated them, she wasn't quite sure of his real age. He watched Winter grow up, and did some growing up with her too. Bren had always been there to help Ramona with anything she needed, which was good, because she needed some sort of man around the house. She and Winter were pretty good at doing most anything a guy could do, but the extra strength and height came in handy sometimes. And Bren had plenty of both. Besides all of those extras, he was a cool guy. Winter adored him in a brotherly way that bordered on idol worship and Bren knew it.

That was probably only a quarter of Tor's problem with Bren.

Bren's brother had married Ramona or something complicated and intangible like that. The two of them were always vague about the details whenever Winter brought it up over the years, so eventually, she stopped trying to sort it out. What she could gather was that when all of his family were killed in a freak car accident, they left Bren and Aunt Ramona everything--which amounted to a small fortune- and each other.

Now, Bren traveled mostly and saw amazing things that Winter could only dream about, He went to exotic places that she begged him to take her to. He never did, though, telling her that her school was more important, but he always promised to whisk her away when she was an adult.

Maybe that was what he had come to tell me? It was her senior year and her 18th birthday was barely a month ago so surely she was meeting all of his minimum requirements.

Maybe he was ready to make good on his promise?

It didn't really matter why he was here though. Whenever he came home, he was always with Winter and that was what she loved best. Being with him was so much better than being with anyone else, even Tor.

Technically, they weren't family, but Winter loved him that way, not caring about how people whispered that their closeness was wrong. Aunt Ramona never had a problem with it, so it never occurred to her that anyone else should. Besides, he and Winter had that unusual common bond.

Her parents were dead too.

Her dad died before she was born, and her mom passed shortly after her birth. She wasn't even lucky enough to get any pictures of them, so Winter just used her imagination. All she knew was that they were best friends with Bren and his family, Ramona had told her. She had, perhaps out of the loneliness of her own loss, taken over her care and raised Winter from a baby.

Aunt Ramona, who regained her normal and less playful composure quickly, backed away from Bren when he stood to greet Winter. He was as entrancing, as always and Winter immediately felt herself blooming like a flower in spring whenever she saw him.

She could sympathize with Tor's jealousy. No one could ever come close to stealing Bren's place in her heart.

He reached out and grabbed Winter tightly against him in a half bear hug. The air in her lungs was forced out in an audible rush.

"Ugh, Bren, come on, not so tight," she laughed. Winter freed herself from his death grip. Bren smiled at her with enough wattage to illuminate the darkest room in the house. Winter stepped back to look at him appreciatively. She swore she could actually feel his heat roll off of him in her direction. His imagined warmth surrounded her, clinging like an echo of their embrace, still holding on.

Bren stood near her still, invading her space even though their hug ended, but she didn't mind. She could smell that scent that was so particular to him. Whatever cologne he wore, it always reminded her of every scent of summer and goodness rolled into one. She caught little whiffs of it coming from his subtle movements: Pine and earth and leather.

She took a deep breath of him.

Because he always smelled the same, that sameness brought memories of her youth with it. Bren was in every good memory she had.

All the while, they stood together in silence, appraising the changes, or lack thereof, in each other, he never stopped smiling at her. Bren always looked at her like she was the best present he had ever gotten, and it was still Christmas morning. Even now, he was practically melting her with his adoration. Winter felt an answering trickle of sweat slide down the groove of her back in the suddenly stifling heat. The air in the sitting room seemed to shimmer with the dying fire of summer that was trapped low to the ground. She gasped in another breath, fighting for a taste of cool air.

"You okay, Win?" he looked at her questioningly. She just nodded, trying to focus. Her vision had gone a little blurry around the edges when she looked at him. Maybe it was because Aunt Ramona always kept the house warmer than Winter was fully comfortable with?

Bren never seemed to notice the stifling heat, or the cold, for that matter. He was always dressed for summer in every season, it seemed. In fact, just being around him reminded her of summers, and the way they would play in the woods when they were younger. Bren was always Winter's favorite companion, keeping a skilled eye on her on every outing they shared.

She shook her head to clear it of not only the flood of memories, but also the strange sensations she was experiencing. The effects of the fever must still be lingering, if that was truly what had befallen her, brought back by the insufferable heat of the foyer.

Maybe she needed some rest.

Winter moved, wobbly kneed, to sit on the edge of the big, overstuffed couch that was her favorite thing in the sitting room. It was the closest thing to her anyway and she didn't think she could make it farther than that without falling over. She breathed in through her nose a few times to regain control. Bren, suddenly concerned, moved over to her and placed his hand on her forehead to check for a temperature.

"You sure you're okay, Win?" he asked again, throwing a worried glance back at Aunt Ramona, looking like Winter just confirmed his greatest fears.

"Yeah. I'm just..." She wanted to say she just wasn't sure what was going on. She wanted to say that he seemed different, better than normal somehow. She wanted to tell him that she met a famous rock star, passed out in his presence, but miraculously, he wanted to see her again and she was on her way to meet him now.

Instead, she only sighed and said, "I was just on my way out. Will you be here long this time, Bren?" Winter leaned into him apologetically, buttering him up so he would be okay with her departure and hugged him warmly. Bren wrapped his arms around her too. He hadn't seen her since her birthday, and she felt like a horrible person for running out so quickly, when he had been gone for so long.

She had to admit she missed him so. Bren looked briefly hurt at the fact that she had other plans, but recovered quickly and produced a devious smile just for her.

Chapter Eleven

"Yes," he said speculatively, rubbing his chin like a detective. "Where *is* your other half? I am surprised he isn't at your heels already. The sun has been up for hours." Bren pretended to peer around to see if Tor was hiding behind her. Winter tried not to laugh, but it was funny.

Truthfully, Bren wasn't sure if he had ever seen her without Tor in tow whenever he showed up unexpectedly, well, at least, not recently. Before, when she was not quite a woman, Bren would spend most of his days with her, being with her, doing whatever she pleased.

But not so much anymore.

Now, he saw her even less. It was probably to his own detriment that he had to leave her so often, and he was afraid that one day he would show up to find that she did not have time for him anymore, or that she would not greet him the same enthusiastic affection as she did before.

Today may be just that day.

She was leaving. It was the first time she had not dropped everything to be with him.

"I have something for you, Winter," he said with sudden seriousness, intent on recapturing her attention.

She, of course, saw right through his pretend fierce demeanor, though, and said, "Well, give it to me," with all the sass an eighteen year old could muster and snatched playfully at the gift he now carried.

Bren held a silver package carefully in his tanned hand. He knew it looked expensive from the wrappings but he was still surprised when she squealed excitedly, just like a little girl, and kissed him on his cheek. That pleased him more than she could know.

Her good opinion suddenly mattered more to him in recent years than ever before. Bren did not think she noticed his growing need for her approval, in his previous visits, so he was determined to ramp up his future efforts. He smiled at her again and swore that this time, the heat he so hoped they might share one day seemed to flicker back at him from inside her like a candle flame caught in the breeze.

And that flicker too, made him happy. He bent down to kiss her cheek, holding his gift for her hostage above her head.

***

His blue eyes, the color of the Caribbean ocean, glimmered with anticipation when he held the gift out to her. That was what she noticed first, before the apparent weight of the package. The contents of the silver wrapped box *thunked* loudly as he held it high over her head. She gave him a narrow stare, then Winter dutifully turned her cheek, presenting it to him so that he could lay one on her. And with just the slightest touch of his lips to her skin, she was ablaze.

That was strangely unexpected.

His lips reminded Winter of the feel of the late summer sun, like it decided to shine a potent ray of its pure, hot light on her and that Bren was only its conduit. Until that very moment, she hadn't realized just how much she missed Bren. Of course, she always missed him when he was gone on his trips, but this time, she felt the pain of his absence more severely in the wake of his return.

And that was strange indeed. New.

Apparently, there were many things she never noticed about him before. He was so handsome. Every woman, and certainly all of her own female friends, not that there were many of those, fell in love with him instantly. Honestly, though, what *wasn't* there to like about him? He was tall, blond, and tan. Rich too. But to Winter, he was just wonderful Bren.

He stretched his hand out, offering the gift to her. As she took it, he slid his index finger gently along the back of her hand, leaving a surprising trail of flame in its wake. She snatched her hand back suddenly, confused about his strange new effect on her.

Winter dared herself to meet his eyes again before opening the exquisitely wrapped package, to see if there was something there that she missed all these years. All of her friends said that it was his eyes they fell for. Of course, the eyes. The strange Caribbean blue of them was impressive. He was looking at her too and he held her gaze as long as she cared to look without making her feel uncomfortable. Yet, it was different.

It was true, somehow looking at him now, touching him now, was not the same as it was when they were kids. Winter dropped her gaze and shook her head slightly, blinking rapidly in disbelief. Maybe the remnants of the supposed fever were making all of her female hormones rage in strange and overactive ways. She took a clearing breath and looked up to see that he still held out his token to her.

"Th... Thanks," she managed weakly. Winter stared down at the small, flat box, taking it from him, barely seeing it but still curious about what was inside. She rotated it slowly in her hands, listening to the heavy object strike the hard, paper sides thickly, wondering if she should open it now or wait until she had more time to give him. Winter wasn't sure when Shade would come for her. In fact, she forgot all about him in Bren's presence. Still, Winter hated to hurt Bren's feelings by taking a gift on the run.

She was still considering her options when the doorbell rang. Winter jumped and dropped the gift to her feet. She bent down to retrieve it and Bren started for the door.

"Should I get it, Mo? That's probably Tor anyway, isn't it, Win?" he asked teasingly. Winter could swear that there was a touch of sadness in his honey coated voice, hiding just below his playfulness.

As he walked, she noticed the room seemed to lighten wherever he went. Winter never realized how graceful he was. He was at the door faster than she could have thought possible and Winter was suddenly filled with the strong desire to keep him away from Shade.

"I can get it," she said hurriedly and brushed ahead of him a little more roughly than necessary, only to catch the door knob as he did. Their hands touched again, setting off the same intense, white heat inside her.

What in the world is going on with me?

Winter's mind instantly filled with the images of pale, fragile flowers and new wheat waving gently in the breeze.

She froze and looked back at Bren over her shoulder. *What the hell?*

All she could manage was, "I need some more room, Bren," in a whisper.

Obligingly, he backed up half a foot, which was not nearly enough distance for her to remain unaffected by him. His body heat and familiar smell enveloped her, blurring her vision and making her head pound uncomfortably with the strange increase in temperature.

Winter fought through the fog and remembering her guest, stood on her tiptoes and peeked out the little window in the center of the front door, but all she could see was a large black SUV out in the street. It looked expensive and she knew who would have arrived in it. Giddily pleased, she flung open the door.

And there *he* was. Dark and gorgeous, calling to her in a way that he most certainly shouldn't.

Shade.

Some dark, undiscovered part of her soul sang joyously at the sight him, pulling her toward him as if they were two magnets held only inches apart. Waves of lust crashed over her. Winter bit back an embarrassing sigh of longing and just stared at him hungrily. Unfortunately, there was no way to conceal the rush of blood that had flowed to her face, coloring her cheeks a vivid red. She tried to rein in her blatant ogling to keep from offending her family, but Bren surely noticed her strange reaction to her guest.

Every bit of her rational self screamed *danger!* and *stay away!* at her. The same way it did when she and Bren came across that rattlesnake in the woods when they were small.

Shade leaned casually against the door jamb, dressed fully in black, of course. He had not looked at her yet, but was staring past her intensely at Bren and Aunt Ramona beyond. Winter hoped he wasn't disappointed to see she lived a tragically normal and decidedly unglamorous teenage life. The absence of his eyes on her felt like it would tear a hole in her heart, ripping her uncomfortably, causing her to suffer in plain view of everyone. She fidgeted, hoping to catch his interest once again.

Winter felt Bren behind her, pushing up against her, crowding her; inadvertently leaving little flame kisses all over her skin where he touched her. She tried to push him back, giving him a signal that personal boundaries were still called for, but he was always right there, always touching her.

What a fine time go all protective, Bren.

"What a lovely surprise to see you waiting and ready for me." Shade glared at Bren menacingly and she could swear that his black eyes flashed a predatory warning. Winter couldn't be sure, but she almost thought Shade wasn't talking to her, wasn't congratulating her on waiting dutifully, at that precise moment.

There was an unhappy period of male posturing at the front door and Winter felt trapped between the two of them, felt forced to choose a side in case a fight were to break out. She was smothering under the weight of their two distinct and opposing personalities.

The air behind her was warm and arid, familiar and inviting. At that moment, trapped in the sweltering heat Bren created, her fear of Shade seemed overwhelming and she almost changed her mind. Winter thought about closing the door right then and there, and forgetting Shade forever. She could be just as happy to stay home, stay with her Aunt and Bren. Somehow, Bren knew she was thinking of him because he put his hand on her shoulder protectively. Winter felt the heat hidden in his skin flowing into her, making her brave. Then, it became too much and she started to sway on her feet drunkenly. Winter was afraid she would faint again.

Shade's hand twitched slightly and it looked briefly like he would like to reach out to steady her, or better yet, reach past her and throttle Bren for trying to lay an obvious claim on her in front of him, but he didn't move. Instead, his stare rested heavily on the silver package she still held in one hand, down by her side. Winter, feeling very guilty, hastily hid it behind her back and he smiled in approval, then lifted his eyes back to Bren.

"Boys," she cautioned playfully and muscled herself free.

Shade turned his full attention back to Winter's face and held her with his gaze the same way that poisonous serpent held her frozen in fear before. It felt like her life was on pause until then and now, the reel began to move again, making the players in this strange drama resume their story.

A strange breeze picked up and darted in and out of the leaves of the big tree just outside. Leaves, fallen to the ground, swirled in a violent dance toward the porch. Winter felt tendrils of cool breeze kissing her face as it snaked around the rock star, through the open door. Its chilled fingers, cooled by the coming autumn, caressed her intimately, driving back the languid warmth that she felt from Bren's touch. The slivers of fall that were carried in the swirling air slinked around her, over her arms and neck and even reaching through the thin fabric of her skirt, cooling the skin on her thighs. Her hair twisted about her face, toyed with by unseen hands and Winter blushed at the strange intimacy. Then she shook Bren's hand off her shoulder.

There would be no claims laid on her.

Not today.

She handed him back the gift, with an apologetic smile and stepped closer to Shade, making her choice.

***

When it was clear her choice was made, at least for the time being, Kieran felt confident enough to deliver a warning. He was going to enjoy this part.

"Back off, Brendan," he growled in a feral way. It gave him more pleasure, putting him in his place that way, than he experienced in a good many years. Winter just stared at him, shocked he assumed, that he would even know her would-be savior's name. He gave her a slightly apologetic smile that he hoped would hold her over. The uncertainty on her face when he spoke earlier, wondering whether he truly had been praising her for diligently waiting at the door did not go unnoticed by him.

Kieran gestured, oddly formal for the situation, for her to lead the way to the waiting car and, as she passed, he placed his cool palm on her back, not on the pretty shirt she chose but he let his hand slide up under the thin fabric to rest on her sweat dampened skin. He felt her shiver with pleasure, or at least he hoped that was what it was, and it buoyed his spirits even more than her choice to leave with him. She loved his touch, and he loved to touch her. This was good. Kieran was happy to let Brother Brendan fume in the doorway if he must.

The battle lines were drawn now, and he was not afraid.

Chapter Twelve

Winter let Shade guide her away from the door, pretending not to notice the way his skin felt on hers as he slid his hand deftly under her shirt, but she paused on the top step of the porch and looked back over her shoulder one last time at her makeshift family. Shade had already made it down the stairs, but he too, turned, to wait on her.

Aunt Ramona was red faced in the doorway, puffing like a marathon runner and giving Winter a look that meant she would be in no small amount of trouble when she got back, but for what, she had no idea. Bren was shaking with the insult and livid beyond necessity called, for the situation. There was more fueling his anger for some unknown reason. She comforted herself with the obviously false thought that maybe it was just a state of profound shock of seeing her accompanying anyone other than Tor out of the house. Especially when that someone was a super-rich rock star who just, in no uncertain terms, told Bren to butt out.

No, Bren would not have liked one thing about that encounter.

And Tor wouldn't like this outing between her and Shade either. His jealousy of Bren led to more than one "mantrum" in the past and her associations with Bren were infinitely more defensible than this one would be. There was, truthfully, no good reason for her to be doing this. The worst she could have been accused of with Bren was that she would merely turn off their cell phones and watch scary movies on the couch. That was hardly the capital offense that sneaking off with the lead singer of her boyfriend's favorite band would be.

Winter told herself she refused to think about Tor. She also refused to look back at Bren's face, trying to forget his ocean eyes, his summer heat and inspired touches. She just really didn't understand what was going on with him either. It was a little off-putting. Why was being in his company so different this time than any other time in her life?

And then, of course, he practically tackled her away from the door when he saw Shade on the other side.

Stupid male protectiveness.

But it was a little sweet that he did so. Bren was always keeping her best interests at heart, she told herself. Besides, Shade was probably a little scary at first to most people, just not her.

Winter banished her fleeting urge to turn back to Bren and nestle into the safety and warmth of his arms. It still felt a little like she was betraying him to leave with Shade this way, but in the end, she decided she did not owe Bren a thing.

Her new companion was still looking at her questioningly. "Have you forgotten something?" he purred at her.

"No, I...I," but she still hesitated before saying, "I'm ready." Winter did not add the *"I think,"* at the end, but it was only because she forced the words back

106

down her throat at the last minute before they could escape and give her away. She looked to the dark and decidedly delicious rock star waiting for her on the bottom step, as out of place on this suburban street as could be, and he gallantly offered her his hand. She took it tentatively, afraid that even the slightest show of affection between them would anger Bren more and he really would come barreling off the porch and tackle her date. Shade started walking toward the waiting SUV, dragging her along behind him. Winter had to run down the three stone steps to catch up or risk falling flat on her face.

That teasing autumn breeze rustled the leaves in the giant oak tree just outside. Winter noticed that their colors had started to change beautifully, filling them with orange and golden fire. A murder of crows had alighted in the massive tree and they called angrily, taunting as she moved quickly down the sidewalk with Shade.

He helped her into the car graciously, touching her in a way that was all-too-familiar for the small amount of time they spent together, but still completely satisfying. Then again, she had tried to take all off all his clothes off in a very easy way last night, so maybe he felt they were already at that place where touching like that was perfectly acceptable.

Shade *had* stopped her though, an unlikely gentleman to her rescue, and even after stopping her, he wanted to be with her, spend time with her still.

So that was something.

Winter did not stop him or force his hands into neutral territory, but let his hand drift down her back as he helped her in and felt him trace the curve of her bottom as he followed her into the car. She sighed deeply; the tremor of need he caused in her was fantastic.

She also secretly wondered if that lascivious display was for Bren's benefit as well as her own.

"Let's go," he directed and tapped on the seat back. His driver started the car that would roll them away from her childhood home. Bren and Ramona were both standing on the porch and they didn't look happy.

***

Bren watched the dark SUV pull away, then turned back to Ramona with his fist balled at his side, the discarded package still in his other hand. He wanted to hit something, destroy anything into a thousand pieces, but that was not his way. Violence was never the answer, but sometimes he couldn't help but think it might make him feel better. He needed to do *something*. Bren spied Kieran's pet crows in the Oakman's tallest branches, still obnoxiously taunting him. The Oakman, a secret sentinel he had placed here 18 years ago to protect the home or provide a warning if need be, waved violently in a breeze that wasn't there, trying to shake the raucous birds free. They clung tight, gripping with jagged claws to the thin upper branches, mocking him. Bren concentrated on them, focusing all of the heat of his anger, his frustration and other pent up aggravations, holding them firm in his stare, until they were blanched of all color. Now, the once ominous black birds were blindingly white, a stilted symbol of purity. They screeched at his offense and took to the skies, finally leaving them in peace.

He felt much better. Kieran would be angry at that; he loved his birds very much. Bren took in a deep breath or three, then turned to his half-sister who was still waiting for him to speak, silently standing by the open doorway. He brushed off his temper tantrum with a shrug and a roll of his head. Ramona put her hand on his shoulder comfortingly and he almost broke down right there, but managed bravely for her.

"We did so well, Ramona. I thought we had done so well." He hung his head in defeat and retreated back into the sanctuary of the home he created for them here. Ramona followed behind him at a respectful distance. He had tried to break her of that habit, since they weren't back at Court, and she was practically his equal there too, but her old ways were not easily forgotten.

She coped admirably in this world, caring for Winter, but he knew she wished she was home again. Perhaps, soon, she would be.

However she felt about her isolation, she never complained. He trusted her, and that was enough for now. Bren dropped the forgotten present on the low table nearest to him and flopped down wearily on the overstuffed couch he always used in the sitting room. This was his favorite room in the house. The light here was perfect, streaming in from the windows at all times of the day. In a way, it reminded him of being back at Court, the way the light was always so bright, so warm.

His comforting thoughts were interrupted by Ramona's pleas for forgiveness.

"I did not know they met, Brendan." Ramona said apologetically coming to join him on the fat sofa. That was true. Fae couldn't lie after all. "I did not even know where she went last night until the boy brought her home and I did not think... She was unconscious, Bren. At first, I thought maybe it was true, that she had been sick. You don't think..?" Ramona wrung her hands regretfully. "I am so glad you came. I should have called you sooner. You were right, you always are, My King."

"No, I *don't* think," he snapped and then thought better of it. He should put on a brave face for her. "I know you are worried, my dear. Of course, I came. How could I not? I should have been here anyway. It is my fault."

Bren silently berated himself for not being strong enough to stay around Winter without losing control. It was getting harder every day, as she grew, to be around her without falling at her feet to beg for her love.

He took another steadying breath and added, "Kieran threatens everything we have fought to protect. I just thought we had more time. I wanted her to love me. I thought I could wait out her fascination with that *boy*." He practically spat out the last word. "We should have stopped her. We should have ended it between them sooner. If we had acted, shown ourselves, we could have kept her from *him*." He sighed deeply and the air suddenly smelled of freesia.

"You did what you thought was right, Brendan. And to manipulate the girl, or cause her sadness, that is not our way, brother." Ramona reminded. "We can't take someone's choices away."

"Did she ever have choices?" he countered wearily. Bren raised himself from the couch to stomp off across the room. "Her parents' choices define her, as our parents' choices did us. I know what it is like not to have choices." He hoped he didn't sound cruel to his sister.

"We were lucky to find her at all," Ramona reasoned. "What if Serah had lived?" She got that faraway look of remembrance on her face.

"Her parents couldn't have lived. Even if they had, they could not have coexisted. They could never have shared a life together," Bren mused. "A Dark and Light pairing! It would have been like a flame that loved ice. And that they should even manage a child..." He shook his head in wonder. "It was so unlikely." Brendan paced the length of the room, working out his frustration through motion. He stopped at the big bay window and looked out for a long while. Ramona sat still as a statue on the couch.

Bren broke the painful silence first.

"What if he wins, Sister? What if he takes my queen?" The sadness in his voice had been building for centuries, compounding his loneliness and his desire to live the best life for his Court and himself. "Our power will be lessened after the equinox. Kieran will be stronger soon. His draw for her will be very great indeed. Fall is already here, and winter, with its long nights, will only make him bolder."

111

"He won't win her, Brother. You have been with her all this time. You have taught her everything she needs to know. She would never be able to love him, after being taught how to love by you. She *loves* you. The prophecy says she has to choose. She would not be the girl I love if she were to choose your brother. It is not in her nature to side with evil." Ramona was always better with reassurances. That was one of the reasons he picked her to guard his most treasured possession for the last 18 years. Winter was the key to everything." Kieran will never put the work in to keeping her happy, and he cannot harm her in any way. He is as much bound by the rules as you are."

"I know what the prophecy says better than anyone," he said angrily. He was starting to lose it and it was showing. "But what if she loves me the wrong way? She could still love me and choose him; no one said that love and duty are the same." Bren could not stand the thought of losing, not only the friend he made in Winter, his potential queen, but also losing the balance between the courts.

He thought Ramona wanted to say that she would not choose him, but that might be a lie, so his sister remained quiet.

Upstairs, the phone in Winter's room began to ring.

***

Now that he was fully awake, Tor realized how strange their conversation was. Normally, Winter would have told him about her dreams first thing in the morning, because lately, God knows they were getting pretty weird. She seemed out of it, distracted. Maybe it

112

was just the sickness, whatever twenty-four hour bug she had caught, just making her feel bad.

He was probably reading too much into it anyway.

But she hadn't invited him over either, which was also strange, as it was a Saturday. Neither of them ever had plans, *ever*, that didn't include the other. Why would they bother?

Tor remembered with an ache that Bren was in town. Surely, feeling as poorly as she did, she would not take off with him on one of his dumb adventures. Somewhere, deep inside him, a small voice told him she would. She always did anything Bren asked.

Against his better judgment, because he didn't really want his suspicions confirmed, he picked up his phone to call her.

One ring.

Two rings.

Three.

"Hi, this is Winter! I'm not here, ob-vi-ou-sly, but I am assuming you're familiar enough with modern technology to know what to do at the beep." BEEP

Tor hung up without leaving a message. Winter was smart enough to use caller ID. He was certain she would know he called. He tossed his pillow across the room in anger, and it landed in a silent heap on a pile of laundry. This day was going to suck.

Chapter Thirteen

Kieran couldn't take his eyes off the queen.

Did she already know?

He felt like he didn't even have to woo her. She had chosen him so boldly in front of Bren that the Dark King was sure that he already won.

Almost.

Kieran stared at her unabashedly now that they were alone and watched her squirm nervously under his intense gaze. Then he turned away to look out the window, bothered that it bothered him that he'd just made her uncomfortable. Outside, he saw that Bren and Ramona were still on the wooden porch glaring daggers at him.

"Drive, Dugan," he growled, tapping on the seat back, "I said, let's go," and the car crawled forward. Feeling a little less unsettled now that they were in motion, he held his arm out to her, never looking at her and still Winter snuggled up close to him, letting her cheek rest on his chest.

She must surely know what she was doing to him?

He wanted to grab her up in his arms, and kiss her right now. If she had been anyone else, he could have, he would have already, but he was afraid of the queen. Of course, Kieran was not frightened that she would harm him, which he doubted she could ever do.

C. B. Cole

He was more afraid of what she could do to his soul, if she were to choose Bren instead.

If she were to reject him, even though he didn't think she would, he would have to be cruel to her. He would be forced do things that would be deliberately spiteful. Kieran let his fingers knot up in her hair, tighter and tighter until she winced visibly and fidgeted to be free of his grip.

He hated to hurt her, but touching her like that was one thing he could allow himself to do without fear of losing control. Much more intimate contact than that, even simply holding her body against his own, could be too much of a temptation. He came so close last night, and he was pushing himself to the limit again by letting her press against him in that way.

"How do you know Bren?" she asked suddenly, sitting up while her small fingers played with a button on his black shirt.

He continued to look out the window, watching the unseen denizens of the city, members of his Court that had come to catch a glimpse of the queen, slink back from his car as they drove by and fan out again in the wake of his passing, rejoicing after they had safely gone.

"We move in the same circles sometimes," he said by way of a reply. He knew it was deliberately cryptic, but he didn't care. If Bren hadn't made a move for her yet, thinking he could hide her from him and seduce her at his leisure, he made a poor decision.

Kieran thought he may have growled just now at the thought of Bren seducing the queen, but it was a natural reaction, a rumble deep in his chest. It was unavoidable when he thought of seeing his treacherous brother and half-sister in the doorway of the queen's home, knowing they already spent more time with her than he could ever achieve before it was time for her choice to be made. But if he did make that dangerous noise, she did not seem to notice.

Kieran was mostly mad at himself anyway, and hated to admit that he felt slightly stupid for not thinking of it sooner. He should have known that if Bren and Ramona had found her they would try to hide her, and that Bren would want take his time winning her affection. It was so predictable now, that he couldn't believe he had been so ignorant of the idea. His brother was never the kind to sweep his lovers off their feet, if he ever had any before at all, or make his romantic intentions known overtly. Bren never did have the gift of lust at his disposal like members of Kieran's court did and for that he was thankful. Bren was always so damned concerned with doing things honestly and fairly. Kieran couldn't begin to see the appeal in that.

***

"He never mentions you though." Her statement almost felt like a challenge. Winter was practically daring him to tell her why Bren wouldn't mention that he knew one of the most famous musicians in the world.

Shade sighed and finally turned to face her. It was the first time since the car was in motion that he seemed to remember that she was there for social interaction. Winter cursed herself for being so stupid to think he truly wanted her company.

116

"We don't see eye to eye on a lot of things, My Dear," he said with a tone of finality that told her that explanation would have to be good enough. Shade stroked her hair as she leaned back into him with a "humph" and returned to watching the empty street. He was warm under her, like a stone that had been in the sun for too long and he radiated an intense heat under his hard persona. He wanted to do things, she could tell, more things with her than they had done with their lips, but apparently he wouldn't until she made the first move.

That had to be it, she thought.

Why would he take me out, just to stare out the window in my presence? Surely, he has plenty of other women who would be content to watch him watch the passing houses.

As if he sensed her disappointment, he turned back to her, wrapping her in a tight embrace that held her motionless against his perfect chest. His dark hair brushed against her face and she noticed it smelled not like smoke, as she had expected, but of the air just before snow. He pressed his lips against her neck where it met her shoulder in a sloping arc.

"So you aren't going to ignore me all day, then are you?" she purred, nibbling on his earlobe as she spoke. She didn't think she had ever purred before. *Who the hell am I? I'm not this girl.*

This new Winter had been lying dormant, waiting for him to set her free.

***

"What would you like to do today, Winter?" he whispered in her ear when he could finally find the will to speak. The words slid out of his mouth like melted butter, pooling hot and liquid fire inside her. He felt her melt against him. He liked that, having that effect on her. He thought he would do very bad things to keep her happy. The Dark King hoped they could do bad things together, not only as a couple but as a ruling pair. Their Court would sing their praises and the balance that had been maintained would tip to the Dark Court for the first time in, well, a very long time.

His pulse still raced from her bold move. Kieran could feel the already poorly contained darkness in him leak out into the air all around them. The invisible tendrils of it, his essence, curled around them both, lessening their inhibitions, intensifying their need for each other.

They already made it this far without bursting into flame, without being consumed by desire, he told himself. He tried to be stealthy as he pushed up the hem of her tank top just enough to see her tattoos on her hips again. It felt like she put them there just to torture him, seeing the marks that bravely broke up the monotony of her perfect, pale stomach. He loved the delicate, symmetrical ink on her skin. When his fingers brushed her exposed flesh she twisted beneath his touch, but he didn't think she was trying to get away. It made him very...happy.

She looked wickedly pensive and then said "What would you like me to know about you that you don't share with anyone else?"

It was such a strange question, but it filled Kieran with more joy than his dark heart had known it could hold. She would make a fine queen if she could rule that way, ruthless and unapologetic.

His lips were on her lips, her face, her hair, tasting her. He pulled her close against him and then laid her back on the seat, hovering over her, not daring to press his body against hers lest the Dark King find a point from which he could not return. All he wanted was to see her beneath him, to give him some memory to hold tight within him at night till he saw her again.

"I would have you know all of me, because I share no piece of myself with anyone else but you," he stopped just short of calling her *My Queen*. Kieran thought she wouldn't appreciate it just yet. Instead, he kissed her forehead one time and sat up, leaving her sprawled, panting and desperate for his touch.

It wasn't time for that yet.

"Dugan," was all he said, just enough to capture the other man's attention and his captain nodded at him and closed the glass between them silently.

Kieran pulled her upright, then lifted Winter carefully onto his lap, her thighs pressing on either side of his own, so that he could look into the clear mountain lake of her eyes. The blue of the shirt she had chosen made them sparkle wildly and he was pleased with her choice. Kieran wondered if she dressed that way to please him.

Her eyes spoke words of encouragement to him, told him how close he was to his goal. He grabbed her face in both hands and kissed her passionately until they were both breathless. When he pushed her away in desperate search for air, her eyes were as black as his, and that, too, made him very happy.

***

Maybe she was just in the shower, and didn't hear the phone ring, he tried to convince himself. Winter had done that before, gone off somewhere about the house and not remembered to check her phone until much later. She always left it on vibrate anyway. If she dropped it down in the covers and forgot about it, she would have never even felt it go off when he called.

It wasn't like her not to keep her phone with her if she was out though. Even if Bren was in town, she would have it with her. If she couldn't answer it, she would at least text him back so he would know she was okay.

Something strange was going on.

Tor fought a compulsion to hop in his crappy Colt and drive over there. Instead, he paced the little, untidy living room, frequently looking outside through the big bay window at the street beyond. It was way past lunch time on a Saturday and the rest of the world was getting on with their weekend. He wanted to get on with his weekend as well, but he couldn't find his damn girlfriend, so things weren't quite working out for him.

He hit the #2 button and held it until it rang her number.

One ring.
Two rings.
Three.

"Hi, this is Winter! I'm not here, ob-vi-ou-sly, but I am assuming you're familiar enough with modern technology to know what to do at the beep." BEEP.

"Uh, Win? Can you call me?" He felt stupid talking to voicemail like that. She couldn't hear him anyway. He quickly snapped the phone shut, effectively ending the call.

Tor plopped down on the old, brown, ultra-suede couch that he and Winter rescued from a curbside two years ago and flipped through the channels, all 800 of them, without seeing a thing.

This was Bren's fault. He knew it. Tor could tell in the way she was acting last night that she would rather be home with him than out at the concert with her own boyfriend. She hadn't even mentioned he was in town, but left it up to Tor to discover on his own when he brought her home.

Bren always had it out for him. Tor felt like they were constantly in an ultimate death match for her attentions, her affections. It really pissed Bren off that Tor had won her. He was glad.

Winter picked him.

Tor smiled, bolstered by his small victory and settled on VH1 Classic. He and Winter loved to watch the cheesy 80's videos.

"See there, Win? That's the *Ashes to Ashes* video by David Bowie. It was one of his strangest, I think. What about you?"

The empty spot where she normally curled up like a ball, didn't answer.

***

Winter felt so small in his lap. He was big, tall, and *dark*. He held her protectively, but not like a child. She let him hold her, just so she could enjoy the closeness of it. She was drawn to him and could not deny it, and she certainly wasn't doing very good job of staying away from him either, so why bother trying. Tor would be so disgusted with her when he found out and that unpleasant thought was enough to bring her crashing painfully back to reality.

Winter slipped off his lap without a word and moved across the seat, as far away from him as possible without actually getting out of the car, feeling suddenly very disappointed in herself. She buried her face in her hands, trying to dig up some sort of remorse or regret over what she was doing, but nothing came. No tears, no screaming sadness, only the subtle uncomfortable loneliness she associated with being away from her handsome companion.

Winter peeked out of her web of fingers to see Shade staring at her. He was smiling at her in a very strange way, like he was contemplating whether mental illness prompted her retreat. She stuck out her tongue at him and he laughed. It was a dark sound that rumbled around the back of the car ominously.

"What *are* you doing over there?" he asked. It seemed like she could be a brat and prepare a multifaceted response to his question, but she lacked the energy and resolve to deliver it in the proper way. Instead, she chose an answer she could manage.

"I don't know," was all she said, then added, "I have a boyfriend, you know." She felt horrible confessing this to him. Shade did not look upset though. Then again, why would he?

"So you said last night." He moved across the seat to be beside her. She was suddenly very afraid. He was all around her.

"You had a *boy,* Winter. Don't mourn for his loss. Now you have me," he added brightly. She should have been flattered, should have felt moved by his proclamation, but instead, Winter felt trapped. Fear welled up inside of her, black and molten, for the first time since she was in Shade's presence.

She fidgeted and gasped like a drowning person, twisting away from him in search of air. Instead of relenting and giving her space, Shade drew his face nearer to hers, doing that weird animalistic thing again, then dipped low and drug the tip of his thin, angular nose along her jugular vein, taking in deep, evaluating breaths.

Inside she was screaming, but it only came out as a soft moan.

"Amazing," he said, the words coming out sensuously, then kissed her ever so lightly on her throat.

"What?" she whispered back, desperately afraid she had just done something truly embarrassing.

"I can tell what you are feeling right now and it is *very* sexy. But you don't need to fear me, Winter. I would never harm you."

He started to pull away, but she stopped him. It was true, she could feel terror and fear and sorrow funnel from her into him leaving her blissfully free of any remorse. Any regrets she may have had about leaving Aunt Ramona and Bren shocked and scandalized on the porch, or acting this way--so blatantly whorish behind Tor's back--was gone. Shade consumed it all and left her with nothing but a willing heart.

Chapter Fourteen

The big, black SUV rolled to a stop long before Winter was ready to get out of the car. She hated peeling herself away from Shade, but when Dugan opened the door for her, looking very much like a mafia hit man, she exited. Shade was out and behind her in a flash, his feline movements measured and sensuous.

They had come to a stop in front of the oldest cemetery in town, pleasantly decrepit in a lovely way. Winter always thought it was beautiful, with the big, old trees dripping Spanish Moss. The graves were that way too, moss covered and in various degrees of disrepair, no longer sharp lined after their repeated years of suffering at the hands of the elements.

She had come here a few times with Tor, to take pictures or just skip school. It was always empty. Most of the relatives of the inhabitants were long since dead, or there had been enough generations between the deceased and the currently living that there was hardly ever anyone there. Winter thought it was a perfect place for them to spend the day in relative secrecy, which, she was sure, was something he wanted. Nothing would be more unromantic than to be besieged by screaming fans while trying to learn more about this amazingly delicious man.

The wrought iron gates and tall fence that surrounded it were gleaming in the afternoon sun and their sharp tips pointed gloriously to the sky. Dugan went to the gate and with a pained look on his face, unlatched it and pushed it hard enough that it swung open under its own momentum, so that she and Shade could enter. When they went through, he closed the gate.

"Go take care of your hand." Shade told him dismissively and Dugan nodded.

Shade grabbed Winter by the hand and led her down the narrow, overgrown walkway that sprung up between the most ancient graves. If there was a heart of this place, then they were following a vein directly to it.

"Is that your bodyguard?" she finally asked, after they were deep in the cemetery, far from the road. She felt safer here, like she could be herself. Now that there was some space between them, Winter did not feel the need to undress him as strongly as she had in the confines of the car or bus. Winter was grateful for the gentle breeze and cool autumn day. It was probably the only thing that was keeping her sane.

"In his way, I guess," Shade said, mentally evaluating Dugan's job description. "He is also a trusted friend and advisor," he added. Winter thought that sounded very patrician of him, but didn't say so. She swung their hands gently between them like she did with Bren on their walks in the woods, but then stopped herself. It didn't feel right for her to compare him to Bren.

They left the low, old graves of the previous century behind and entered an even older area, filled with slender monuments to civil war heroes and the

126

beautiful, crumbling angels for children lost too early. Winter found a low roof of a massive marble mausoleum and climbed up to sit on it. She patted the clean space beside her and Shade obliged happily, clambering up in a very real way, not like a rock star would at all. She was glad that they were past that, glad he could be himself with her too, not a famous musician, but just a guy with a girl.

After he was settled to his liking, legs hanging, long and lean, over the dull and rounded edge, he leaned down to nuzzle her neck. She lifted her chin so that he could have full access to the soft skin he seemed to favor. It struck her as a very submissive thing to do and she could tell it pleased him.

They never had to talk much, she noticed. They were both happy just to be with another person that understood them. Winter thought that Bren was the only person that she could do that with, sit in a companionable silence.

Another wave of shame crashed down on her at the thought of comparing Bren to this man. Still, the similarities between them were just as shocking and blatant as their opposing qualities.

"You have me all to yourself," she said softly. "So what is it that you want me to know about you?"

"Whatever you want to ask me, I will answer," he said simply. He put his hand on her knee, drawing shapes on the thin, black cloth with a long finger.

Winter leaned back, supporting herself with straight arms and her palms flat on the cool stone and watched the clouds go by above her, white puffs with periodic tinges of gray, while thinking about what she could say that would not make him find her irritating or typical. The changing shapes rolled by at a pleasant speed, not too slow nor too fast and Winter thought that the day could not get any more perfect.

Tired of living with only the touch of his hand on her knee, she pulled him down with her so that they could both lie on their backs and watch the sky together. The cold marble pressed through the thin fabric of her shirt, making her shiver against the strange chill of the grave so she shifted her position and draped herself on his warm body, resting her head on his chest. Shade toyed with a lock of her dark hair, humming some tune to himself and she thought of things she wanted to ask him, things she wanted him to tell her, but she did not want to pry.

Winter decided on her first question.

"What is it like to tour and perform for all those people? Why do you do it? I mean, aside from the money and fame, obviously." She sat upright, cross-legged, facing him and turned her focus away from the sky to his face, waiting for his answer. She let her hand drift up and down the seam of his shirt, counting the buttons that held on the black fabric. Winter kept telling herself she did not really want to take his clothes off, it was just an infatuation. Still, even in a sitting position, she noticed how she pressed her body against his, letting her thigh and knee and shin rest against him.

"I do it for the fans," he said automatically, no emotion in his voice.

"Everyone says that," she said sarcastically. "Don't you watch MTV? Tell me the truth. I want to

128

know why *you* do it, not what your PR person tells you to say. There has to be a reason that would make you want to get up there every night. The view seems like it would never change."

"No, it never did. Until you." He too sat up, echoing her own twisted form and kissed her sweetly on the top of her head, letting his hand glide comfortably up and down her back.

"It is amazing to see that more people every day love what I do. They are definitely drinking the Kool-Aid, if you know what I mean." He was starting to become more passionate about the subject and Winter watched his hands, gesticulating as he talked. "I love that I affect them in that way. All those people are there because of me. My shows break up the monotony of their boring lives. I give them license to be someone else, even if just for one night." He said each word of the last sentence carefully, as if he was trying to be very selective about what he told her. She wondered why he was so guarded about some things with her, and had absolutely no inhibitions about others.

"And in what ways do you want to affect them?" she asked slyly. He gave her a half smile and she felt like it was her reward for asking the right question.

"I *want* them to let go of their inhibitions and just do what they want to do for two or three hours out of their miserable existence. You were there. You saw them. They were happy to be there. They didn't care about appearances or rules. At my shows, people can be who they want to be, do what they normally would not, because I make them feel good about it." He shrugged, as if the thought just occurred to him.

"But not me," she said as an afterthought. He laughed, low and wicked, at her observation.

"No, not you."

"I must seem very strange then," she mused.

"Not strange, Winter, special." She leaned back again, looking to the sky for inspiration, wondering what she dare ask next after that revealing glimpse into his mind.

A few birds flew overhead, calling mockingly down to them. Winter thought they were crows at first, but then their light coloring made that impossible. They circled angrily above for a minute, calling raucously, then flew away to where their home for the night may be.

"Did you see those birds?" she asked him incredulously. "That was strange. They looked like crows at first, but they were white. I think that's what they were though."

"Hmmmm," he rumbled in agreement. It came out more like a growl than an affirmation.

Winter stared up at the blue sky again and dared herself to ask the question she really wanted the answer to.

"Is Shade your real name? I don't see how it can be. No one's parents are that cruel," she added with a laugh.

Winter felt him stiffen; holding his breath as he seemed to shut down and she wondered what she did wrong. She waited long seconds that bled into minutes until it was clear he was not going to answer her, before she decided she was a fool to think he was treating her any differently than he did any other stupid girl.

***

She got up so quickly and unexpectedly that the loss of her warmth caused him to shiver. Kieran was surprised that she asked the question so soon. She was much cleverer than any of the others were.

He had lain there for a minute, thinking of how best to answer her without lying. He wasn't entirely sure he wanted to lie to her anyway, even if he could. By the time he decided that he would tell her the truth, she was so angry with him she was already walking away.

"It's fine. You don't have to tell me anything," she spouted out quickly over her shoulder, her face flushed with anger and embarrassment as she stomped off down the path. "I know that you probably don't tell people you don't give a shit about things like that. I was such an idiot for thinking that I was different, for believing you when you told me I was special. You probably never stop performing do you?"

She hopped neatly over a gravestone that had fallen into the path, worn down with age and, without missing a beat, kept walking away. He smiled to himself at her brave tirade. Kieran could honestly say no one dared stand up to him before. Well, no one but Brendan, but he didn't matter.

At least, not the way this delicate, dark angel mattered.

The Dark King could not help but let her get a little bit further ahead before he went after her. He wanted her pain of rejection to grow to something so palpable that when he scooped her up in a minute, the sensation of it would be overpowering. But he would go after her. He would always pursue her, wherever she went, forever.

He counted her steps mentally, listening to them grow fainter as she retreated angrily and weighed the virtues of his decision to tell her his name again.

He doubted she would tell anyone.

Who would she tell, besides Bren? He already knew it, so that would hardly matter.

He wasn't really worried about her telling the boy either. If things went the way he hoped, she would never see him again anyway. And besides, what if she needed him?

But then, if she knew, would she use it against him? He hoped not. Naming things gave the speaker power over them. Kieran eventually decided she already owned him body and soul. It probably wouldn't matter if she knew, though he wasn't ready to give up his own secrets just yet.

He finally, after making himself wait an extra minute beyond what he was comfortable with, sat up, then swung his legs over the edge of the marble roof and hopped lightly down without so much as a huff. He was much faster when he wasn't trying to be human and caught up to her before she even got to the gate. Kieran didn't know if the iron would affect her, but he didn't want her physically hurt. It seemed improbable that iron would bother her now, if Bren had been hiding her in the city this long, but all of her recent association with Fae royalty may have awakened some long-dormant aspects in her so he was not going to take any chances.

Winter was a woman now, no longer a child, even by human standards. Things would start changing for her if they had not already. No matter how Bren may try to downplay it, Winter would grow increasingly bored in her human life. Kieran had already seen the way the fae of his Court were drawn to her, once discovering her existence. She would find out soon enough, even if he wasn't the one to tell her that Faerie was waiting for her with open arms. Kieran wanted very much to be the one to tell her about it, but not just yet.

She just wasn't *that* ready.

He slyly motioned to Dugan to open the gate, just to be sure she wouldn't be harmed. If he ever found out that someone hurt her, his queen, he did not want to give voice to the things he would do to them.

"Winter," he called softly. He was already at her heels. The Dark King put his hand on her shoulder and used her forward momentum to turn her around to face him. Unexpected tears poured down her face, and he felt a flicker of shame for being the one to cause them. The shame was immediately buried under a new, and this time, definitely expected feeling.

His heart swelled, like he knew it would, at the rush of anger and sadness she emitted because of her twisted and misguided interpretations of his previous silence. His Court would love her passion. Winter reeled back away from him, apparently reminding herself she was still angry. Yet she remained in his arms.

Winter refused to look at him though, as some sort of last act of defiance. He felt a laugh threaten to burst through his lips at the sight of her, wounded and weak over something that was really nothing at all.

"Take me home," was all she said. Her voice was so quiet, he wasn't sure if he heard her correctly.

Kieran thought that maybe she was not even angry anymore, but possibly just resigned to leave.

He couldn't help himself when he bent down to kiss some of the tears off her damp face, tasting the salty sadness, rolling it around in his mouth like a fine wine. She was exquisite. He leaned in to do it again, but she jerked angrily away.

Could she really not see how much he wanted her?

The taste of her tears in his mouth only made him want more of her, but he would not take from her what she would not freely give.

"Dugan," he called softly, "Do as she asks."

He let her go and she stumbled without his support. Kieran turned and walked away, back into the cemetery, disappearing behind the older stones, leaving her there. Dugan waited at the entrance with his hand freshly bandaged and, when she drew close enough, reopened the gate.

***

Winter watched him turn away from her, turn his back on her and leave her there. In his wake, reality stepped in to fill the void his absence created. She thought of Tor, and how she should just leave, go back to her boyfriend and never see this conceited man again. Shade was probably so used to people giving

134

him his way that she didn't matter to him at all. She had blown her chances with him by proving her intelligence, then stupidly daring to stand up to him. Winter could never be like the vapid groupies he was used to, and she never would be.

And she *did* matter.

She mattered to Tor, if he did not leave her over this, and to Aunt Ramona and even to Bren. She would go back to her normal life, receive her scolding for running off with a rock star from her very disappointed guardians and never see Shade again.

Winter comforted herself with the thought that she was merely star-struck, and resolved to forget about Shade. Decidedly, she began her trek to the exit, but her newfound resolve brought her to a stop, doubled over and frozen on the pavestone path, suffocating with regret.

Bren.

She was cruel to leave him like she did. And Bren's face, the way he looked right before she abandoned him and his gift to take off on a whim, consumed her. It was strange that she should think of him now and be so affected by his hurt when it wasn't an issue before. Yes, they had always cared for each other intensely, but now, she wanted nothing more than to go back to him and make things right, however she could.

She was wrong to come here with Shade.

Winter steeled herself with the thought of Bren and the forgiveness she hoped to garner. She started to walk away again, more confidently this time, keeping her eyes firmly on Dugan as he waited at the gate.

There was something so familiar about him, but she couldn't put her finger on it. She told herself she wouldn't look back, not try to find Shade again, even though a tiny part of her was telling her she should.

Dugan watched her, and then his face twisted into a devious grin. Winter got the impression he was watching something just behind her.

That something caught her hand, pulling her to an abrupt stop. Shade was behind her now, pressed up against her indecently, his arm wrapped across her chest and curved around to cup the back of her neck. Using his free hand, he bent her head to one side so he could whisper softly in her ear.

Winter was terrified, trapped, and ready to flee all at the same time. But all of her trepidation brought something else with it, a wave of pleasure so intense that it escaped through her lips as a soft moan. Her sound encouraged Shade to tighten his grip on her and he pressed his body hungrily against hers.

"Kieran," he whispered to her, "My name is Kieran and that is your first gift from me. Remember it when you are thinking of what gifts you receive today from others. Mine is of infinitely more value to you. Think of me by my name and I will hear it. Call for me when you truly need me, and I will be there." He kissed her ear, running his tongue possessively along its lobe. She wasn't sure, but she thought he might have growled with the pleasure of tormenting her. Winter couldn't see the expression on his face, but if it was anything like she imagined, and Dugan's face led her to believe it was, what he was saying was something that should have been more private between them.

And then, he was gone.

Winter spun around, looking for him, but all that was left was Dugan, waiting for her just past the gate. She left the same way they came, but this time Dugan did not shut the gate behind them.

He held the car door open for her and she got in wordlessly, shocked by the recent events. Thankfully, Shade's bodyguard did not speak to her at that moment. If he had, she probably would have burst into a fresh round of tears. The back seat of the SUV was so vast and cold without Shade's, well, Kieran's, heat oppressing her, that she almost missed him. Dugan finally said he would drive her straight home and did not speak another word for fifteen long minutes. Eventually, Winter couldn't help but wonder why.

"Why don't you speak to me? He does let you talk, right?" she asked curiously when they were less than a mile from her aunt's home on Ashe Street. Suddenly, she was feeling very prickly and mean.

"I mean, I know you *do* talk. Is it because I am just another stupid girl who is infatuated with a rock star? I'm not that stupid girl, you know." Acid coated her voice, though she didn't mean it directed at him. He hadn't done this to her, but Kieran was not there for her to yell at, now that she was recovered enough to be able. Still, she silently raged at the thought of being regarded like that wretched creature she saw backstage the night before.

But Kieran just made it abundantly clear that he didn't think of me that way.

137

Why was she still fuming? Maybe she raged at the thought of anyone else touching him. Her strange descent into this insane obsession with him, a frightening aspect of her newly discovered self, certainly would have been all for throwing jealousy into the fresh mix of emotions.

"No, Winter, that girl, you are not." Dugan said finally, then smiled the most terrifying smile she had ever seen. His eyes, reflected in the rearview mirror, flashed like a great cat's in the dark. Now, she really was afraid, more than she had ever been with Kieran.

She barely waited for the car to stop moving before she threw open the door, not even letting him come around to open it for her. Not bothering to close it behind her, she ran as fast as she could up the walk, onto the porch, then slammed the heavy wooden door behind her. She heard the soft *thunk* of a car door closing, and the great big SUV purred away down the street.

***

One ring.

Two rings.

Three.

"Hi, this is Winter! I'm not here, ob-vi-ou-sly, but I am assuming you're familiar enough with modern technology to know what to do at the beep." BEEP.

"Seriously, Win. You're starting to freak me out. Can you call me back? I don't care if you are out with Bren.

Whatever.

I just want to know you are okay. Call me when you can. It's almost 3 o'clock. I haven't heard from

138

C. B. Cole

you since 10 a.m. Just starting to worry. Call me. Please. Love you, Babe."

Chapter Fifteen

Winter was panting, slumped heavily against the front door. It woke Bren from his nap on the couch. Normally, he stayed in his own room, but he wanted to be there when she came home. He wanted to know if he had lost the war before it had begun, and if she came home damaged in any way...

"Winter? Is that you?" he asked, even though he knew it was. Her heavy breathing stopped suddenly and he realized he must have surprised her. His first instinct was to run in and scoop her into his arms, but she would not understand his sudden irrational concern.

Instead, Bren stretched himself on the couch before getting up to go to her. He felt older in the past few days than he ever had in the long centuries of his life. The worn wood of the floor in Ramona's sitting room felt good against his feet, warm and smooth. He went to her slowly, keeping his eyes fixed on her and his movements deliberate, like he would have if he were meeting a new creature for the first time. And this fragile new creature was Winter, staring at him like a wild thing caught in a trap.

Damn him. Bren thought.

Her beautiful blue eyes shimmered with tears that refused to fall. Those big, wide eyes held his attention. They reminded him of the sky. She was so pure, so perfect. He wondered what she would be like if she were to say the words he wanted to hear. Would it change her personality, her true self, everything he already loved? What would she be like unbound, as a Fae, ruling the Court of Light as his queen? The thought of their future sent a shiver of anticipation through his bones. She looked at him quizzically.

"Rabbit ran over my grave," he shrugged by way of an explanation.

Bren sat on the floor in front of her, cross-legged, like he did when he wore the glamour of a child to be with her. It must have made her more comfortable, to see him sitting like a kindergartner, because she slid down the door and landed with a thump, looking for all the world like a broken, gothic Raggedy Ann doll. She stared at him for a minute, never really seeing anything and he wanted to believe she was composing herself, rather than possibly reliving her time with Kieran. Taking the opportunity presented in her silent moment, he pulled back out the discarded present he brought and offered it wordlessly to her.

She took it from him and smiled. Bren saw the regret and the implied apology it held. Winter continued to hold his gift in her lap for a minute turning it over and over in her hands. Now, more than ever, he wanted to scoop her up in his arms, hold her and smooth her hair and tell her that he loved her, but instead, he did just the opposite.

He did nothing.

"So, Winter," he said calmly, still seated at her feet. Bren knew he would have to play this new role just right so he didn't scare her away or break her trust in him. "I see you know my friend, Shade."

He rolled his eyes and said it in a voice that contained just enough sarcasm that she could interpret their relationship as either a positive or a negative one. Bren wasn't sure what Kieran said about him.

She too gave him a cautious look, wondering what she should reveal of their encounter, he thought. He desperately hoped she would tell him everything.

"He says you aren't really friends," she countered, but said it with little emotion.

"No, I guess we are not that." Bren smiled at her again, letting the full power of his Lightness shine on her. He didn't notice it as a perceptible difference in the appearance of the room, more as just a gentle warming of the air around them. It felt like a softening, a relaxing, a settling of the space around them. There was the slightest scent of cut grass in the air.

Winter responded to it promptly and let the tension she was carrying release just a little. That gave him renewed hope that all was not yet lost. He watched her stretch out, uncurling like a flower in the warmth of the sun. If Kieran had already won her, the benefits of the Light Court would be lost on her. And the fact that she was here, in the home that he made for her, meant that she felt safe here, not with the Dark King.

There was still time for them yet.

"We have known each other for a long time, though," he added as an afterthought, it came too late, sounding disjointed from their conversation, but Bren needed some way to break the oppressive silence. The silence was so different from their usual peaceful quiet

142

they shared. If she wished to question him about his relationship with Kieran, he would be honest. That might be just enough motivation to move the conversation into the trials and tribulations of Faerie, and their bachelor kings. Soon enough, she would need to know everything, and he would much rather be the one to tell her than leave it all up to his brother to spin the tale. Bren knew that in Kieran's version, the White King would not come out looking like the hero.

His spirit lightened to see her relaxing in his presence. Things were getting better now for her; the darkness was fleeing, not able to last here in this place. At least he could offer her that small thing. Bren reached out and carefully pulled a sandal-encased foot toward him. Winter immediately gave in to his intent and stretched her feet into his lap. He slipped off her shoe and held a delicate foot in his hand. Bren stroked the arch of her foot and she giggled. While his broad hands were wrapped about her feet, he focused on spring and summer and heat and white and the smell of rain and let it all flow into her, letting her skin absorb some of his Court. She sighed as he started to rub her feet.

"You have the tiniest feet, Win," he teased, "They have to be aching at the end of every day to haul you around. It is good I am here to rub them, or they would probably pack up and move away while you sleep."

"Hey, my feet are fine. They're perfect." He laughed and she threw the other shoe at his head, which he caught.

She was right.

"Yes, they are perfect." She sighed again and rested her head against the door while he continued to rub, just for the sheer joy of touching her.

Bren, for that moment, allowed himself to believe that she would do well at his side as queen. They had an easy, agreeable way together that would help them lead their people well. The good things in this world brought her so much joy that he thought it not unreasonable to believe that he might too, if she would have him. They were happy when they were together, and that was important. He did so want to make her happy.

"You going to open that?" he asked finally.

The tiny package still lay in her hands, resting on her lap. He gamely tried to put on a hurt face to entice her to do it. He pushed his bottom lip out like she did when she was little and he or Ramona did not give in to her way.

"Sorry! Don't pout Bren. It doesn't suit you at all. Your face is much too handsome to look like you sucked a lemon," she said and gave a halfhearted laugh before quickly opening the package.

Winter pulled the glittery paper off in one fluid motion and tossed it carelessly to the side. She held the white, flat box in her hands, softly as if it were a bird with a broken wing. It looked like she was trying to decide whether she wanted to open it or not.

Bren didn't push her. He never pushed her to do anything. He always wanted her to have choices when they were available to her. He had tried so hard over the years to ensure she had choices, and now, he feared that doing so might be his downfall.

C. B. Cole

Winter slowly lifted the lid off the flat box, not truly feeling worthy of any gift that Bren could give her after her previous behavior. She gasped quite audibly when she saw what it contained. Bren couldn't help but smile at her bewildered expression.

With the care one would use to handle glass, she carefully lifted the thick, silver braid out of its box. It was the most beautiful thing she had ever seen. A wide, glittering rope that twisted like a living thing through her fingers, the weight of it surprising, even though she held the box for a long time before opening it.

"Do you like it?" he asked cautiously. "I have had it for a long time and always wanted you to have it. It was my mother's." Bren looked wistfully at the coil she held gently in the palm of her hand.

She had to swallow many times to clear her throat before she told him, "I love it."

Winter held it up to the light and the sun sparkled beautifully on it, catching each individual hammered strand. The smaller silver twists were pressed with symbols. The five unique strands were then braided together to form the rope. There were flowers, vines, an antlered deer, the lean shape of a cat and the twining branches of a tree. The symbols were small, pressed into a repetitive pattern that reminded Winter of the Celtic knots she saw at a jewelry store downtown. This piece of jewelry was not from anywhere around here. Winter knew it was old, not just because Bren told her it was, but because she could *feel* it.

She turned away and held it out to him so he could fasten it for her.

***

When she lifted her dark hair away from the nape of her neck, he was hit by that most delicious fragrance she always had about her. He leaned closer, pretending to peer thoughtfully at the clasp, but really, he was just finding a way to be nearer to her.

The clasp was easy and he only pretended to struggle with it so that he could look at the graceful line her neck made as it met the top of her back. She moved subtly and Bren jerked back, the licorice and sandalwood smell he always associated with Kieran wafted off her. They had been close today, too close to make Bren comfortable. He dropped his hands from her neck and pulled away. She turned back to him and her face was aglow with the light of a thousand suns.

She may have been close to Kieran earlier, but she was here with him now. He smiled at her, pleased she was happy with his gift.

"You look lovely, Win," he told her.

"Only because of you." She leaned forward and kissed him softly on the cheek. She lingered though, and he thought for a second she was going to kiss him again, but she didn't. She patted his face instead and smiled. "Thank you, Bren. You know I love you."

"I love you too, Win." She leaned back against the door again and fingered the still cool, new jewelry that now adorned her.

The necklace was thick and heavy, a silver braid at least an inch wide that sat close to her collarbone. Bren was afraid that it would be too

146

overwhelming on her small frame, but he was pleased to see it suited her just fine. The silver reflected the perfect whiteness of her skin and made it glow even more, if that was possible. Her eyes, too, were enhanced by the gleam of the silver rope.

They sat there that way, silent, him soothing her tired feet and she gently touching his generous gift, for a long time. The longer they stayed in their companionable stillness, Bren grew certain he could spend the rest of his life soothing her, and do it gladly, if she would choose him. The thought of forever warmed him and the heat from his desire to see it happen, rolled away from him toward her, seeking her out. Winter lounged languidly against the door and began to hum some tune he didn't recognize. She looked at him contentedly and he let himself believe that she would be happy with that life too.

Their beautiful moment was interrupted by the furious ringing of her cell phone.

"It's been doing that all afternoon," he told her in an annoyed voice. She heaved a sigh, lifted herself off the floor and padded up the stairs to her room.

Chapter Sixteen

"Hello?" It was a question, but Winter knew who it was.

"Hey, Babe," Tor greeted her coldly. It was the same greeting as always, familiar, yet not the same. The next question, however, was one she didn't think he ever asked her before. "Where have you been? I've been calling you all afternoon."

He didn't sound angry or accusing, he just sounded like Tor. She reminded herself that she loved him and he loved her. Guilt swept over her, crashed down on her and she could no longer stand up. She fell miserably onto the bed.

"I, uh, I went for a walk." She let the weariness that always came with tears seep into her voice. It seemed wrong to lie to him, and she didn't really want to, so abridging the day seemed wiser. She almost thought he would be excited if she told him who she was with, but then the other questions that might follow would damn her. "Sorry. I missed you." That, too, came out like a question, but it wasn't a lie either.

"I missed you. Should I come over?" he asked. He sounded worried, she thought, but there was something else there, too, that she couldn't yet identify.

She wanted to tell him yes, but instead said, "No, maybe not today, I'm not feeling great and Bren just showed up out of nowhere yesterday like he always does. I think he wants to do something with me while he's here, so, maybe tomorrow?" None of those things were untrue and yet, she felt strangely deceptive.

"Oh, okay. Right, Bren. I forgot." He sounded hurt that she didn't extend an invitation to him. She knew she probably should have, since he was intensely jealous of Bren.

Knowing Tor, he already knew Bren was here, he probably knew it last night, if he was paying attention when he brought her home. In fact, Winter was pretty sure that his poorly-hidden jealousy was providing the strange tinge to his voice. Tor had the silly idea that he and Bren were competing for her affection somehow. Winter couldn't believe that of Bren though. He was more like family. She had never even thought of him that way. Until...

"Hey, Babe?"

"Yeah?" She tried to sound tired, which wasn't too difficult.

"Thanks for coming with me to the show last night. I feel so awful that I dragged you there and then you got so sick. Are you mad at me?"

God, he was such a good person.

He would think that. He would think that her distance was his fault, not hers. He would never imagine that she was making out with his idol in a cemetery downtown. Her betrayal stung that much more now, with him practically thanking her for cheating on him.

"No, no, of course not, Tor. I am just...a little out of it," she admitted. Once the words were out, she

149

realized how true they were. Things were so far from the ordinary today, this week, this last month, that she hardly recognized herself anymore. She was not the same girl. It had just taken her this long to admit it to herself.

Winter swallowed hard, then choked out a jumbled "I love you, gotta go," before she hung up and burst into tears, face down on the quilt. She sobbed and sobbed into the wrinkled, unmade bed, the pale green comforter pressed into her face so that she saw nothing, heard nothing, until she felt Aunt Ramona's warm hands on her back.

***

I love you, gotta go, and the line was dead.

"I love you too, Win," he said, though there was no one but himself to hear the words.

She did not want him.

She did not want him around because Bren was there. That was the only explanation. She said so herself, confirming his suspicions. So now he would sit here and wonder why he could never measure up to Bren in her eyes. It was probably because Bren was rich. Bren lived like a king while Tor lived like a pauper. True, he could not lavish her with gifts the way Bren did, but still, Tor treated her like a queen, or at least, he thought he did.

They were probably together right now, curled up on the couch in the sitting room, planning the adventure Bren always promised her when she turned eighteen. He always said he would take her away when she was legally an adult and he never mentioned that she was welcome to bring Tor.

150

Of course, he wouldn't, Tor thought. They would probably go somewhere really exotic and romantic and when they got back, Winter would have suddenly remembered that she and Bren weren't really related after all and it was perfectly acceptable for them to have a more serious relationship. Tor would be forgotten, cast aside, like she had grown out of him the way a child outgrows a toy.

Tor got up and punched the wall three times, sending flakes of sheet rock flying, then kicked an offending recliner that had the misfortune of being too near. It helped a little.

Bren would not take her away from him without a fight.

A small voice in his head that sounded an awful lot like Winter said *I love you Tor,* and he told himself he was overreacting.

Tor told himself she was fine and resting at home after an eventful night that was *his* fault. She would call him when she was ready and her obligation to be with Bren while he was in town was over.

Winter loved him, and she would never leave him.

***

"What's the matter, Winter girl?" Ramona asked sympathetically while she worked her hands deftly over her niece's back, working out the knots that the tension and stress had formed. That is exactly what she would always be to Ramona, no matter which of her brothers she chose. It was not fair, what this poor girl had to go through. Most girls merely had boy problems. Winter's problems were men problems, and those men were centuries-old kings, no less.

Men or no, they can still act like children, Ramona thought. She didn't envy the child for the decision she would be forced to one day make. That day seemed to be growing closer far too soon.

Ramona was always fonder of Bren. She could relate to him better than she could with Kieran, but they were all still family, even if Kieran left them for the guiles and intrigues of the Dark Court. She was secretly glad that she didn't have to deal with the intense rivalry they shared; brothers, opposing Courts with opposing interests and the simple desire to claim the queen.

If Winter was not the girl she was, so interesting, dynamic and beautiful, maybe the boys would have had an easier time of it. They wouldn't want her so badly, or rather, they would want her as a queen, but not desired the rest of her so badly. The competition over this dear child was too much. It wasn't their fault, any of them. They never had a choice in the matter, Light and Dark, friend or foe. It was all decided for them.

"Oh, Aunt Ramona!" Winter wailed again, a muffled sound escaping the covers, and Ramona let her cry it out in racking sobs.

She always felt bad for the girl. Winter never had a choice in any of this either. Her parents were not her choice. Her life without them was not her choice. The life they left her with was unfair, and what choice she did have left to make for herself, would not be an

C. B. Cole

easy one. What she was and what she would become was nothing Winter could control.

None of it was up to her.

"I think I messed up everything with Tor," she cried, sounding truly miserable. At least she was sitting up to face Ramona now. Winter was beside herself with guilt and Ramona didn't know what to do.

"It's ok, Baby," she said in her most soothing voice. "It will all be ok in the end."

Ramona often wondered if she had done the wrong thing from the beginning by allowing her to be friends with the boy. Even with her true nature bound as it was, Winter had such a potent mixture of the two worlds, Dark and Light that could not be denied. The boy was practically addicted to her; whether it was the goodness in her or the wickedness Ramona didn't know.

What Ramona did know, was that nothing Winter could do would ever be enough to free him of his fascination with her. She leaned toward the girl, offering her arms, wide open and comforting. Winter collapsed gratefully onto her shoulder in a new fit of emotion.

Bren was upset with her for allowing it to continue, but how could she deny the child even the joy of true friendship? Bren barely had the strength to be around her anymore and still maintain his control and his glamour, especially after wasting so much of his time by remaining near her in her youth. How could he ask her to deny the child a companion who was not asking the world of her? Her brothers already claimed Winter's future, one way or the other. It seemed wrong to be so cruel.

Ramona stroked Winter's back until she stopped crying, long minutes later. She never asked exactly what she had done to cause her to think that her relationship with the boy was over. She didn't want to know if the battle for her affections was won and lost in a single day. When Winter regained some composure, and clamored back to an unsupported sitting position, she looked at her Aunt with red and bleary eyes.

"What am I going to do, Aunt Ramona?" she croaked.

"You should go for a walk with Bren. You never have the time with him anymore and it will make you feel better," Ramona suggested. She may be the sister to both kings, but she would much prefer to see Bren triumphant, for both hers and Winter's sakes.

***

Winter agreed with Aunt Ramona on most things she said, because it was clear that she put time and thought into every word she uttered, so when she suggested Winter go back down and spend time with Bren, it seemed like a fantastic idea.

"You're right." Winter's hand flew to her neck subconsciously and touched the silver necklace he had given her, now warmed to her body temperature.

"Oh, that is lovely," Aunt Ramona told her. "Was that Bren's gift?" Winter thought Aunt Ramona must have known that it was, because the look on her face told Winter she had seen that necklace before.

"May I?"

Winter nodded and Aunt Ramona stretched a slender hand out to trace the thin strands of silver. Winter saw in the mirror behind her aunt that Ramona's fingers lingered on the piece that was covered with the flower pattern.

"It is very beautiful, Winter. You are a lucky girl," she added with a motherly smile.

"Yes, it is," Winter agreed. "And I am lucky." She looked down at her clothes and frowned. "I should change," she added.

She scrambled off the bed and scoured her closet with a new determination. Her previous outfit of skirt and tank top would never do for the woods. Besides, it only reminded her of everything she was trying to forget. Settling for a pair of old jeans and a faded flannel that Bren tossed her way several years ago, she padded down the stairs again.

She picked her Chaco's off the floor at the foot of the stairs, still waiting where Bren had deposited them during his very gracious foot rub, one slightly farther away since it was unceremoniously launched at him. Winter slipped them back on and checked her face in the mirror in the foyer. She was still red cheeked and puffy, but it was only Bren and he had seen her in worse ways. She peeked into the sitting room, where she knew he would be holding court.

He was sitting in the big, extra wide chair by the window, practically glowing in the heat from the late afternoon light that beat its way in through the glass.

Winter

He is so handsome, she thought proudly, watching him bask like a cat in the sun, his eyes half closed in pleasure and a slight smile on his face.

Tan, lean, all-American looking, he was practically a walking ad for Abercrombie and Fitch in his plain T-shirt and jeans. And barefoot, he was always barefoot in the house. If he did have to wear shoes, they were invariably some form of sandal. He personified warmth and summer. She always thought he looked like he just came inside from the most wonderful day, with his perfectly-tousled sandy blond hair and ruddy cheeks with a secret spattering of freckles hidden carefully below his tan. He lounged in the chair, a long leg slung over one arm, flipping slowly through the pages of a book of some kind, though he wasn't reading it, merely keeping keep his hands busy.

Winter turned to sneak out, not wanting to disturb him, but a creaky board confessed her presence for her. His head snapped in her direction, but he was all smiles when he spotted her. She tried to hide behind the wall playfully, even though she knew he had seen her.

"Where are you sneaking off to?" He tossed the book at her lightly and it smacked her squarely on her retreating backside. She jumped high and then fell to the ground dramatically, closing her eyes and playing dead. He came closer to examine her prostrate form and she stared at his feet unblinking. Winter let her head loll to one side with her tongue hanging out and then the ground was gone from below her, with nothing but air and Bren's strong arms around her. One

156

of her sandals dropped loudly off her foot, landing with a thud on the wood below.

"Hey! Put me down, Bren!" She laughed though, and he never hesitated for a second before dumping her unceremoniously on the couch. She quickly recovered and twisted into an upright position so that he could sit beside her. When they were both properly situated, she leaned her head on his shoulder as she had done a thousand other times before. It still fit perfectly in that notch just between his clavicle and the ball of his shoulder. And he still smelled the same, like pine and sun and light. Winter drew in a breath full of him and sighed happily, glad to be free of her guilt for the moment.

"Did you want something from me, Little One?" he asked. She couldn't be sure, but she thought something changed in the set of his face after he called her that. Maybe he finally realized she wasn't a little girl anymore.

"Would you walk with me, Bren?" she said it very quietly, like she was asking something impossible and that the refusal she expected was imminent. Winter stared vacantly out the window. "Like we used to?" she added, this time with a little more enthusiasm. She lazily returned her focus to him. "It seems like things aren't like they used to be anymore." Bren kissed the top of her head sweetly.

"Of course. For you, My Dear, I would give you the world."

Chapter Seventeen

Bren could not, in fact, think of a single thing he would be able to deny her, no matter what she asked, when she looked at him with those beautiful, blue eyes. Her eyes held so much promise, so much hope for him.

He took her hand in his own and stroked her palm gently. He let a little extra heat of passion into his fingers and let it flow into her when they touched, to help buoy her happy mood. She was finally over her encounter with Kieran and he wanted her mind off him for as long as possible. If he could keep her thinking about the good times they always shared, maybe she would forget his brother altogether.

Bren was also mad at himself for falling back in to the familiar habit of treating her as a child. She certainly wasn't anymore. Winter was so close to becoming a queen, his queen, and he would need to remember to treat her as an equal. He found her dropped shoe and rose to put it on her small foot.

Bren knelt to replace her sandal the way he remembered seeing Prince Charming do it when they had watched Cinderella so many years ago. She giggled at him and his drama. He imagined the notes of her laugh landed on him like butterflies. He was eye level with the shimmering twist of silver he had presented her with, the first of many of the royal jewels he wished to give her. He reached out and touched it gently.

"The necklace compliments you, Winter," he said, his voice thick with the pride that came with her choosing to wear one of the symbols of his Court.

"I love it," she told him happily. "What do the symbols mean?" Her hand rested over his and she stared at him like she was seeing him again for the first time.

"The vine represents my mother, because she was the thing that held our family together," he said, stroking that strand thoughtfully. "The flowers are my sister, because her beauty and grace bloomed as she got older. The cat is my brother, who was very skilled at the hunt and relentless when it came to the pursuit of his goals."

It was true, Kieran was ruthless, but he thought the way he described him sounded better.

"The stag was me, I guess, because I was strong and the stag protects his herd?" He laughed a little, and she smiled at him fondly.

"I can see that about you," she said. She inspected him and added "And a stag is noble too, like you. He is like the king of the herd. You think you are the king of this house, that's for sure," she teased. She had no idea how close she was to being right. Bren was born to be king, the first-born son of the royal family of the White Court.

"Maybe you're right," he said agreeably.

"What's the last bit? I can't tell. It looks like a tree." She tried to pull the necklace away from her neck so that she could look at it again, but it lay too close. Bren reached back, undid the clasp, and dropped it into her hand so that they could look at it together.

"That is the tree of life. See how there are branches above and roots below? The tree of life is a depiction of how all life is connected, birth and death, winter and summer, dark and light. One thing cannot exist without the other."

"That's beautiful, Bren. This is amazing, the artwork, how did they get the designs on the silver that way, so small but so detailed?" She stroked the necklace affectionately, then handed it back to him so that he could put it back around her neck.

"My father made it for my mother, just before my brother...went on to the other side. He was always good with metals. He died not too long after he gave this to her, and then she died a few years later of, well, I guess you could say of a broken heart. She never did know how to live without him." Bren did not like talking about them, and he hated to give her a deliberately vague explanation of Kieran's defection and subsequent murder of their father, but she wasn't ready for that. He reached around her and deftly secured the clasp.

"What do you say we get out of here, Win? Find some happier times?"

He pulled her to her feet, not because she needed help, but because he was happy to have the excuse to touch her. The heavy door in the hallway was their escape and he moved her to it quickly, wanting to be alone with her and away from this place so badly, he could taste it. He had to find a way to

C. B. Cole

undo what Kieran may have already done to reduce his chances with her.

Bren worried about that too, though his main concern was her. Not only was his future and the future of his Court in jeopardy, but Winter's was as well. In the future he wanted, he hoped he could he treat her the way she deserved. Winter was so precious, like a tiny snowflake in the palm of his hand. If he did not find the perfect balance of his heat or the time he could safely hold her, she would be gone in an instant and he could never find another like her.

Kieran would still try for her though and if he were to suffer her loss, then his people, too, would suffer. It was Bren's greatest hope that he could make everyone happy and in that, find happiness himself. Love and duty were not the same thing, but with Winter as his queen, they could be. He had been alone too long. Of course, Ramona was there for him in a sisterly way, but her main care was Winter.

Now, he wished Winter could find a way to care for him in a manner that she never would've considered until now. Things were changing in her rapidly. The last 24 hours had been intense.

She led him down the sidewalk, and turned to cut through their neighborhood toward the woods they used to play in. She swung her arms back and forth happily, skipping every so often, just as she had when she was small. Bren knew she was not able to think of him as a man worthy of her affections yet. He had made the decision to grow with her, appearing only five years older than her and now, he feared it may have spoiled everything.

Bren wanted desperately to change that.

"Hey, Win! Wait for me!" He jogged to catch up with her and put his arm around her shoulder to hug her closer. She may not feel that way about him yet, but he would try every way he could, to make her see, until he won her heart.

Chapter Eighteen

Kieran sat miserably in his private chamber. He was on the prowl ever since he got back from his doomed outing with Winter, lashing out in anger at anyone or anything stupid enough to get in his way. He pouted in the main room, ranting and raving loudly and kicking the hounds that strayed too near his perch. He even took it out on some of the Fachan, miserable creatures with only half a body, which were too slow to escape his temper. The Dark King was angry, to say the least, when he saw what Brendan did to his beautiful birds, now a sickly white. His response was restrained when he was with the queen, not wanting her to see him erupt, but now, he had too much time to think on it and his opinion of Bren was at an all-time low.

He brought them with him, the birds, to his rooms here in the Royal Wing, lest some of the braver members of the Court torment them. They were still his treasured pets, even if Brendan had changed them.

They were hideous; their brightness unbecoming in this place where darkness was desired above all else. He kicked a few errant brownies out of the way. They had snuck in behind him, delighting in the foulness of his mood, to grovel and dance merrily at his feet. The tiny pack scattered under the bed and into cracks in the walls, leaving the room in a silence that was only punctuated by the infrequent caws of his birds and the heavy breathing of Dugan crumpled in the far corner.

He looked at the crows and then at Dugan, unconscious in a heap, and sighed. The whole Court practically rejoiced when he lost his composure and pounded Dugan into the ground after he reported the details of his ride back with Winter. Dugan should have known better than to scare her, but it wasn't his fault. He could have had no idea what he was walking into.

Adding to his anger was his self-loathing. He hated himself more every minute for what he did, more than he hated any other of the offenses that had affronted him. He was so arrogant and gave away his name to the queen without demanding anything from her in return. Kieran sighed remorsefully. And she wasn't even *his* queen, yet.

It was the right thing to do though, that she should know it in case she ever had a need for him, but he should have bargained. He'd received nothing, and in return had given her much.

A groan from the corner of the room echoed in the cavernous expanse of the royal chamber.

"Shut up, Dugan. You deserved it for scaring the queen." Kieran didn't even look in his friend's direction, didn't attend his crumpled form, but merely sat in a huff on the bed and resumed his obsessive self-flagellation. Dugan deserved his punishment. He practically sent the queen running into Bren's arms and that was unacceptable.

The Court needed to see that I can still deliver justice, Kieran told himself. They needed his anger and

164

his rage to feel alive again, to know that the queen would not change him, if she were to join him. Everything had been so tempered, so balanced, for so long. The White Court was too strong for them to really live the way they would. This perfect balance was killing them.

Kieran provided them enough darkness to survive, with the concerts and the groupies. Those who wished to be a part of the poison he was offering were always best. The sin and wrongness of the acts those stupid humans would commit while he sang were enough for the last few years, but only just. The Court needed the vile side of humanity, just as his brother needed and depended on their goodness.

There was still some darkness and evil in the world, but barely enough. Kieran hated to admit that he was beginning to wonder what would happen to the Dark Court if he had not found Winter soon. Even the most evil residents had begun to wither without the proper violence and upheaval they required. He had been afraid that after this last rising of their power, brought on by the shortening of the days and the approach of All Hallow's Eve, that it would be the last for some of the oldest creatures if he could not sustain them.

But the queen, she would give the Dark Court the extra push it needed, the extra authority they had lacked to act out against Bren. With her, they could run unchecked through the world and the White Court couldn't stop them. They would not be strong enough to push them back anymore.

Kieran flopped back on the bed, and pressed his face into the opulent coverings. He refused to let them be changed or moved in any way since she left, so that he could keep some small piece of her with him. Kieran wanted to *be* with his queen; her memory consumed him in her absence. For the first time in his life, he had a need that he could not immediately fill and it was torture; a glorious, painful torture.

In his frustration, he pounded his fists down silently on the big bed and Dugan stirred again in the corner. It would heal him faster if Kieran could keep up these strong emotions. The presence of these feelings, the jealousy, anger, wanting and lust, were all fortifying necessities that the members of his Court must have to survive. He supposed he owed Dugan that much, a little help for suffering his beating in silence.

Dugan, like the king, knew that the greater good of the Court came first; the Court and now, Winter. Kieran got up and went to him, kneeling at his side. He placed a hand on his shoulder.

"It will be better soon, friend," he whispered. He felt Dugan rally beneath his touch. He was pretty sure he would be back on his feet within the hour. Kieran rose and went to pour himself a steadying glass of wine. He rolled the liquid in his mouth, savoring the flavor. Its sweetness reminded him of Winter again.

He would go to her, if she called for him. He already decided that he would, even if she was not in any danger. The thought of his name on her lips caused goose bumps to race across his flesh. He thought she

C. B. Cole

should know that he would drop everything to be with her.

If she was foolish enough to be with that *boy* when she thought his name, he would crush him just to get him out of the way. And if she was with Brendan, well, he could crush him too.

"Dugan, my friend, let's have a little fun, shall we?" Dugan managed to twist his body into a sitting position and faced his king.

"What did you have in mind, My King?" The words came out slurred through the puffed and swollen lips where Kieran had broken the skin with his fists.

"Set the hounds out for the boy. Let us see how much Brendan is willing to do to keep Winter happy. I sincerely doubt he'll go out of his way to protect the competition." Kieran drank down the rest of the wine, then smashed the glass on the stone floor.

"And when they locate the boy?" Dugan croaked. He was crawling on his hands and knees to be closer to the king. Kieran presumed it was so he wouldn't have to speak so loudly to be heard.

"Have them turn around and come home without him," Kieran could barely believe what he was saying. Dugan's face confirmed the irrationality of his statement.

"Why?"

The Dark King glared at his friend for daring to question his pronouncement. He did not bother answering him; it was none of his concern.

Kieran knew Brendan's people would be on guard for the Dark Court to act out. They would be expecting it. If the White Court spies found out what the Hunt was after, they would leap into action and secure the queen and her boy, if they chose to protect him, long before the hounds could ever find him.

Besides, whether it seemed weak of him or not, Kieran would not be the one to harm Winter's pet either.

He looked up at his birds again; winter white, pure as snow, in his world of darkness. When he thought harder on their loss, and what occurred, he decided they could live. They would be a bit of Winter in his world, and a reminder that Brendan was angry enough to fight for her.

That was just fine by him.

***

He should have asked her what time she was going to be free today. If Bren and she had plans, surely they weren't going to last all day. Tor really wanted to see Winter, hold her in his arms and comfort her. She was sick and he hadn't even stayed to take care of her. It was wrong of him, to leave her in the care of Aunt Ramona without even offering to stay and keep watch over her.

He doubted Aunt Ramona would have let him spend the night anyway.

Tor had hoped that after the concert last night they could have...well, been together, since they never had. It would have been the perfect ending to the perfect night, but it didn't happen that way at all.

He should call her; see if they could get together tonight, even if to watch basic cable and make fun of crappy movies while he served her cocoa and refused to let her up off the massive couch in her sitting room. He should be doing that for her, not Bren. And if she wasn't resting on the couch, like she should be, then Bren should know better than dragging her all over when she was feeling poorly.

Yes, he would call her and see if he could come over.

"Hi, this is Winter! I'm not here, ob-vi-ou-sly, but I am assuming you're familiar enough with modern technology to know what to do at the beep." BEEP.

The phone went straight to voice mail.

"Uh, hey, Win. Just wanted to see if I could be your personal nursemaid and feed you soup and hot chocolate on the couch and watch some Mystery Science Theater? Okay, so um, call me. I guess. I love you."

Chapter Nineteen

The woods were the same as she remembered. It had always been their special place, hers and Bren's, and she was pretty sure that he came here without her, too, just to be alone. Winter swore she could feel his presence here, as fresh as if he had been there only hours before. But, of course, that was not possible. He only arrived late last night.

Winter spun around in circles, with her head tilted up to the sky, watching the light filter through the trees and their thick branches. The sunlight was starting to fade and it dappled the ground beautifully, making everything look as if it was gilded for their arrival.

She spent time in these woods without Bren, of course. She and Tor would walk here in the summer, right after a rain, and look for turtles that came out in search of food. It was never the same though, not really. All the magic this place held was saved up until she and Bren could come here and unlock it together.

Winter loved coming here with Bren. It was the most special thing they did together. When they were here, it was like this was their own secret kingdom. It seemed whenever Bren was near, animals would come out just to stare at him. It was a weird thing for her to think, but she just always felt that way, that he was so special everyone adored him.

It's probably because he's the most handsome thing to ever enter these woods, she thought with a laugh. Bren gave her a sideways glance, obviously appraising her sanity.

As if to prove her point, even now, the birds twittered happily at the sight of them, dipping low as they flew from branch to branch alongside them. Chipmunks and squirrels that normally would have fled at their intrusion, stopped to watch them as they passed, then resumed their foraging.

Once, they even saw a deer. The doe was standing guard over her fawn and though Winter thought that the she would run from them, she merely stared at them with her big, dark eyes and then lay down next to her baby.

The thought of the deer caused Winter to touch the necklace again, to make sure it still sat securely around her neck. Even though she had not worn it long, already, it was a part of her, warm and alive. She traced her finger along a thin strand of silver to see if she could identify the pattern on it, but they all felt the same.

Maybe in time.

"Hey Bren?" she called in a stage whisper, not wanting to disturb the peace. He had ventured a few steps in front of her, letting his palms pass over the bushes and clumps of late autumn blooms that crowded the edge of the trail. He turned back to answer her, walking backward while waiting for her to catch up.

"Yes, My Darling?" he said dramatically.

171

"I was just remembering that mother deer we saw a few years ago. Do you remember?"

"I do."

"If you are like the stag, do you think that I am like that doe?" she asked uncertainly.

"How do you mean, Win? Do you have an illegitimate fawn I need to know about?" he clucked his tongue disapprovingly.

"No, Bren, seriously! I mean it; I used to feel like I was like her. I knew when I should be afraid and when I should trust someone. I mean, she didn't run from us because she knew we wouldn't hurt her. I don't run from you, because I know you would never hurt me." Winter stopped in the middle of the trail and toed a deep rut in the path while she thought of how to say what she wanted.

"Sometimes, though, lately I feel like I'm not scared of the things I should be very afraid of. Does that make any sense?" His brows knotted in concern, but he didn't answer. "Bren, do you think you will always be here, to tell me when to be afraid and when it's okay to trust? Things have been weird lately and sometimes, I... just..." She couldn't get the rest out in a comprehensible way, so she just gave up.

"I will always be here Winter. I will be whatever you need me to be, don't you ever forget that." Bren pulled her close in a tight hug, then whispered in her ear, "Don't ever be afraid of me, my love." She nodded in his arms, ended the hug, and linked her arm in his.

"I'm sorry for being depressing. Let's keep going."

As they ventured deeper into the interior of that magical place, she felt better. Flame colored leaves dropped down on them like a ticker tape parade, welcoming them home.

*The woods are lovely, dark and deep...*she thought.

The trail snaked windingly between the tallest trees in the forest and their branches formed a dome over their heads worthy of even the grandest cathedrals. She smiled at the sight of the beauty hidden deep in the wood and dropped her arm from Bren's. Winter held her arms out away from her body and spun around, faster and faster like she would grow wings and float up to the sky.

Then promptly tripped on an exposed root and went down like a stone.

Bren was there, quick as lightning, checking her for injury. His hands were all over her; warm, steady hands. When he was satisfied she suffered no permanent damage, he sat down and laughed at her.

Winter grimaced at him, making a face, but it was all exaggeration. She was lucky he had always been her guardian, always been there for her. Winter was suddenly very grateful that he was there. She threw her arms around his neck and squeezed him close. He crashed into her with a *whuff*.

"Thank you, Bren," she said sincerely. He pried himself free and she noticed he was blushing. "Bren! You're blushing!" she teased. He knelt and pretended to reexamine her ankle so that he didn't have to meet her eyes.

She watched the concentration on his face as he looked her over for wounds again.

He's so kind to me when he really has no reason to be.

They weren't related after all. That he cared enough to bother with her still, after all these years, spoke volumes of his character.

When he was satisfied with her wellbeing, he looked back at her. Winter liked his face, so sun kissed and perfect. Before she could stop herself, she reached out and touched his strong jaw. There was just the slightest hint of roughness under her fingers, the beginnings of a beard. He leaned into her caress, pressing his face into her open palm and closed his eyes.

Winter took his head in both her hands and tilted it gently to the left and right, examining him, watching the red of the sunset catch in his most golden of strands. Bren's blond hair was shaggy and it fell perfectly across his face. She took some between two fingers and rolled it around, so that she could feel the texture of it in her hands.

Bren continued to kneel before her and let her quietly evaluate him. It was so curious; when she touched him, ribbons of flame seemed to crawl up her skin from his, the strands of it wrapping around her wrists and pulling her closer, urging her to touch him. The heat grew between them, becoming an invisible fire so intense that it forced her to let him go for a moment so that she could roll up the sleeves of her flannel to cool her overly warm skin. He watched her, saying nothing.

174

Winter worked methodically, touching every part of him gently; judging the broadness of his shoulders, the perfectness of his ears, and the straightness of his nose. She picked up his hand and held it palm up in her own so that she could look at the lines that crossed his smooth palm. She let her fingers drag up his wrists to the inside of his elbow and watched him shiver at her touch. Winter dared not meet his eyes until she was finished. When she let herself look at him again, he was smiling.

"I feel like I have never even seen you before."

***

Bren couldn't believe that he was going to get his opportunity to prove himself so soon since resolving to make a firmer effort to win her heart. Her ankle, while badly strained, was not broken, but he was glad to have a reason to touch her nonetheless. And when she took his face in her cool, small hands, he felt a satisfaction, a completion, like he never felt before.

It was working.

Bren radiated happily with the heat of the White Court, pulsing softly under her gentle touch. She brought it out in him like no one else ever could, but then, that was exactly why he was forced to leave her so often, because of what she could do to him. Wanting her to be everything to him without being able to even try to convince her to want him back was torture.

Bren was sure she could feel the growing connection between them now in a way she wasn't able to before. Things were changing so fast. He continued to focus on the Court, letting her feel the power it contained. He saw her hands start to shake the longer she touched him and when she paused to roll up her sleeves, he could actually feel the heat of light trapped just beneath her skin. Bren knew everything between them would be just fine.

Even though the coming of fall had begun to erase the virility of summer from the earth, had begun to swallow all living things into the darkness of winter, he could still hum with the energy of what was left of his reign in seasonal power.

Unfortunately, he was running out of time to use it to his advantage. After the equinox, when the Dark Court would have its strongest months, he thought he might not have as good a shot at convincing her of his worth.

It was the trade between the Courts, using the tilt of the Earth to influence the strength of their reigns.

Somehow, Bren doubted it would take her that long to make her choice. Winter was already beginning to feel the pull of her destiny completely. She *looked* like she was feeling it too, and honestly, she looked like hell. Her human body was dying as her fae self was struggling and yearning to be free. Bren wondered if the effects that he and his brother would have on her, the things they would make her feel--all those strange new experiences and emotions--would pull her apart or drive her insane before she could choose.

And her choice would change her and the state of Faerie forever.

Never had there been a ruling couple, not in all these millennia. There was only a lone monarch to rule. His father may have been king, but neither his mother, nor Ramona's was queen. They were merely consorts.

Winter would be the first queen ever to rule jointly.

The rules of Faerie were all about balance. Bren was the counterweight to Kieran, his White Court , the antithesis of the Dark Court. But Winter's parents had been so foolish in their love affair. Dark and Light could not possibly coexist peacefully, he and Kieran were proof of that. Were they really so enamored they thought they could survive the pain of their union? Bren could not imagine that Winter could love Kieran without being injured by his hate or broken by his malice. She did not deserve to suffer that way.

Surely, Winter's mother, a member of his own court, must have known the dangers involved in loving a member of the Dark Court. He remembered her and he would never have thought her capable of it. Bren wondered who, and what, her father must have been, and what she would look like unbound. He knew her mother, as did Ramona. Serah was one of the most beautiful Dryads in his Court. Dryads were the thin, willowy, lovers of nature that generally favored the White Court. They were peaceful as a race and as individuals, and it made her mother's inclinations that much stranger.

That history, that gift from her mother would certainly explain Winter's love of the forest.

Bren looked at Winter. She was quietly tracing random lines with a stick through the leaf mold not minding that he was lost in his own world. He loved that they had always been able to remain in silence, not needing to break the stillness with idle words. It was one of the most wonderful things about them, he thought, that they didn't have to interrupt their time with meaningless talk. Bren believed that each word, each sentence should be delivered with the utmost care and that small talk and wasted words were a human trait that he was glad Winter never adopted.

In the end for her parents, they were parted by death. Bren hoped that they found each other again in the Land of Ankou. They at least deserved that much for creating the beautiful creature that Winter was and would surely become. She was the perfect balance of Dark and Light, the essence of both Courts filling her veins, swirling magically, gorgeously within her, to create the promise of a stronger Court. Unless she could remain between the two worlds forever, which was almost impossible, she would always be dangerous to either he or Kieran.

His mother told him, in fact, the last thing she ever said to him before she, too, went to the Ankou, was of the prophecy of the Undecided Queen. After Kieran stole the throne, she told him of the long forgotten tale. She said that if were to come to pass, and he was to find her before the Dark King, he would need to bargain with the Ankou, the king of the underworld, to hide her true nature. It written, she had said, about the brother kings.

She had known all those centuries ago that this would happen. Bren had waited, patient and focused, waited so long, that he began to doubt.

Luckily, Serah had relied on Ramona and trusted her with Winter. They had given her somewhere safe to hide; somewhere she could try to be happy for at least a little while.

It wasn't Winter's fault that she was born into a world of danger. She was never going to be truly safe until she made her choice. That was the only thing that could make her strong.

Bren wanted her to be happy; he always wanted her to be happy. That was his most basic wish for her.

He wasn't sure what he was about to do was make her happy at all, but he was resolved to do it anyway.

The king of the White Court, placed his hand under Winter's chin and turned her to face him, then pushed back a strand of black hair from her perspiration-damp face and tucked it neatly behind her ear, letting his hand linger on her face. Before she could think of stopping him, he leaned in and kissed her questioningly on the lips.

They tasted sweeter than he ever could have imagined.

She froze at his touch and he briefly thought she was going to pull away. He saw her eyes go wide with surprise, but Winter did not push him away. Her mouth burned beneath his, unmoving at first, but finally, willing, answering his unspoken question. Bren felt the heat and passion of young love lying just beneath the surface of her soft skin. He deepened the kiss, and she responded.

It was working.

Their first kiss was better than he imagined it might be, and after eighteen years, he had plenty of time to imagine.

Chapter Twenty

Winter couldn't believe that she was kissing Bren. More than that, she couldn't believe she was actually enjoying it. She was inexplicably drawn to him, almost lost in him, his earthy smell, his warm body near hers and his soft, able hands covering her, stroking her arms and legs slowly. It was so strange, he never had such a powerful draw for her as he did right now. She eventually had to pull away to keep from getting kiss-drunk in his arms.

"Was that ok?" he asked so quietly and unsure afterward, like he thought she might suddenly run from him if he were to allow his words to end their fragile moment.

Truthfully, Winter wasn't sure what she felt. True, she was extremely attracted to Bren, but she had also been pawing all over Kieran as well, and neither of them were her boyfriend.

She successfully cheated on Tor, whom she loved, she reminded herself, with not only a rock star, but also the one man he was most intensely jealous of, all in a single day. She felt like she was going for a Worst Girlfriend of the Year award.

Winter stroked Bren's arm absentmindedly, reassuring him without words. She didn't think she could talk right now even if she wanted to.

"Tor hates you."

Apparently, she could.

Her hand flew over her mouth after the words escaped, but she couldn't take them back.

Not now.

Bren looked at her, totally shocked at the unbidden admission, then burst into uncontrollable laughter. Relieved, Winter laughed too.

"Maybe he should *now*," he said when he regained his composure and gently took her hand in a very familiar way. Winter was still giggling stupidly, then he burst into another loud hearty laugh that sent the birds that were asleep in the trees, careening to the sky. He shifted from his knees so he could sit beside her. Winter rested her head against his warm shoulder while he kissed the top of her head; neither of them speaking, but not existing uncomfortably either.

That was good.

He was good.

Good to her, good for her, good through and through.

The light was almost gone when she heard footsteps, the approach of something large in the bracken beyond.

***

Bren shifted slightly in anticipation of having to get up when he heard the stranger approach. He knelt into a defensive crouch, ready to spring into action if necessary. He was so foolish to have brought the future queen out here without any guards.

What was I thinking?

Now that Kieran knew about her, he would never stop coming for her until she had chosen one way or the other. And even then, if the Dark King lost her, his brother would never give up on her.

He never gave up.

Ever.

Staying in his low crouch, Bren kept his hand on her shoulder, pushing Winter slightly so that she would know to stay down. He peered into the new darkness, using his Fae sight to push beyond the natural limits of human vision.

A tall, lithe form stepped out from the shadows, into their little clearing and Bren's hand tightened on Winter.

Then relaxed.

"Sorry, Sir," a woman's voice addressed them. He let out a relieved sigh.

"It's okay, she's with me," he told Winter, reassuring her first before addressing their guest.

"What is it, Fiona, and for God's sake, I hope you are presentable," he chided. Bren hoped his warning was enough to keep her from stepping out of the shadows without her glamour.

"Milady," Fiona nodded to Winter, who said nothing, but made a strange face at the greeting, as she came into the clearing. She had, indeed, made herself presentable for the queen, but her glamour could not hide the wildness of her. She looked like she had sprung up with the vines and weeds from the forest floor.

"What," Bren asked more forcefully than was his usual style, but he was unhappy with Fiona for interrupting his most eventful evening with the queen to date. She cleared her throat.

"Sorry, Sir, but he has sent the Wild Hunt after the boy, Sir. We saw them rise not long after the sun set. One of my informants in the D...um, well," Fiona winced as she said it, knowing she was divulging something that the queen may only vaguely understand. The look that Bren gave her confirmed her suspicion.

"Yes, well I do understand. Thank you." He gave her a withering look. Forced into action by Winter's comprehension of the subject matter and the mention of the boy, Bren bent low to kiss her one last time before heaving her to her feet, and hoisting her higher again into his arms. Bren wasn't sure whether she could walk or not, but he was more than sure he could carry her. He held her like a child, tucking her head under his chin. When she was settled, he kissed her forehead gently and smoothed her hair with his cheek.

The king of the White Court started to walk back toward the house on Ashe Street. It was not far, but it would be slower going than normal.

"Gather him and bring him to the house," he told Fiona over his shoulder. "And tell the Oakman to prepare. Ramona, too. We leave tonight." Before he could finish speaking his orders, Fiona was gone, disappearing without the slightest rustle of leaves into the blackness of the forest.

Bren moved stealthily through the woods, sticking to the level ground of the trail, bearing the future queen back to the home she'd always shared with Ramona. It took Bren until the edge of the woods to look at her.

He didn't want everything to end tonight.

He wanted more time to woo her before Faerie was forced on her.

"Something is happening, and you are not safe here anymore. If you trust me, I would like to take you somewhere else. Somewhere you will always be safe."

She nodded once, but said nothing.

***

He finally looked at her when they were at the edge of the woods, but his words were not what she expected. She thought he would first speak to her of the moments they shared, and how it would change things, but instead he delivered bad news.

Still, she trusted Bren. He had yet to let her down.

"Who was that?" she asked calmly after the initial panic caused by his warning had subsided.

That was the first of many questions she had for him. None of her potential questions involved asking whether she was in jeopardy. She knew enough about him to know he wouldn't let anything harm her.

"That was Fiona. She works for me." He wasn't even breathing hard, though they were moving through the dense foliage fast and Winter secretly delighted in how strong Bren was. His body, pressed close against her own, was warm and comforting, which was good, because she didn't think he was going to offer any more information than that to soothe her.

"The boy she talked about was Tor, wasn't it?" She was sure she knew the answer he would give her. Winter looked up at him as he walked and couldn't

184

C. B. Cole

help but think that, at that moment, he looked like he lived lifetimes longer than she would ever know.

Bren looked like he didn't want to answer her, but he did anyway.

"Yes, he is the boy she was talking about." She could see it pained him to admit that to her. Maybe Tor was right all along. Maybe Bren didn't care for Tor after all.

"You will always tell me the truth, won't you Bren?" It seemed stupid to ask.

"For the rest of our lives," he said matter-of-factly.

"So you will keep Tor safe from whatever she was talking about? Keep him safe from whatever is after him? That is the only question I have for you, for now," she qualified.

"If that is what you wish from me," he said softly. Winter pushed the hair that had fallen over his face from his eyes, watching him and waiting for the pulse of heat that they had shared before to comfort her. When it finally began to move through her, it wasn't the ribbons of writhing flame that she felt in the clearing, but a soft, gentle blanket that kept her warm from the coldness that seeped into her heart.

Bren held her tightly and the repetitive rocking motion of their movement soothed her enough to keep her inside her own skin. It was not unpleasant to be there in his strong grip. She was safe with him. Everything about him assured her of that.

That was why she couldn't believe it when it happened.

But it did happen.

185

The only name that she could think of, the only face she could see while wrapped in the safety of Bren's strong arms, sick with worry over Tor's safety, was *his*.

Winter could already see Aunt Ramona on the wooden front deck, bathed in the yellowed light of the porch lamp, waving at them to hurry, when Kieran's name flashed like a lightning bolt in her mind.

Chapter Twenty-One

Ramona was all at once concerned and thrilled to see Winter in Bren's arms. Bren, for his part in the matter, was radiant in his joy, practically lighting his own way back to the house. Winter was nestled safely in his arms, her face pressed peacefully against his chest, absorbing his heat.

This was good.

They were feeding off each other, sharing their gifts.

She held the door open wide for them as Bren climbed the few porch stairs up to the house. He gave a triumphant smile meant only for Ramona.

It practically screamed "We've done it". Ramona was not as confident as Bren, but she could admit it was a good start.

"Is she okay?" Ramona asked in a worried voice, not bothering to ask Winter herself.

"She's fine, Mo, she just tripped." He was brusque with her, so she knew there was more to it than he was admitting.

"The hunt is coming for the boy," he said hurriedly. He deposited Winter on the couch and knelt at her side, checking her ankle once again. "Are you much better?" Bren asked her gently.

"I'm fine, Bren," she reassured him. Looking to Ramona this time, she asked, "What's the hunt? And what about Tor? Is he going to be okay?" At the same time Winter patted Bren's face softly as she spoke and it made Ramona swell with pride, and hope.

Their need to touch each other was definitely a beginning.

Bren turned away from the queen just long enough to give his half-sister further directions.

"Ramona, I am moving us to my room. Bring the boy when he arrives with Fiona and meet us there."

"Does she..." Ramona couldn't believe she heard him right.

They were all going home.

"Winter knows she trusts me, and that it is not safe for her here anymore. Right, Win?" The girl nodded in solemn, shell-shocked agreement.

Bren looked Winter over one more time before hefting her back into his arms. Ramona couldn't help but notice how adroitly he ignored the girl's questions. That was something he couldn't make a habit of, if he wanted her to continue to trust him. Winter was not a child anymore. Ramona was always afraid he would forget that.

Before she could say so, Bren had already walked to his room down the hall.

***

Bren was forced to do this he told himself. Forced into this moment that might make her hate him. Kieran was probably laughing about this somewhere right now. The king hated feeling like a pawn.

He kicked the door to his room open, shattering the wood and sending the handle to the floor with a clang. Bren carried Winter across the room and, without giving her so much as a warning of what was coming, stepped into the mostly empty closet.

With just the slightest hint of a breeze and a flash of light, they emerged on the other side in a gleaming white hallway with a *pop*. He had done this so many times he didn't even miss a step.

Marble was everywhere, floor to ceiling, on all sides of them, surrounding them with golden, flowering vines dripping from every surface. It felt like a beautiful, controlled jungle with the leaves always just out of the way, no matter how big or small the creature passing may be. The open flowers followed their passing, turning as if Bren was the sun. The temperature here in the Court of Light was perfect and every so often, a lightly scented breeze would waft down the hall to welcome him home, smelling of a hayfield in summer after it rains. It felt good to be back here again.

"Gilroy, get me food and drink for the qu... For this young lady," he shouted down the hall. He didn't see his valet anywhere, but Bren knew Gilroy heard his order. There were some benefits to being king.

He put Winter down in the middle of the seemingly endless corridor so that he could have the use of both his hands. After helping her steady herself against the vine covered wall, Bren released her and opened the door to the room he prepared for her. Barely remembering to breathe, he turned the golden, handmade knob to reveal the room within.

Bren hoped she would like it here; he spent almost two decades trying to get it ready for her.

Whenever he would use up every ounce of willpower that he possessed to be with her in the world above, he would flee back here and try to busy himself by finding ways to add details that he discovered about her to the décor. Bren thought he had gotten it mostly right.

The white wood door swung open to reveal a massive room, a chamber really, easily as big as the bottom floor of the home he provided for her up until now. Bren hoped she would choose to stay here with him after she knew that it could be her new home if she wanted it.

And that her boy was safe.

Bren helped her into the room. Winter's eyes grew large with surprise as she quietly took in the scene before her. She hadn't asked him how they got there or where they were and honestly, her silence scared him a little. Bren put his arm low around her to support her as they moved to the couch that he had placed against the wall.

It was exactly the same as the one in Ramona's house. He hoped she would notice. It had been no easy thing to get it here. He fluffed the pillows and settled her onto it, not feeling comfortable enough around the queen here in this place, her royal rooms, to put her on the bed, lest she feel that he was too forward with her. Bren found a blanket and wrapped her in it tightly. Winter just stared at the couch, rubbing her hand disbelievingly over the light colored fabric.

It was subtle, but it was there.

Bren knew everything changed between them when he brought her here. Everything that he waited

190

all his life for was now real. His Court would be expecting her to stay once they found out she had come, expect her to join him.

The thought of letting them down seemed too much to bear.

Bren, finally satisfied that she was comfortable, lifted her legs and sat down beside her, lowering them gingerly back into his lap. He did not look at her just yet, but drew in the all strength of his Court that he could--and there was certainly a lot here in his home-- to bolster him.

They had to know she was here now.

Nothing stayed a secret long. Bren tentatively placed his hand on her bare foot, the shape of it still familiar. Her shoes were long since lost between there and the woods. To his silent delight, she didn't shake off his touch, so they must not have destroyed all the fragile bonds they created together.

"Say something," Bren prompted.

***

Winter laughed.

She laughed like she was going crazy. She felt like she was certifiable at any rate. Bren did not look at her, but she watched his patient face transform. His handsome visage changed expressions from something she thought might have been hope to the most delicate look of hurt. That was enough to bring Winter back to reality, or wherever they were.

She shook her head vigorously several times, clearing it of failed attempts at questions, and finally settled on, "Where are we?" That was the first question.

Of many.

Things were strange lately, and she felt, somewhere deep inside her, that it had a lot to do with her. For days, weeks, she felt herself distancing from her friends, Tor, Aunt Ramona. Everyone, it seemed, was operating on a different wavelength from her.

Except for Bren. He was always her constant.

And then she acted so wantonly last night and even today. *Was that today?* It seemed lifetimes ago, that car ride with Kieran. It was wrong. It wasn't like her at all. She was changing and she thought Bren knew why. She also felt that Bren, the patient and loving man beside her, knew the answers to every question she could think of.

"We are at my home, well, my real home. This is where I am when I am not with you. Probably not as exotic as you had imagined is it?" he gave a dismissive laugh. Winter didn't think his scorn was directed at her, but more toward himself, as if he let her down somehow.

"This is all my fault, isn't it?"

"No, Winter, oh no, of course not!" Bren said stricken with regret and leaned across her, very carefully, not wanting to hurt her. He shimmied down beside her so that they lay side by side on the couch. His size made it hard for them to share it easily and he had to turn on his side and press himself flat against the back of the couch to make room for both of them. He draped his leg across her to keep her from falling off the edge.

The proximity of him was intimidating. Bren was everywhere, all around her at once. They had never been so close. Winter couldn't remember feeling the press of his body that way, even when they hugged. She couldn't contain a sigh of pleasure the heat of him caused. He was warm and safe. Winter let herself relax into him.

"What do I need to know, Bren? What am I missing that will make all of this make sense?" She asked, exasperated. Winter felt a rising hysteria creep into her voice. "First, I black out at the concert, and then you show up and have that weird confrontation with..."

Winter stopped herself before she called Kieran by his real name in front of Bren. She didn't think Kieran would want that. She didn't think Bren would like it very much either, judging by his reaction to seeing the rock star. Winter wanted to keep some part of their secret friendship, their strange closeness, to herself.

"With...Shade, at the house this morning. And then you want to kiss me! Which you have never wanted to do before, I might add and that thing with Tor...Oh crap. Tor!" She pressed her forehead against his white tee shamefully.

Instead of crying, which was her original intent, she found herself breathing him in with deep, gulping breaths. The familiar smell of him seemed stronger now, and the fresh, clean scent of pine cleared her head of the hysterics that threatened. Feeling a little more gathered, she braced herself and asked what should have been a hard question.

But wasn't.

"It is all over with Tor now isn't it?" She knew the answer before he even gave it. Her heart told her it couldn't have room for Tor anymore, he had been replaced: Unwillingly, but it had happened all the same. Bren opened his mouth to tell her what she already knew, but her hot, shameful tears started anyway.

***

"I am afraid it has to be," he said, giving the answer he knew she already figured out on her own. "I'm sorry, Winter." Bren stroked her soft, black hair reassuringly. He could not fix the hurt she was feeling, but he could be there for her, if she needed him.

He shifted down, sliding lower so that he could rest his cheek on her chest. His feet hung over the edge of the couch. His six foot frame was already awkwardly situated and now, he had even less room, but he didn't mind. Bren played with the hammered rope he had given her, noticing the way it rested on her pale skin and moved slightly with each beat of her heart.

When his fingers brushed her skin, he noticed those heartbeats grew closer together. Knowing he could speed her pulse with just a touch and that she wore the things he had given her, filled him with a joy he didn't expect. That she accepted his formal gifts, like the silver rope, were important, of course, but he also thought it was terribly sexy that she wore his old clothes too. Knowing that she retrieved the things in his drawer just to be near him, and wore them with the same grace and dignity, was making him feel things that were very un-kingly at the moment.

Bren unbuttoned a few of the top buttons of her shirt so he could press his cheek to Winter's bare flesh, then lay still and listened to her breathing. It was contented and soft. Moved by their closeness, he turned to kiss her.

Winter did not reject him. Emboldened, he moved slowly, supporting himself so that he would neither hurt her nor scare her, all the while, letting his lips find hers. This thing between them was too new to spoil with hasty fumbling. Even when he shifted so that he lay above her, she did not squirm or refuse him. Instead, she kissed his chin, his neck and even that small place; the super sternal notch he vaguely remembered it was called. It should have been called something else, something sexier, the way her lips on that part of his skin made him feel.

He wound his arms beneath her and pulled himself closer, but held the bulk of his weight on his elbows, away from her tiny, still fragile, human body. He kissed her again and again and stroked her soft hair and whispered words blurred unintelligible by passion in her ear. Still she did not stop him.

What did stop him was when she asked softly, "What am I?"

Bren stayed frozen in that precarious position for a long moment still stretched over the length of her, trying to decide what to say. Winter stared back at him amusedly, with her wide, blue eyes waiting for his answer. Then she started to rub his back in a maddening way, letting her small fingers dance across his skin. He couldn't think of the answer, couldn't think of anything but her.

Winter nipped at his lower lip again and whispered, "I know you know I am different and I know you know why. Tell me what I am, Bren." She was teasing him, not the way she did when she was younger, but the way a woman teases a man. In that moment, Bren could see how wars were waged over women such as Winter.

"Winter, you," he kissed her lips, "are something so special. You are one of a kind." He leaned in, gathering the courage to whisper that she was queen into her ear. He could feel every inch of her beneath him, soft and warm through his clothes. He gently pushed the hair away from her ear and touched his lips to the delicate skin.

He didn't want to do this.

What if it ruined everything?

He was grateful when Gilroy knocked softly.

"Sir, may I?" he called from the door.

Not bothering to take his eyes off Winter, or move in any way, he answered quickly, "Of course, come in," His valet brought in a plate of food worthy of his queen.

"Your sister and the human are here, My King," he said briefly when he deposited the tray on the coffee table in front of them. His servant then turned and left just as quickly as he had come, making sure not to show any emotion on his face, even after seeing the king in such a precarious position with the would-be queen.

While Gilroy's face didn't betray his thoughts, Bren was sure the rest of the Court would know Winter was here within minutes. He shuddered to think what else Gilroy might tell the gathered assembly about this first meeting.

His gaze found Winter's again.

Her eyes were wider, if possible, after hearing Gilroy's report. The look on her face spoke volumes. There was no more playfulness left in her features, just a confused expression. It made him afraid of what she might think. He was forced to call upon every strength of his Court, felt it flooding inside him, reassuring him. It was all that was keeping him afloat in the wonder he found he lost himself in.

"He said sister," she whispered, "And he called you king, Bren."

Chapter Twenty-Two

Tor lazed on the unfortunately colored brown couch in his living room, watching *So I Married an Axe Murderer* for the thousandth time.

It was the first time he ever watched it without Winter.

She loved that movie.

He missed her today, missed her more than he thought possible. Tor wondered if, despite her reassurances, she wasn't really a little upset with him over the concert the night before. She didn't want to go, not really, and he knew that, but she went because she loved him. He loved her too, God knows he did.

The music he loved never moved her the way it did him; it was one of their only true differences. Tor wasn't sure just what moved Winter into action anymore. She had always been, a different creature, more so than any other person he had ever known. Lately, he felt like she didn't even belong to this world anymore.

What killed him, then brought him back to life again, was the fact that she chose to shine the pure light of her love on him and him alone. Tor wasn't sure what would happen to him if he lost her.

He had never truly lived, not one day, without her.

She had saved him. Winter saved him from the nightmares that tortured him after his parents died. She saved him from his brother when he was in one of his drunken rages. Most amazingly, she helped him keep his home, albeit with some creative assistance from her Aunt Ramona, when Sean left for good.

A knock on the front door behind him jerked him roughly out of his memories and Tor jumped so high he practically levitated off the couch. It was so unexpected at this late hour.

Maybe Winter decided to come after all?

Brightened by the thought, he bounded to the door to let her in, his once leaden heart now in flight at the anticipation of her skin on his skin. They had never, well...but Tor would wait for as long as she wanted. It could have been last night, but life got in the way.

Maybe tonight?

Even if not, everything else with her was almost as good anyway. Tor paused with his hand on the latch to clear the impure thoughts from his mind. He didn't want to come panting to the door like a Neanderthal. He opened it with a smile on his face.

But it wasn't Winter after all.

Aunt Ramona and another blond woman waited on the stoop for him.

Aunt Ramona said, "You must come with me," and took his hand without waiting for an answer. His immediate thought was that Winter was worse than she was before.

What if Aunt Ramona came because Winter had gone to the hospital? He was already grabbing his coat and twisting the lock behind him as he pulled the door closed.

"She will be ok, right?"

"*You* will be ok," Ramona answered cryptically, and led him to her car. He got in complacently.

"Where is she?" The car door slammed behind him and the blond woman, in deference, opened Aunt Ramona's door for her . When Aunt Ramona was secure in the car, the blond got in and drove them to Winter's house.

They ignored him completely.

"That's him?" the blond asked after a few minutes. "Hmmm. I thought he would be different somehow." Ramona just glared at her and the rest of the ride was silent.

He watched the street lights periodically illuminate the women's faces in the front and couldn't help but think they seemed improbably stoic if Winter was doing poorly.

When they pulled in to the drive, Tor noticed all the lights were on, but there was no sign of Winter or even Bren inside, though his car was still parked in the other space. His blood boiled at the thought of Bren with her. If she was ill, and Bren was the one caring for her, sitting patiently and holding her hand at the hospital, Tor didn't know what he would do.

Tor knew down in his bones that Bren wanted her for his own. He wanted her the way Tor had her. Winter never believed it whenever he mentioned it to her, claimed she never even saw it, but Tor knew the truth. Bren was not a good liar. In fact, Tor didn't think Bren tried to hide it at all. Winter was just blind to his faults.

C. B. Cole

The car came to a rough stop and they all leapt from it simultaneously. Ramona ran to the door, Tor did the same. For the first time, he thought there was truly a reason to be afraid.

"Fiona, what now?" Ramona asked uncertainly. For the first time, panic seeped into her words. Tor couldn't remember a time that she ever faltered from her perfect intonation.

"Aunt Ramona, what's going on?" Tor grabbed her arm, forcing her pay attention to him, but Fiona immediately pried his fingers off and gave him a menacing look.

"Do *not* touch her again," she growled.

They both proceeded to ignore him completely again.

"Take him and go. I will follow you soon." Fiona told her, then shoved Tor into the foyer and pulled the big wooden door closed behind her. Fiona remained on the porch and Tor reluctantly followed Aunt Ramona down the hall into Bren's first floor bedroom.

He was secretly glad this room was not on the same floor as Winter's.

Tor stood in the middle of the sparsely decorated room, confused. Aunt Ramona went to the closet and opened the door. "In here," she said hurriedly.

"Someone needs to tell me what is going on first," he said firmly, digging in his heels like a mule.

"I would, but there is no time, boy," Ramona said curtly. "We need to get you safe." Tor walked closer to Bren's closet and peered in at the collection of clothes and shoes that lived here permanently.

"Why?"

**

Ramona didn't want to argue with the boy. She didn't have the time or the patience. He would have more questions than just that one in a few minutes, so she just pushed him in the closet.

When he went through to the other side, she too stepped into the closet and pushed through the thin, invisible, skin-like barrier until she stood in the familiar hall that led to Bren's rooms. Ramona supposed that now, there was a good chance they would be Winter's rooms as well.

Then, of course, here in the royal wing, was her chamber, too. Beyond that, further down the corridor was the White Hall, where she spent so many happy times. It was the heart, the lifeblood of the White Court and she missed being there more than she admitted, even to herself.

Ramona took a deep breath, sampling the air that was so particular here.

Everyone smelled something different on the subtle breeze that drafted down the halls. Bren always said he smelled hay or grass. Her mother said that she always smelled apples, ripe and ready for harvest. Ramona, though, always smelled lavender, and that lavender smell relaxed her. She felt years of stress and worry fall away from her. She was home.

The White Court always had the largest piece of her heart. It contained a sense of belonging that she

C. B. Cole

could never find back in Winter's house. It was never really Ramona's home, not like Court had been.

Her thoughts were interrupted by the whimpering boy who had landed in a heap on the floor and still remained there after crossing the barrier. He looked bewildered, slightly scared and she did not envy him for the strange thoughts that were probably running wild inside his mind.

Ramona felt the slightest tug at her skirt hem. He was looking at her questioningly.

"Aunt Ramona, where are we?" he whispered.

She stepped over him, not bothering to answer his question. She was done with humans.

"Put Tor somewhere safe," she told a pixie that hovered excitedly nearby after witnessing her arrival. The tiny winged creature was flittering happily at the sight of her and she reached out to stroke its tiny ice blue cheek. The pixie nodded joyfully at her instructions and before doing as she asked, merrily dove into her thick, auburn hair tying, knotting and braiding it up into an intricate up-do that was fashionable in the Court. It was done in seconds, and then the giddy creature, zipping to and fro like a hummingbird kissed her lightly on the nose. Shimmering dust from the pixie drifted onto Ramona's cheeks and lashes and she smiled happily. Ramona supposed that was as much of a grand welcome that she was going to get. It did not matter, she was home.

"Thank you, my dear one," she told the retreating creature. "But remember, *not* with the queen," she added as an afterthought. The pixie nodded again and, with glittering wings, flew over to the boy.

Even though she was much smaller than he was, she moved him down the hall at a proficient speed, belying the tremendous strength she possessed. Ramona watched to make sure he was well past the queen's doors before she turned to find her own room across the long and vine hung hall from her brother's entryway.

She had not set foot in there for eighteen years, since the night Serah had borne Winter.

Ramona never dared leave Winter for one second, even though the gateway was so close. She was afraid that if she did, even for a few minutes, that Kieran would find Winter, or members of the Dark Court would take her. Besides, time was different here: The days were not in sync with the human world.

For a long time, Ramona stood outside her old room, studying the hand-carved doorknob that Bren had made for her so many years ago. It depicted a leaping stag carved into the wooden ball. It was one of the nicest gifts he had ever given to her. She turned the knob slowly, pushing the door with some trepidation. Part of her thought her things would have been moved out or her room given away to a more important member of the Court in her absence, but it was all still there, just as she left it.

Once she made it all the way inside and found everything initially safe, Ramona closed the door quietly behind her and leaned on it, breathing heavily and keeping it closed since there were no locks here. She didn't want to be disturbed for a very long time.

C. B. Cole

A low table, made of heavy granite and driftwood sat near the settee. It was just the thing. It took some great effort, and her Fae muscles were weak from lack of use, but she managed to effectively block the doorway.

Now, no one could disturb her.

Silent tears slid down her cheek, but she could not will them away no matter how weak they made her seem. Ramona dropped to her knees, breaking down with the stresses she had borne silently all these years. The room was so quiet that she heard the quiet *plop* when one hot, fat drop rolled all the way down her thin face and fell to the warm marble floor at her feet. She kicked off her shoes and let her skin press against the smooth stone. She was not human, and she didn't need their accoutrements any more. She wanted to be herself again, not the human version, but her true self.

Have I done the right thing? Have a done as Serah would have wanted?

Her thoughts consumed her, doubt and fear filled her as they had so many times over Winter's short life. But what was done was done and she had to move on.

Ramona had to take some deep breaths and concentrate very hard to remember how to shed her glamour. She had worn it for so very long. Her eyes slid closed, and she held her shaking hands out in front of her. Heat seeped into her, from the floor below, from the air all around, pulling at the heavy coat of magic she had worn every day of Winter's existence. When she opened her eyes again, Ramona's skin glowed with a light from within.

205

There was nothing dull, nothing human about her anymore.

Her hands flew to her face, probing, examining and she felt that her features were sharper, more defined. Ramona practically danced to the mirror at her dust covered dressing table.

Copper and brass reflected in her individual strands of hair, making it look thick and regal in its intricate style that the pixie created. Her eyes were wider, more almond shaped now, slanting just so and the color was the deepest ice green of glaciers. She could never be mistaken for human again. Using a trembling finger, pale and thin, she pushed back her gilded hair to reveal her ears, which now had a slight point at the end.

Finally.

Ramona clapped her hands happily, and smiled even more brilliantly when she saw the echoing movement of her wings reflected in the dirty glass. They were still stretching and reshaping after being contained for so long, but they were there. The purple transparent flutters of her delicate appendages were the final confirmation she needed. She was truly home.

Trying them warily, she lifted herself a foot off the ground, sending dust motes swirling into the air. She lowered herself back to the ground and turned away from the glass. Sighing happily now that she was herself again, she turned to her pathetically neglected, once radiant chamber.

Ramona's room was made in the purest whites of summer clouds and the light pinks of the early sunrises. Her bed, which was her favorite part, was wound around every driftwood post and beam frame of the canopy bed with the deepest purple morning glories she was able to find. They bloomed for her now as she watched, waking for the first time in all these years. They had lain sadly dormant, devoid of her care and untended for so long. Ramona stepped to the closest drooping tendril of the vine and toyed with a flower between her pale fingers, encouraging it to burst into life for her. Hovering slightly off the ground, she bent and blew a thin coating of dust off the waking bud.

Ramona resolved she would not leave her home here in the Court again. She did her duty and that was enough.

***

The white crows were doing what little they could to cheer Kieran in the great hall of the Dark Court. He brought them out so that the others could enjoy them, witness the proof of Bren's fracturing patience, but still guarded them with a watchful eye carefully just the same. He wanted the Court to know how close Bren was to doing something truly stupid.

The malicious birds swept down from the rafters to claw at the Ly Ergs and Redcaps and assorted oddities that drank themselves silly in plain view of the Dark King. The simple minded beasts just squealed and covered their heads every time they passed, but refused to give up their seats. He figured if they were foolish enough to become incapacitated in his presence, then they were as good a target as any. The Court needed action.

Desperately.

Every member, from the smallest sprite to the wizened grogoch, had become weary and complacent with the lack of any real violence or devious acts committed against the White Court or even the humans for that matter. The stalemate that came with the discovery of the queen was killing them.

Kieran threw raw, red meat, dripping fresh blood onto the floor as it flew, to the Hounds that snarled and snapped at his feet. They took less time to return from their task than he expected, but he rewarded them anyway. The Hounds did their job sufficiently and Dugan was happy to report that Fiona, Bren's captain of the guard, was stationed ominously close to the *bruig* entrance. She saw them as soon as they were set loose, and questioned Dugan immediately on the Dark King's intent, which he was more than happy to supply.

Kieran hoped Fiona would not be too much of a problem. She always did seem to have too many of her own ambitions to be truly loyal to Bren. She was too familiar with the members of the Dark Court to make her completely light.

Dugan, back from the hunt as well, pulled a chair up to sit next to the king. Kieran had his leather boot encased feet propped on one of the ancient wooden banquet tables that lined the great hall. The assortment of tables, long and much abused, were hardly used any longer since there was little cause for the great feasts that once lasted for days here in this room. There was nothing worth celebrating anymore.

Kieran.

Her voice coiled around him like a snake, sinking its fangs deep into his flesh and injecting her particular venom into his veins. It burned.

She was thinking of him.

She thought his name as clearly as if she spoke to him aloud, with her lips centimeters from his ear.

He stopped moving, frozen in shock when he realized he heard her call to him and one of his Hounds almost took his hand off to get to the meat he still held. The near miss startled him back to reality. Angrily, Kieran grabbed it by the scruff of its neck and hurled it back to some hungry looking glaistigs to have for their dinner. Then he tossed the remaining blood soaked mess, platter and all, across the room for the remaining Hounds to fight over.

He put his hand on Dugan's knee, slapping it down hard and smiled at him before rising to his feet. His queen was thinking of him, needing him.

"Dugan!" he shouted boisterously. "Our queen desires my presence. Call for our ride!"

Dugan nodded solemnly, but then, he rarely showed emotion, for any reason, not that his face could have expressed any feeling at the moment. Dugan still looked like hell, his left eye was fully black from their previous encounter that evening, but the rest of him healed enough to handle their outing.

Sometimes Kieran thought that Dugan had locked everything away, his conscience, his opinions, even his emotions when they came to the Dark Court. He certainly didn't dare pass any judgment in front of the king since he questioned him earlier over the deployment of the Hounds.

Kieran pulled his favorite rock star glamour back over his skin, like water settling in a pool, feeling the subtle changes soften and dull his true self, then he nodded back at Dugan.

They were ready.

There would be a day soon that he would not need his glamour anymore, but until then, he would just have to be what she thought he was. Dugan started out ahead of him, his thick boots stomping through the vast hall, the leather soles slapping angrily on the stone floor.

Kieran hoped that his Winter had not fallen prey to Bren's practiced and perfect routine. He doubted it, but in the event Bren took any small piece of his Winter from him, he decided he would be very annoyed.

They left the Great Hall with its residents happily toasting the future queen's imminent return to their home.

Chapter Twenty-Three

Kieran and Dugan arrived late that night at his half-sister's home on Ashe Street to find all the lights inside and out ablaze. He could detect no motion in the house and there was not a soul in sight.

They were already gone, but he knew that.

Kieran started up the walk, but jumped back immediately, barely dodging a huge branch from the massive oak that crashed to the ground in front of him, blocking his way. There was a short, delighted laugh at the sight of his narrow escape and he could now see Fiona waiting for him on the porch, lounging apathetically in one of the weathered rocking chairs. Kieran gave her a plastic smile, then peered back up at the massive tree. The branches above him swayed and whipped in an invisible gale. It was gearing up for another attack if he came any closer, which he fully planned on doing. That belligerent tree, that angry vegetation, was one of Bren's stupid guardians, the barely useful Oakman.

Oh, well.

He should have known that he could not expect just show up without any alarms or surprises. But Oakmen, while big and imposing, were by and large, slow moving: One trick ponies. It would be a small matter to rid himself of its involvement.

The Dark King put his hand on the cracked branch that blocked his way and let his anger fuel the frost of the coming winter, letting it sink into the living wood and wind its way into the Oakman's quick. While broken, the thick limb still remained connected to the powerful trunk, pulsing with the magical life within.

It would be the creature's downfall that the branch didn't sever completely. Kieran stayed with his hand on the wood, pumping fear and darkness into the gentle creature until he heard the last breath of the dying Oakman rustle the leaves above him. For all of the centuries it had lived, it took less than three minutes to end its life. The once beautifully colored leaves, so fiery earlier that morning when he last saw his birds in their true state, were now dry, dusty husks. They drifted down in a mass exodus and piled all around him.

Kieran laughed.

Fiona grumbled.

He looked up at Fiona, remembering she was there. The wild looking woman of the woods was looking up at the wasted trunk of the great tree that already withered down to nothing. The final leaves were floating on the breeze as they broke free of their branches and drifted away. She looked like she was mumbling something to herself.

A prayer for the departed perhaps?

She turned her attention back to Kieran with a wicked gleam in her eyes. In the darkness, they flashed the way an animal's would in the night. They were so similar to Dugan's eyes. Before he found Winter, he would have been really turned on by that and she knew it. She blew him a kiss.

212

"They're gone, but you have to know that already," she said sarcastically. She was happy to have a reason to talk down to him.

"Have you missed me, Dear?" he mocked. "You truly are too wicked to belong to my brother. You would have done well with me," Kieran couldn't help but taunt her.

She had been his lover behind Bren's back for years. For a long time, it was one of his greatest victories, tainting something was so close to his brother. He liked thinking that his own darkness could infiltrate the White Court without anyone knowing. Maybe he could have used that to his advantage eventually, but he thought that now that he began to pursue the queen, his ability to count on Fiona's help was over.

Kieran's gaze narrowed at the WhiteCourt fae. She obviously knew the queen was here all these years, and never mentioned it to him.

Lying bitch. Was I so blinded by lust that it never occurred to me?

That thought curdled in his stomach like sour milk, and he stared at her with a new and unclouded perspective. Like she was reading his mind, or merely his face, she smiled sweetly at him. Fiona reached up and absentmindedly picked at a loose house number on the wall.

"She *is* a lovely girl, don't you think?" she asked innocently. "I mean, she has really grown into something beautiful. Even when she was little though, you could see it. She always had that hint of our world

213

about her. The king is very pleased." She smiled sweetly at him and Kieran wanted to rip her head off.

"He is not *the* king. He is a king, just like me, and you would do well to remember that, *Oread*,"

"Maybe so, but Brendan was to born to be king, and you killed to be one. Surely, that is something of a difference, don't you think, dear?" She winked at him and his blood boiled.

The Dark King was furious. There may have been a time when he had thought there was a chance he could eventually woo Fiona over to the Dark Court, but now Kieran realized that he had been the one being played all along.

Maybe Bren was laughing with Fiona over this whole ordeal after all. Would Bren have had the deviousness to ask her to come to the Dark King as a means to keep him away, or did she do that much on her own?

Kieran eyed her speculatively. The smile on her face was all the confirmation he needed. She deceived him and now that he knew it, she was giddy with it.

He kicked the wasted shell of the Oakman's fallen limb angrily and it shattered into a million lethal shards. Most of them flew like daggers into clapboard walls of the big, white house, sticking with deadly precision into the old wood. Others cracked windows, or broke them completely, with the glass landing like tinkling chimes on the deck below. The best part, though, were the few that struck Fiona, jabbing deep into her dark skin, which was even more alien looking than normal here in the sickly, yellow light of the porch.

214

Fiona, scowling at him in an incendiary rage, pulled a particularly nasty looking splinter, jagged and rough, from just under her collarbone and threw it down on the porch angrily where it skittered off the edge and into a bordering boxwood. Black blood oozed from the wound temporarily, managing a three inch drip of blood, then sealed itself.

Her jovial tone was gone when she said "The White King took her to his home, to *our* Court, but surely you are not so *stupid* to not realize that for yourself. He will not bring her back to this world if there is a chance she will run into *your* arms again. You may be aware that the White King is not over fond of you, Kieran. His focus is on the queen now, as it always has been." She put extra vitriol in the final words of her pronouncement, reminding him how long he had been in the dark. "Even now, he is probably wooing her in ways that someone with a heart such as yours could never imagine. Did you think that you would, or even could, win the Undecided Queen by lust and showmanship alone? You truly are a fool." Her sharp words could have cleaved the flesh off his bones, cutting him deeply with the malice infused in its delivery. If she had ever spoken to him like this before he had found the queen, he probably would already be taking her clothes off.

But that was before Winter.

The difference that shy girl made in him since their first meeting was slight, but Kieran knew it was there, crawling just below his skin. Things would be different because of her, whether he won her or not.

215

"She won't love him," Kieran said confidently. "He is too tangled in the threads of her lifelong deception for her to be with him. I've seen it. She loves me, or very soon will."

He hopped over the very few remains Oakman's branch and glided up the concrete walk then calmly sat on the step below her. If she truly wanted to strike him, it would be the perfect opportunity. The Dark King had no fear of her retaliation, though; Brendan was the only one who could actually kill him. Possibly Ramona, too, though she never would raise a hand to him.

Or now Winter, if she so desired. The fae magic prevented all others from making fatal wounds.

Fiona could still hurt him though, and with his back turned to her, it would have been easy, but she wouldn't dare, not with Dugan here. Injured as she was, she would never raise a hand to a monarch, even if he was her ex-lover, under penalty of death by the laws of Faerie.

And Fiona would have to know how much Kieran enjoyed death.

The wood-fae scooted her chair nearer, scraping loudly across the wooden porch, and leaned closer to him.

"Even so, she is in the White Court now. Would you go there, Dark King, with no invitation? You have no friends there. Anymore."

Kieran knew that was the closest thing to an admission of her pain, her true feelings about the end of their relationship, as he was going to get. Unable to help himself, the cruelty of it not to be missed, Kieran winked at her and watched her eyes narrow with rage. She stood angrily.

"Only a fool would go to his Court and cause a war to take what is not even yours!" Fiona turned to leave, stomping away from him in a funk of rejection. Her shoes made angry reverberations on the wood slats of the porch. Without a further look at the man she had, on many occasions, shared a bed with, Fiona crossed the threshold into Ramona's home and disappeared down the hall, slamming the door in her wake.

"Yet," Kieran whispered after she was gone. "She is not mine, yet."

The Dark King leaned tiredly against the worn wooden banister and looked out at the dark street beyond. He wished Winter was with him so that they could create the chaos he knew she held inside her. It was there, he had seen a tiny, yet illuminating glimpse of it hidden deep in her soul, last night. The darkness he saw within her, curled in on itself like an angry serpent, , coiled and ready to strike, reassured him.

That small thing was the spark that erupted into the all-consuming flame when they kissed.

And then the fire that Winter started inside him, devoured him completely. He burned, sitting there on her porch, as he thought of the possibilities for their future. Kieran could not see from that minute forward when he would not need her by his side to be complete.

When he was sure that Fiona had gone to join the others, Kieran rose unsteadily and turned the brass knob on the main door. He motioned for Dugan to remain outside, then crept in. Softly, he entered the house that Bren had hidden the queen in all her life. He smelled her, sensed her in everything here. Worse, he felt the goodness of Bren and Ramona on every surface and in every room.

It disgusted him and Kieran shoved his hands deep in his pockets for fear that he could possibly contract an ounce of decency through an errant touch.

The Dark King realized he would have a hard fight ahead of him if he wanted her to recognize she belonged with him. He may have seen the darkness inside her, but it was cowering before the overwhelming goodness that also lay just below her surface, smothering it into submission.

Damn Bren for keeping her away.

He climbed the stairs two at a time, to where he knew she stayed. Winter called to him, like a ghost, haunting him, telling him where to find her. Kieran felt the breath from her unspoken words fall hot on his ears.

Kieran located her room easily and he steadied himself against the door frame, digging his fingers in hard, to keep from falling to his knees. He steeled himself against the onslaught of the residual Winter inside, gasping as tremendous waves of passion and lust washed over him. Walking slowly, guarded lest some unexpected piece of her take him unawares, he crept to her bed.

Once there, he gently lowered himself onto it, as he would if he was creeping into their own bed late at night and he wished not to wake her. Then, he lay back with his head on her pillow.

Kieran wrapped the thick blanket that warmed her body nightly around his own. He breathed her in; the darkness of the summer, the coldness of her purity, the wickedness of her absolute reason. The bedding he clutched tightly to his chest, was all he had of her until he could figure out how to go after her.

Her room was everything and nothing like he imagined it. Winter had stacks of books on every flat surface.

Books, books, books.

There was lots of music too: Mostly artists he'd never heard of, so they must not be his competition. He shuffled through bands like Pela, Bon Iver, and Iron and Wine. He flipped them one by one onto the floor. No, this was nothing like the music he made.

"What the hell is a Frightened Rabbit?" he said to no one.

Kieran tossed the final CD. It landed with a click against the others, sliding off a pair of her jeans.

Clothes were everywhere, and he tried not to notice that some of them smelled like Bren. There were photos everywhere too; Ramona holding her as a baby, Winter as a toddler in the snow. She was with a boy in every picture, not more than a few years older than herself and he wondered if that was how Bren had gotten to her. Kieran couldn't even remember much of what Bren looked like when they were small. It should have bothered him more that Bren was in every one of her memories, he thought, but he was too utterly fascinated by her life playing out in front of him to care.

219

Of course, there were pictures of her as she got older too. Winter in school, Winter at concerts. It was the picture of her kissing Tor though, that jerked him violently out of his perfect moment.

Enraged in an instant, and insanely jealous of anyone who could compete with his affection for the queen, he dropped the blankets he was holding and went straight to the dresser, picked up the image, and threw it through the closed window, sending a hail of glass down to the lawn below. He watched the chunky silver frame skid out into the road and come to a stop face down in the street.

Momentarily satisfied, he angrily balled the sheets and blankets up and carried them with him as he marched down the stairs. The Dark King closed the front door quietly behind him, but left it unlatched and joined Dugan in the SUV.

"Our queen is really gone," he said, trying not to sound sad. It would not do for him to sound weak.

"Do we ready ourselves for war, My King?" If Dugan thought that it was strange that he was stealing sheets from Winter's house, he said nothing.

Kieran looked out at the yard beyond, and watched a Dark Brag circle the house. It pleased him that the dark ones were drawn to her. He wondered how many more circled the house in the last 24 hours.

There was still time.

"Let us see how our queen fares on her own. If she calls for me, Brendan cannot refuse me entry to the White Court. We may be able to do this without violence." The words were barely out of his mouth when he realized his mistake.

Of course, his Court would want war and violence. He should want it too.

Dugan merely nodded, painfully aware of the torment his friend was enduring, and held the door open for him. Then, his captain drove them away, backing over and crushing the remnants of the picture in the frame

***

Tor silently sat in the room to which he had been sequestered. It was opulent, over the top and if he was honest, if one *had* to be confined, he could think of worse ways to live out his sentence. He sat now, cross-legged on the bed because the door was sealed, though he saw no locks, and he was worn out, his, fists bleeding from all the door pounding he'd done. He had called out too, but no one answered.

Maybe they heard him and no one cared.

What was worse was that he hadn't seen or heard anything about Winter since coming here. Tor was so afraid she was hurt or sick. What if she was calling for him, needing him, and he couldn't go to her? She may never forgive him.

Tor raged at the thought that she needed him and he was ineffectual. This was all Bren's fault somehow.

Of course it was.

Tor spied a beautiful, handmade, twisted wood and vine side table near the bed, and, after considering its artful merits, promptly smashed it and all it represented, violently into a thousand splinters.

When he made sure that the biggest pieces left were barely the size of his pinky finger, he stopped to survey his work. He felt oddly gratified at the sight of the destruction. It was better than sitting by idly, or being consumed by worry over Winter. Tor carefully pulled a sliver from under his fingernail and popped the finger into his mouth to suck the blood that came rushing to fill the void. The scattered wood looked irreverent and vulgar on the floor of this beautiful room and Tor was almost pleased.

Then he spied the coffee table.

Chapter Twenty-Four

"Yes, I guess he did call me king," Bren said sheepishly. He gave a dismissive chuckle, but Winter saw through his attempted evasiveness.

"I think we better start talking, Bren," she suggested firmly, leaving no room for avoidance or negotiation.

Bren knew Winter wanted answers from him, of course she did, and he knew he would have to tell her what she wanted to know. It wasn't as if he had a choice, he couldn't lie anyway; it was contrary to his fae nature.

The king of the White Court had always ruled by example, and his example should fall firmly on the side of right and good. Now was no exception, no matter how much he dreaded this conversation. He thought many times over the years about what he might say to her, but none of those conversations ever began with him stretched out over her small body.

Bren wanted, more than anything he ever wanted in his long life, to make her happy.

She deserved that.

Bren knew he would have to move again, though he wanted very much to stay in Winter's embrace and kiss her again and again. But she had also heard Gilroy say that the boy was here and Bren thought the time for kisses was momentarily over. He sighed heavily, wearied by his imminent task.

Bren carefully shifted and adjusted himself, moving slowly to not burden her with his weight as he began the precarious job of disentangling his body from hers. He folded her legs back on the couch after he was free and fixed the blanket around her.

Free of her, but not happy to be so, he knelt on the floor at her side and put his face very close to hers, so close that he felt her breath on his face, ruffling his hair. Bren was so close that he saw himself reflected in the pure light blue of her eyes; the eyes that, for him, held every wonder that the White Court knew, and could realize in the future.

Bren sucked in a steadying breath and brushed his lips against hers one last time for courage, before saying what he had always wanted to say.

And what he had never wanted to say.

"I love you Winter," he began unsteadily. It seemed like a good place to start. "I don't know if I have ever told you that. Or maybe I have, but I mean it. I have loved you unendingly for every year of your life. I have gladly given you safety and security so that you might grow up in a world away from where we are now, where you were born. Because I loved you and wanted your choices to be your own, I have kept you from your home here and for that, I am eternally sorry." Bren kept his head down; not meeting what he was sure would be a shocked and disgusted gaze.

He was about to continue when she interrupted him.

"What are you trying to say, Bren? That *this* place is my home?" Her voice was calm and questioning, but not accusing. She was not angry, not yet. That gave him some hope.

"I am saying...Winter," he sighed deeply, "...that you belong here with others like you." Bren squeezed her hand, wanting her to understand. "Your parents were from this place, well Faerie, just like me, and my sister, Ramona. And here, like Gilroy said...I am their king." Again, he waited, expecting at any minute for the dawn of realization to cause her to strike out against him, curse him for his concealment.

But she did nothing.

When he could take the suspense no more, he raised his eyes to Winter's perfect, pale face.

***

It took a minute, but Winter eventually processed what he was saying, though admittedly, she didn't know whether she believed him or not.

Bren, who had been part of her only real family, was telling her that he kept her from her true home and the life she could've had here in this place, if she could bring herself to believe him...oh, and that he was in love with her, but she would process that later.

Surprisingly, she wasn't angry at him.

Fitting in, after all, was always a problem for her. She never really felt she belonged anywhere and Tor always made a big point of relaying every time he felt that she ceased to act human.

Maybe that was why?

No, Winter was not all that surprised, or angry, as Bren seemed to believe she should be, at finding out that she was different. But she was definitely having a hard time accepting the details of her supposed

225

differences, mainly because Bren just admitted he was a king in fairyland.

Winter briefly wondered if Bren happened to be wrong, or crazy, and they were not indeed in Faerie as he claimed, if all of his money could buy him a good therapist, one that would consider treating both of them for temporary insanity.

"So," she said slowly, echoing the absurdity she felt for having to say them, "We are in a fairy kingdom, Bren?" she asked carefully, trying not to sound too ridiculous or disbelieving, lest he get angry with her for mocking him. Crazy people could do strange things if they thought others didn't believe them. Winter tried to press as far back into the couch as she could, and Bren noticed.

"No, we are in *Faerie*, Winter. It's not a kingdom, really, but a place that exists because we exist. I am not crazy, Win, so quit scooting away like I am the Boogie Man." He dropped his hands in exasperation and settled into a more comfortable position on the floor, "This is my home, the seat of the White Court, the Court of Light. Books have called it the Seelie Court, though we don't ourselves. I am the king here, the ruler of my fae the White Fae, as was my father before me. Ramona is my half-sister, and she lives here as well." He stared into her eyes, hoping to make his last words stick. "We are not insane and I am not lying." He looked back down at the floor and muttered, "This was one reaction to this conversation that I was not expecting," he said to himself, further confirming Winter's suspicions of mental instability.

"Wait. Ramona is your sister?" She could let him talk like a lunatic all he wanted but now he was messing with her real life. "Bren, stop this. If you're joking, it's not funny. What's going on?" She hated to admit it, but she was actually starting to get a little scared.

"Yes, Ramona is my half-sister," he said dismissively, "Win, listen to what I am telling you, please. Does it matter who she is to me? Or to you? I am telling you that everything that you have known up until this point has been false and it is my fault. Does that not upset you?" Bren tested her forehead to see if she was feeling well, but Winter pushed his hand away.

"No, what upsets me is that you expect me to *believe* you. So, what, you think you're a fairy?" it came out a little more incredulous than she meant it to. Bren rubbed his hand over his face and took a deep breath.

"We are Fae, and so are you, Winter. Generally, our kind lives apart from the human world, most of the time, but not you. We are older than the human race and we live by different rules, different laws and different customs. You belong *here*, with the rest of your kind. You. Are. Not. Human, Winter." He said the last part slowly, loudly, like she was hard of hearing.

"I'm not *deaf*, Bren, or stupid, you know. Although I'm not quite ready to rule out crazy for either of us at the moment. Do you want some sort reaction from me that I'm not providing? If you did what you did, and everything you say is true, then you

227

must have had a reason. If not, we're both nuts," she couldn't believe what she was saying, "Because I trust you, and until I wake up and find out this is all a dream, I guess I'm going to believe you. My life has been too weird lately for me to rule anything out."

Yep, I said it; I'm just as freaking crazy as my new boyfriend, who happens to be practically my brother.

Bren, for his part, was looking a little more relieved, but she couldn't help but notice the pained expression he wore either.

"But that's not all is it, Bren? Because if fairyland was so flippin' wonderful, I would have grown up here right?"

"Oh quit being so dramatic, Winter, please. I am not trying to pick on you. I have done something that has removed you from your true home and robbed you of the chance to grow up as you should. Aren't you the least bit angry?" Bren kept looking at her like all of this new information would click into place and she was going to lose her mind.

Either she was still teetering, undecided, on the edge of insanity, or there must be more to this confession, because she was failing to see what was so horrible about what he had done. Bren certainly had a look of uncertainty about him that said there was more to this wild story.

Sure, if he was telling the truth, he probably should have told her before now, that she belonged to an ancient race of nonhumans. But then again, it wasn't so hard for her to believe right now, not after everything that happened in the last 36 hours. She had never really fit in anyway, so finding out she never belonged in the first place wasn't too much of a stretch.

But if it was so wonderful in Faerie, or wherever they were, that he remained here still, why would he remove her from this place? He wouldn't have done it for fun, surely? Winter was certain there was a good reason for what he did.

She tried to appear very calm and collected even though she was coming undone on the inside and Winter thought that she was accomplishing the illusion of it nobly. If she was going to freak out about walking into a closet and popping out in an alternate plane, or discovering she was Fae, or that the king of the White Court was in love with her and wanted to be her boyfriend, she guessed she would do it later, because nothing was happening right now.

Winter shrugged in a bewildered way and opened her mouth to speak, but then realized she had no idea what to say.

That too was a new development.

More bothersome still, was that she couldn't stop herself from touching his sandy hair while she thought, brushing it from his face. It could not be helped. Bren was upset for some unthinkable reason and Winter felt obliged to reassure him. Strangely, in that moment, she felt she was born to do it. He too leaned into her hand like her touch was magnetic. She felt a gratifying surge of intense white heat pulse between them.

Finally, Bren spoke.

"There was some danger for you to be here, Win, but it is no longer. I could keep you safe here now, if you would choose to stay. We could be strong together, you and I, for each other, if you would want me like I want you. It is no small promise for me to make to you, but there is more you need to know before you decide that I am above reproach." After that last statement, he lifted his eyebrow questioningly, then raised his hand and placed it on her forearm, pushing downward and effectively lowering her hand from his face.

"But you didn't keep me here, Bren. Why? What was the danger that has passed from this place, only to appear in another? Are you sure I'll ever truly be safe?" She thought of their flight from Ashe Street and let her hand drag down his arm, stroking the tan, smooth skin that showed below his short sleeve, down to his wrist. Winter felt him tremble slightly and a pulse of light rippled below his skin. It was subtle, but she was sure she'd seen it. Winter felt her surprise reflected in her expression. Bren gave her a sad smile and continued.

"Because...because of who you are. Your mother was a member of the White Court, my court," he paused and checked her face for any sign of comprehension or possible terror before continuing, "And your father was aligned with the Dark Court, our opposite. Do you remember what I told you? Everything is about balance, Winter, like the tree of life on your necklace." He touched her neck again, smiling at his gift that she wore. "You cannot have one thing without the other, Win. Everyone chooses a side.

C. B. Cole

Those who try to remain solitary risk living a life without protection from either Court, a life of danger. Solitary Fae can be tortured, or forced to live alone in fear all their lives. I would not want that for you, even if you could choose it." Bren paused again, this time to kiss her fingers solemnly.

He spoke the last part very slowly, like he was talking to a child.

"I could not wish that for you, My Love. You have not chosen an alignment, Winter, so you are at risk," Bren sat there, silently regarding her, then sucked in another deep breath for his next, and possibly most dangerous, words. "You *must* choose, Winter, because you are royalty too, in your own way." He smiled at her reassuringly, and she thought she must look like she needed it.

"The Dark Court upholds the laws of chaos and disorder. They require evil and violence to stay alive, as my Court thrives on goodness and respect. Just as the White King rules the White Court, the Dark King commands the evil of the Dark Court."

Winter knew that her face betrayed her confusion.

She wasn't exactly confused about the nuances of good and evil, so much as she was confused about how she had gone from a normal girl, to a member of the royal family of Faerie.

Winter hoped Bren would get to his point soon because she had yet to see how this history lesson was related to her other than that she needed to pick a team. She was never a good student; he of all people should know that. Bren sighed again and resumed his teaching.

"Win, I rule this Court, and my brother, Kieran, dictates the other. He rules the darkness, while I make my way in the light." He shrugged as he said the last words, like it was not a thing that could be controlled, just something that was.

But she knew that name, even if it was the first time Bren spoke it in front of her. A tiny shiver of longing that she hoped he didn't notice, or if he did, found a way to attribute it to himself, danced through her veins at the sound of his brother's name.

Now, she really did have some questions.

"I thought your brother was dead?" she countered. She hoped it wasn't too stupid of a question to ask, but she had been through a lot in the last few days and didn't feel like she was firing on all cylinders. Then again, Bren was full of surprises. Ramona had just become family for real, not some imagined connection they forged out of loss. Brothers...

"He is dead to me," he said matter-of-factly. "We grew up together, but he was jealous that I would be king one day. He joined the Dark Court and killed the old king to take his place. Then, he killed our father when he dared to confront him. That is how I came to rule, because of him. In some small way, maybe I owe him, because, without his deception and eventual defection, I would have never met you." Bren patted her hand gratefully, then added the final nail in her coffin. "You met him, Win. Shade is my brother, but his real name is Kieran and he is the Dark King."

Yeah, she got that.

Just now.

She may have been slow on the uptake until then, but that part didn't go by unnoticed this time. Brothers competing, kings in an intense rivalry, and she was in the middle of their childish tug of war.

Fantastic.

Bren, oblivious to her mental deterioration, pulled her close and rested his chin on her shoulder so that he spoke with his lips treacherously close to her ear, sending new little tremors of lust down her spine.

Those were definitely his fault.

"Your parents should not have loved each other, Winter, they were foolish, and it was dangerous. It goes against every principle of both Courts. There are very few of us that could even manage that; Me, Kieran, Fiona maybe, but I doubt it, Ramona, if she wanted to, but no one does. It just doesn't happen. And there are those of us that can change affiliation, like Kieran did, but why would lovers separate themselves willingly? No one knows. It is just as much of a mystery as you are. That they could have maintained a relationship at all was almost as unbelievable as the birth of you. They had to have been very strong indeed, and you are stronger because of it. You are so unique. There has never been a Fae born, who lived this long, undeclared." He let his tongue flick out and tease her earlobe and Winter was afraid she would melt into him right then and there.

It was not a very Bren thing to do.

"So I have to decide between darkness and light? Doesn't sound too tough? And if I do, I will be safe?" That seemed easy enough. Then she considered further."You protected me all these years from...myself, Bren?" She thought it was a noble thing to do, but unnecessary. Thankfully though, she realized that maybe he had just given her time to make a choice. "This was about what I wanted? All along?"

To her surprise, he didn't look particularly proud at that moment.

"If I had not hidden you, Winter, you might have been forced to grow up in the shadow of the Dark Court, subject to Kieran's whims. I know he has spoken to you. I saw your fear. Do not fear me, Winter. I will never do anything to hurt you." His eyes burned with an honest sincerity and she knew Bren meant the words he spoke.

He really did love her.

And she didn't fear him, she never had.

"So, it's easy, Bren. I choose my family." She threw her hands up in the air, exasperated. "It isn't a very hard choice, Bren. Seriously. You and Ramona are the only family other than Tor that I have. Oh! Oh my god, Tor!" She covered her mouth, horrified. She had forgotten all about him.

Again.

"Is he okay?"

***

Bren ignored her last question. The boy didn't matter. *This* mattered, their conversation mattered. He was so focused on her choosing that the rest could wait forever.

Bren pulled back from her, but kept his hands on her small shoulders and shook her a little as he said, "Winter, you don't really know what you are saying.

C. B. Cole

To really choose? As much as I have dreamt of the day that you would choose to remain here with me, I can't believe you know what you are truly saying."

And Bren didn't know whether he wanted to be the one to tell her that there was more to choosing than just saying the words. Somewhere in the back of his mind, he knew he could be happy to play her paramour. He thought in another life, if he was not so focused on doing the right thing, or if he was Kieran, he could live with her and love her until the words that would set him free finally escaped her lips.

No, he would wait for as long as it took until she was able to change them both forever, until she could agree to be his wife. If she was not ready to be his queen yet, he would not force her to live yet another lie. Kieran was the one capable of hiding the truth. He could tangle it in his hands until it was so unrecognizable from its real meaning, but not Bren.

He couldn't do it. As much as his heart desired her affections, how much he craved it, he could not hide this last thing from her. Kieran would never stop looking for her until her choice was made. It was because of Kieran, and his ability to be happy to live a lie with her, that Bren would have to tell the truth.

Winter watched him, witnessing the internal battle he was waging play out on his face. She put her hand out and smoothed the wrinkles on his forehead, then let her palm rest on his cheek.

"Bren," she said quietly, "It's okay. I think I know what I'm saying. I choose the good Court, *your* Court. I could not live my life in a world of evil. You should know that."

His heart raced when his name left her lips, poured out for him like honey, sticky and sweet in her mouth. She looked so innocent and he believed very much that Kieran's world would crush her if she would ever venture into it.

"I believe that but, there is more, Win," This was the part he feared. "If you choose a Court you must choose to be their queen, Winter. You are royalty by virtue of your birth. You were born the first Fae capable of tipping the balance between the two Courts. You are unique, to hold the Dark and the Light in you the way you do. It is so unparalleled that in all the history of forever, that we, *our* kind, have never known another like you. The fae can so rarely have children, you see, and you are fae born; born of the good and the foul in our world. You are amazing, of course, you are amazing." He said the last part softly and smiled, thinking about how lucky he was to share so much time with her already. He would have that, if nothing else.

"There was a prophecy called the Undecided Queen that spoke of you. It had almost been lost to the annals of history, forgotten. Very few of the old ones even remembered, but my mother knew. She told me that you would come. So we, Ramona and I, were lucky enough to find you after your mother died and hid you where no one from Faerie would ever look. It cost us much, and we took great pains to bind you, hide what you were, so that you could live your life as you wanted until it was time. You deserved a life, Win. I know what it is like to have no choices and I did not want that for you.

236

C. B. Cole

"So until you choose, you won't realize your true Fae nature, Win. Until you align with one Court or the other as their queen, to rule, you will be human until you say the words that will free you."

"There are words?" she asked incredulously, as if this situation could get any more complicated. "How do you know?"

"Wedding vows, I think. Though no one is actually certain." He blushed as he said it, then gave her a look that questioned whether she was paying attention, "It says that you must choose, and that you will be set free. No one knows exactly what will happen, Win."

"Well, what *did* it say?" she asked. "The prophecy, what did it say specifically?"

Bren pulled out a dusty book, from the low table near where Gilroy had placed the tray behind them. He opened it, letting dust motes drift down to the stone below.

> *An Undecided Queen is born of chance,*
> *From an opposing lover's dance*
> *To test the wills and thrones of kings.*
> *And the balance that has always been,*
> *Will fall with the Choice she brings.*
> *In her choice one king will rise,*
> *The other will find his rule's demise.*
> *Her true form freed with a king's kiss,*
> *Sprung from her cage with a touch of his lips.*
> *The decisions made out of love will bring,*
> *A new life to a brother king,*
> *And then will rise the one true queen,*

Whose years in waiting, removed from her home,
Have made her ready to ascend the throne.

He shut the book without ceremony and replaced it. Winter could take what she would from the words. He knew what it meant to him, and to Kieran.

Bren rose, leaving her to her thoughts, and paced the white marble floors of what could be his queen's chamber. She seemed so close to understanding. Bren hoped his words would comfort her, guide her. It was his dearest wish not to alienate the woman before him.

Chapter Twenty-Five

"So, what you're saying, the whole point of this convoluted confession, is that I will be a queen when I choose my king, and then marry them, but until then, I stay human?" That seemed the easiest way to say it.

Talking about the discord between him and Kieran seemed like a waste of time. It was clear to her now that the battle for her affections began for the so-called Dark King at the concert. Again, she suddenly felt very foolish for thinking Kieran could have ever really cared about her. He just wanted her so he could be powerful.

Asshole.

That was the least colorful thing she could think to call him right now.

Winter felt dumb having to ask Bren to confirm her recent knowledge, but she was having a hard time wrapping her brain around it all.

Bren, excruciatingly handsome and patient, gave up trying to enlighten her and left her side. Was she so pathetic? Winter shivered under the loss of his all-encompassing warmth. Without him, the world around her seemed colder, darker.

Without him, she was afraid.

"Yes, Win, you will shed your human glamour and become queen when you marry." He stopped by a golden fountain that was built into the marble on the far wall. He was running his fingers absentmindedly through the water, watching the ripples they created.

"And I would have to choose between you and K... your brother? And as queen, I would be your equal?" She could hardly imagine the blow that he could single handedly deliver to her psyche if he told her she would have to get married and then play housewife. Besides, it seemed a safe question, to ask if they would rule together, as partners.

Bren looked surprised at the question, so she felt that she was mostly right about her expectations. He would never ask that of her.

"Of course, you would be my equal, Win!" Then he blushed and snapped his mouth quickly shut in embarrassment. "I mean, I would think that you would rule equally with whomever you choose," he added in his more formal voice. She smiled playfully at him and stretched out lazily on the couch with her arms behind her head.

"And then I suppose I would be required to fulfill my wifely duties as well?" she asked rather archly. Winter suppressed a wicked giggle by pressing her face into the arm of the couch when she saw Bren's body stiffen at the mention of physical intimacy. If she had thought he had been put off his game by her previous question, he out did himself this time. The color of his normally tan skin turned a scandalized shade of red, and that was just what she could see of him from behind. His face, she was sure, was probably a new and unnamed color.

He turned around and confirmed her suspicions. He was, indeed, very red.

Brick, she decided, was the closest color she could think of. It was the first time throughout this whole ordeal that he gave her a look that seemed reminiscent of her old life.

Winter didn't think that she and Bren ever had any sort of conversation concerning sex.

Why would they?

That responsibility fell heavily onto Aunt Ramona shortly after she announced her and Tor's change in relationship status at dinner a few years ago.

The gimlet stare he gave her now was terribly similar to the way he would look at her when she was younger and wore a particularly revealing Halloween costume to school, or, come to think of it, when she told him she was no longer friends with Tor, but instead, dating him.

Bren coughed, fighting for air through his embarrassment. He looked like he was trying to regain control of his voice, then cleared his throat meaningfully.

"Winter, it is my firm belief that marriage and duty are not the same as love. If you do wish to sleep with your husband, whoever he may be," she thought it possible his blush deepened, "I would hope that you do it for love, even if you are his queen. You have no responsibility here, other than to ascend the throne." Without further comment, he turned around, gazing into the fountain again.

After his pointed remark on love and sex, Winter felt stupid for thinking her next question, let alone uttering it. But, of course, she did.

"And I have to let Tor go now, don't I? He can't be safe with me anymore? I mean, should definitely say goodbye, especially if I am never going back, right?" After the words were said, she immediately knew how he would take them, but it was too late. Winter knew Bren was going to assume that she slept with Tor, if he didn't think that already. It would not have been a wild assumption on his part; she loved Tor very much.

She wasn't wrong.

The muscles in his jaw tightened immediately and she saw him grip the thick lip of the golden basin tighter. If he was any stronger, he probably could have bent the metal under the force he was exerting.

Damn it, now I'm going to have to go to him and make it all better.

For a king, he was suddenly acting very much like a child.

Winter flexed her ankle warily, testing it in anticipation of her trek across the room and found that the pain had gone. She tentatively tried her weight on it, supporting herself on the arm of the couch until she was sure that it would hold her. The marble was just barely cool beneath her feet, but it felt like secret warmth might lie below the surface, heating it from deep within the earth.

If she was alone, she probably would have dropped to the floor so that she could press her cheek against it, to see if it was truly warm, cool, or neither at all. But at this particular moment, Winter thought that action would probably make her look as crazy as she felt she was becoming. Thankfully, Bren still had his back turned to her, and he didn't hear her coming closer over the gurgling sounds of the fountain. His calculated silence upset her.

Winter felt the most desperate and unsettling need to reassure him. She never cared so much what he thought of her as she did right now. Winter *needed* to make Bren believe that Tor had not taken that most special gift from her.

While she knew Tor very much wanted to make love to her, Winter had never been able to go through with it. There was always a reason not to, and up until now, she thought that perhaps she was just saving herself for a better time, or a more romantic moment. Now, she thought maybe she was just saving herself for someone else.

Hell, maybe I was just saving myself for someone of my own species.

Winter crept closer to him, moving slowly so that she could watch him. Something about the tightness in his neck and shoulders that developed after her question about Tor bothered her. For some strange reason, Winter needed, more than anything, to ease his fears. She felt all wrong with him upset. Still unaware of her approach, Bren began to answer her. His voice was hard, and it betrayed the hurt he felt.

"I guess you are right, it is not safe for him to be with you anymore. The boy is here now though, and we are holding him safely until Kieran calls off his Hunt. Then, you must say your *goodbyes*." On the last word, delivered with more sarcasm that necessary, she knew he was insinuating that she could have sex with him one last time, if that was what she so desired. It stung a bit, to hear him address her with such vitriol.

How dare he give me permission to sleep with someone after he professes his love to me? she thought, outraged at his suggestion. She wanted to slap him, or maybe kiss him for being willing to let her say goodbye to her first love however she saw fit.

Winter was close enough to see the water ripple out in waves from the place where it filtered melodically into the fountain before him. Bren had his hands cupped, holding the clear liquid hostage in his palms. His passionate heat and his years of well-hidden adoration were pulling her toward him like a siren song. She wanted nothing more than to be wrapped in his arms where he could tell her again that she was safe.

That she was not alone in this strange world.

The water gurgled in a pleasing way. Winter noticed that in Bren's hand, dancing in the water he held in his broad palms, was a tiny woman, undulating seductively to an unheard tune. The fragile creature froze at once when she saw Winter appear behind Bren, and dropped into nothing, leaving the water just as uninteresting it was before it became the water fae's liquid stage.

"She was beautiful, Bren," Winter whispered into his ear and, when her breath caressed him, his entire body stiffened at her words, but this time, she didn't think it was because he was either scared or angry with her.

And that left only one exciting possibility.

It was wrong for her to feel powerful with that knowledge, with that ability to turn him on with just a word, but she secretly did.

"Will she come back, do you think?" Winter let some of her excitement over the thrill of her minor victory color her words. He shivered as her whispered question tumbled softly in his ear. She was so close she could hear his breath come out raggedly as he tried to ignore her nearness. Briefly, she considered trying out "My King" at the end of her question, but then decided that blatant flattery delivered like that was not her style.

He shook his head uncertainly to answer her question and Winter suddenly felt very alone. She stood beside him for a moment before working up the courage to speak again.

"Bren?" she asked quietly, no longer playful. "Will you remember to tell me when to be scared? I feel like I am not myself anymore. I need you to remind me, sometimes."

He looked at her and his eyes were filled with so much sadness that she was quite sure he was breaking inside. "Of course, Win. For you, I would do anything you asked of me. I would do anything to be worthy of your love." Bren stared at her for a moment, searching her face for some mysterious sign.

But Winter didn't wait for him to find it.

She reached out to Bren now, pulling him into a hungry kiss that yesterday, would have felt all wrong. Today, tonight, he was her savior, her faerie king and she thought that maybe she could love him the way he wanted her to.

Better yet, she could love him as maybe she always had, and she could try to love him as his queen, or his wife. The thought made her swallow. Could she live up to the expectations he had for her?

If she had to choose a partner, Bren would be just fine. At least she knew he would never hurt her like she feared Kieran would.

Winter tried to nuzzle against him, mold her body around him but he was still holding back. The strange tension he carried in his shoulders seeped into his kiss. It was a hard, punishing, unyielding version of its former beauty. She knew she was suffering the consequences of his wounded pride, bruised from thinking she was no longer a virgin and that he had no real prize left to claim.

Who was he to assume I would save myself for him?

Affronted by his anger she retorted "You should know I never had sex with Tor."

Winter was facing him, her arms still wrapped around him in a tight embrace. They faced each other, staring, daring the other to reveal any emotion first. She was defiantly holding her ground, and he his.

Bren said nothing, but his lips twitched just a bit, betraying his pleasure at hearing her say so. Those deep blue eyes of his flashed strangely and Winter swore she saw lightning streak across his crystalline oceans. She twined a finger in his shaggy hair.

"I guess I was always saving myself for someone better," she added coyly. Winter felt a little evil saying so, but the last bit was too good to resist.

At that, he rewarded her with the most radiant, triumphant smile she had ever seen. She started to release him and walk away, but he grabbed her back to him, smashing his lips against her own in a way that was not sweet or gentle at all.

Winter very much liked that side of Bren. He was kissing her and kissing her. Bren pushed her back up against the cool stone wall and shamelessly explored her body over her clothes. When she thought they might be too close to reaching that place where stopping was not an option, she pushed him firmly away. He leaned back against the wall beside her, both of them breathing heavily. He grabbed her hand and gave it a reassuring squeeze.

They looked at each other for a moment, holding hands, just staring. Then, he smiled at her and said, "Asrai, will you come back please?" The dancing tiny fairy returned shyly at the king's command, peering speculatively at Winter.

Bren bent down so that he was eye level with the little water creature and said, "This will be your queen one day, my dear."

The water sprite curtsied daintily, balancing on the water's surface.

Winter nodded back to her as regally as she could imagine how. Then, Asrai turned away and began to move again to a tune that only she heard.

Winter watched her fluid dance and wondered what it would be like to feel so liberated, so free. She thought that leaving everything she had ever known to join her real family in Faerie might be like that. A new freedom, if she chose to view it that way. If she could find a way to be happy here, she told herself, the petty problems of her human life would vanish and she, too, could be free.

"I want Tor to forget me," she said suddenly. "I don't want him to remember anything about being here. I want him to hate me so much that he won't miss me if he has to remember anything," she told Bren very seriously. "And if you can help me with that, Bren, I will try to love you the way you want me to."

Bren bent formally at the waist, then righted himself and kissed her cheek. Winter hoped that the fire that passed between the two of them might be enough. It might just be enough to melt the snow covered chunk that she discovered still remained, frozen in her heart.

That great ball of ice held her feelings for Tor, and surprisingly Kieran, rolled neatly into their own special place. They were safe there, contained and immovable, until she could find a way to be free of them too. If she always followed what was right, everything would be fine.

It had to be.

Aunt Ramona had told her that all her life.

"My Queen," Bren nodded to her, then called out, "Gilroy, take the Lady Winter to the boy, whenever she is ready." Then he gave her a thoroughly disapproving look and gestured to her appearance.

"You look like you have been filming a zombie flick, Win," he taunted. He seemed so much more like the Bren she knew, rather than the odd faerie king she just met.

Winter looked down at her dirty clothes and frowned. "Thanks, I guess in Tor's eyes, that's much better than looking like I've been making out with you."

***

"Here. At least change out of those. You look like you have been mud wrestling." Bren went to the gilded bureau that rested along one edge of her room and pulled out a gold silk dress. It was one shoulder, Greek style with gold vines embroidered on the bodice. It was fancier than anything he had ever seen her wear, but it would have to do. It was what would be expected of her from now on anyway.

"This will be comfortable, Win. Sorry, there aren't any jeans in Faerie," he shrugged, "Although we could try to get some made for you. Or you could go back and get some of your clothes in the morning?"

"No, this is fine. Thank you, Bren."

He dutifully turned his back while she changed; he could hear the different sounds the flannel, and then the denim, made as they fell to the floor. There was a shuffling and some frustrated sighs before she spoke again.

"Okay," she called.

He turned at her words.

"I'm mostly ready. Could you help me, Bren, do you think?" she pointed to the laces under one arm. "I can't quite tie these I'm afraid." She looked like she was trying to put on a brave face, but he could tell the attire intimidated her.

Bren came over to her slowly and took her face gently in both of his hands. Touching her nose with his

249

own, he said, "You look beautiful, Win." He tied up her laces swiftly and spun her around so that he stood behind her. Burying his hands in her hair, he twisted and pulled and braided until he was satisfied.

"Put your hand just here," he told her and indicated where she should hold. She did and he dashed to the dressing table and came back with a few jeweled wooden pins that he inserted deftly into her dark mass of hair.

"There. Now, you really don't look like you have been making out with me all night," he said with a smile, then he kissed the back of her neck and the hand that she raised to feel the design he created.

"Thank you, Bren," she said softly. Winter turned around and kissed him gently. She did not tell him she loved him, though. He wondered how long it would take her to say it.

"I'm ready, then," she said with heavy sigh and sadness in her voice.

Bren opened the door and gestured for Gilroy to lead the queen down the hall.

The door clicked shut behind them as they left. He did not envy her the task she had; though he was secretly glad to find out she never shared her body with that boy.

She was whole.

She was his.

She told him she wanted to try to love him.

That was all he ever wanted.

Bren could hear them retreating down the hall, her bare feet making soft slaps on the stone floor. Finally alone, he sighed contentedly at how well everything had gone. She had not yelled or screamed or berated him, but trusted him as always. And now she went to close the final chapter on her human life.

Bren was glad though, to have some time alone, to have a chance to recover from her. She was driving him crazy in the most wonderful way.

After having years to wonder what she would look like as she grew into a young woman, then more years watching her become even more lovely than he'd imagined, he had almost used up all of his self-control in just the act of waiting. Now, she was an adult, aware of her history, and the role she could play in his own, and she still chose to be with him.

Bren was trying very hard not to go too far too fast, but she wasn't making it easy for him. Never had he expected her to want to kiss him so much, so soon, not that he was displeased.

Bren chuckled to himself, maybe the truth of it was he didn't know what to expect at all. He lingered in her room for a minute longer, remembering their time twined on the couch, then crossed to the bureau that he filled with clothes he thought she might like.

She looked so lovely in the dress he had chosen for her just now, and the thick silver braid she wore around her neck made her look regal. He moved long dresses and frothy clothes to find the wooden bottom of the dresser.

There in the bottom of the closet, in a small, black chest, was his mother's jewelry that he saved. He picked out a gold ring, set with a large mine cut ruby. It was the same ring that his father had given his mother so long ago when she became Queen Consort.

Bren thought it would soon be time for him to give it to Winter, when he finally said the words that would make her his queen.

Bren tucked the Queen's Ring into his jeans pocket, then shut the door to the bureau and began to think of ways to ask Winter to be his wife.

***

The hall outside her room was as equally well appointed and exquisite as her own chambers were. She thought it shouldn't have been surprising, but it was. Winter followed the one Bren called Gilroy down the hall, passing several ornate doors she thought must be the entrances to Bren's own rooms. They were by far the grandest entryways in the small corridor and they certainly looked worthy of a king, which, of course, she now knew he was.

And Kieran is his brother and a king too, she thought. *Can it get any weirder?*

The problems she faced seemed infinite, and Tor was just another problem that needed addressing.

Immediately.

The larger issues, thankfully, had more time before they must be handled. Winter hadn't asked, but she got the impression that human life spans were not a hindrance in Faerie. She made a mental note to ask Bren about it later.

Or Kieran, if I ever see him again.

Winter caught herself in a reluctant sigh, then straightened her back and kept moving forward. If she couldn't stop thinking about him, the least she could do was have the decency to conceal it.

C. B. Cole

And the brothers are so different! Winter guessed, by virtue of necessity, they had to be. She remembered vaguely what Bren said about balance. Winter knew she did not envy either one of the men for having to be king.

Crap.

Normally, she would have followed that thought with one that reaffirmed the fact she was glad she didn't have to do their job, but then it occurred to her that she would, indeed, have to do just that. Winter wondered if she could find the fortitude to rule an entire people and do it well. She felt certain that, with Bren there to guide her, she may have a chance. She believed what he said; he *would* love her for his whole life.

Then it hit her rather belatedly.

God, have I come so far so fast that telling Tor, my boyfriend, the person I loved since I was ten, goodbye, is now classified as a minor problem? What is wrong with me?

She let out a weary sob and her escort turned back, alarmed. Winter shook her head to indicate that she was fine, then Gilroy stopped in front of a new door, plain and hidden in a recess in the wall. If Winter wasn't paying attention, she wouldn't have seen it, or she would have thought it was merely a closet.

She hoped Tor was okay. Winter took a deep breath and nodded to Gilroy, who opened it for her. Thinking better of it, she immediately pulled it closed again.

"Milady, if you should need me at all, I will be just outside. When you are finished here I will take care of the rest of your wishes." He said reassuringly as he bowed low and she giggled. He smiled at her graciously. Winter noticed he seemed genuinely pleased that he was trusted to escort her. She wondered if she should say something, but what would a queen say?

"You honor me," was all she could come up with, but Gilroy bowed low again and smiled gratefully, so she was pretty sure her words were sufficient.

Winter gathered up all of the courage she could muster, definitely not wanting to face Tor. He was her best friend all her life, and now she had to let him go.

She would miss him, of course she would, but Winter bravely told herself that the human part of her that loved him was no more inside of her than human blood was ever in her veins. Winter turned the knob and pushed the door that would lead her to Tor.

Chapter Twenty-Six

Tor had destroyed almost every piece of furniture in the room he was in when she finally came to see him. It surprised him that the first thing he would feel when he saw her again was not joy, but, interestingly enough, irritation. He spent the last few hours distraught with worry over her, and here she was, with not even a scratch.

She didn't even have the decency to look ill.

In fact, Tor thought she looked very vital. He watched her, unmoving, from the bed like a hawk watches his prey. Tor noticed the pink flush to her cheeks that seemed achingly familiar, reminiscent of the blush she would wear when they spent lazy days kissing on the couch. Her hair was pulled back and secured with pins in a style he had never seen her wear before. She had changed too, into a floor length gold silk dress that probably cost more than his Colt and was wearing the thickest, heaviest looking necklace he had ever seen. It looked like she might struggle under the weight of it. No, life had not been hard on her these last few excruciating hours.

Eyeing her thoughtfully, Tor was willing to bet Bren had given her those things and it made his blood boil. Winter wisely stayed away from him, he noticed. Perhaps she was letting the wildness in his eyes fade. Or perhaps she was trying to navigate a path through the wreckage to reach him.

"You're fine I see," he stated blandly. It seemed like he was saying it for his own benefit more than hers. She gave him a questioning look, but still didn't come closer.

"Yes, I am fine." She tried to echo his brittle tone, but failed. Then, she absentmindedly tucked some strands of her dark hair that had fallen loose, behind one of her ears.

With that familiar gesture, Tor was no longer angry, but in agony. Part of him wanted to run to her, and smother her with kisses and affection, and tell her he had missed her more than she would ever know.

But he didn't.

The other part of him wouldn't let him. It would not allow it, because some small voice inside him that sounded strangely like Winter told him they might not be at that place anymore. The small voice told him not to be concerned about her, she would be fine.

She had always been fine without him. He eyed her steadily, preparing to fire off his next questions. Winter wouldn't like what he was going to say because he was going to ask about Bren.

"And this place," he gestured grandly, "It is Bren's I assume? What kind of panic room is this?" Tor tried to put a little humor into his attack, but in reality, he didn't find a thing funny about it. She fidgeted uncomfortably.

So did he, for that matter.

Winter stared at him for a long time without answering, but then she must have seen something on his face that encouraged her. He watched her as she

256

moved delicately through the rubble of the room like a dance. She picked her way barefoot through the splinters and broken stone until she stood before him. Still, Winter did not reach out for him. Now that they were face to face, she spoke.

"Yes. This is Bren's home. And my home too, Tor." Her words came out strangely clipped and detached.

That small part of Tor that sounded an awful lot like Winter *was* right; they weren't at that place anymore. He realized that at no part in this conversation would she reach out for him.

The part of him that knew she was gone rejoiced in its uncanny ability to see things for what they were. The other part, the part that was in love with her, was in shock, preparing for what he knew was coming next.

It was always the same.

He'd seen a thousand romantic movies with her over the years, and this next line was always the same.

"I love you, Tor."

And there it was; the dagger in his heart. To her credit, sadness colored her words that time. He thought that part might have been true. Winter was never the type to lie. Now, all he could do was wait for the *but*.

"I love you too, Win. Since we were ten, I have loved you." He saw her wince when he said that. Her momentary weakness emboldened him, so he ran with it.

"Please, Win, I don't know what he said to you, or told you. Don't tell me goodbye, Win. Not like this." Without thinking Tor fell to his knees, pieces of shattered wood jabbed angrily into his skin but he held onto her, begging for his life with her not to end. "I can give you the things you need, Win. Is it his money? His houses? His clothes?" Tor tugged roughly on the dress and he heard a rip. To her credit, she did not step away or yell at him because of his assault. She did nothing but place her hand in a quiet benediction on his head. He knew she was done.

Done with him.

"I love you, Tor, but," and there it was "We can't be together anymore. I am so sorry." Silently, he climbed to his feet and slipped his hand into hers.

Winter didn't take her hand away from him this time. Still, she did not look at him, but graciously gave him time to recover from his desperate act.

They surveyed the broken room and all the damage he created and she laughed. Tor laughed too, and they laughed until big tears rolled down their faces; tears of laughter hiding the tears of their ending.

It was massive, the amount of destruction that he found time to cause while she was away from him.

Tor was glad he had done it though. Bren didn't deserve to have nice things when he had taken Winter away. After their laughter subsided, they sat down on the bed and talked about the shapes of all the broken things that lay there on the ground.

Tor told her that he thought all broken things could be fixed. This was a good thing, if they were talking about their relationship. His now ex-girlfriend just shrugged.

Winter surprised him by saying that people needed broken things, needed the chaos they bring. If

C. B. Cole

things were never broken, and always stayed the same, how would one know that the things they had needed replacing.

Ouch.

He was nothing but a broken thing to her.

She was kicking at a piece of smashed coffee table with her bare foot, contemplating it. It might have well been him, lying there on the ground.

"I can't stay with you anymore, Tor," she said finally, after she worried the stone with her toe until it drew blood. "You don't deserve what I would do to you. I have to be with Bren now. It's the only way."

She stroked his hair, but he thought that this time was different. It was not the way she would have done it when she loved him. He had seen Aunt Ramona do the same thing to her for years, whenever she needed comforting.

And then, in another painfully maternal way, she bent to kiss the top of his head goodbye.

***

Winter felt his grip on her hand tighten when she told him she was staying with Bren. She knew it would hurt him, but she said it anyway. Some strange, dark part of her wanted to watch his pain play out before her. She knew it was his greatest fear, that she would leave him for Bren, and now she confirmed it to him as she told him goodbye. Winter wanted to laugh, and dance while he withered in pain. She really wanted to.

But she didn't.

What the hell is wrong with me? Doesn't the one man who loved me without motive my whole life deserve more than that?

Winter turned to leave, determined to bury her new hateful feelings by drowning in Bren's kisses like an alcoholic, using drink to forget. She would use his passion to sear these strange new feelings of darkness away.

Strangest of all though, was the absence of any regret. Winter didn't regret leaving Tor for Bren. She didn't regret letting Bren think, for no matter how little a time, that she was no longer pure. In fact, she didn't even regret letting Bren think that she never even considered choosing his brother.

Winter never even truly thought she had a chance with Kieran, until Bren told her she did. And that small knowledge made her happy.

And yes, she wondered if the Dark King would love her, and treat her well, but something inside her told her he would if she went to him with open arms.

Kieran was passion and lust embodied; so different from Bren's unwavering adoration. He made her feel like she was the only one in the world in the time they spent together. Winter believed Bren when he told her he would keep her safe, and love her for his whole life.

Strangely, she felt Kieran would do the same thing for her too, only he would love her dangerously, to the edge of reason and sanity. If she wanted to misbehave with Kieran, she thought he would revel in it with her. Part of her wanted that very much.

Winter couldn't imagine Bren being naughty. If he hadn't earlier kissed her with the angry ferocity of a man who had thought his prize had been stolen, she would not have thought him capable of even jealousy.

But it was there, hiding behind his goodness and that was enough for Winter for now.

Kieran was capable of jealousy, though, in a way Bren could never fathom. She knew it.

Immediately, Winter hoped that the Dark King knew she was here with his brother and the knowledge of it devoured him. She hoped it made him want to come get her, just so she could see his desire for her on written on his face. There was a facet of the darkness inside her that he awakened and she so very much craved it in her life.

On her way to the door that would lead her away from Tor, Winter briefly caught her own reflection in a shard of the shattered mirror. Frozen at the sight, she stared horrified at the image of herself. It was a shocking contrast of her normal visage. Her eyes struck her as alien, her irises solid black, just like Kieran's eyes were when he wanted her so badly, back then on his bus.

Maybe, she thought, she was not so much like Bren with her emotions; maybe she was more like the Dark King when it came to love. She had to put her hand on the doorjamb to steady herself against the rush of desire she felt at the thought of Kieran's mouth on hers, his strong hands never straying from her face or hair. His intensity for her held a passion that Bren was unable to convey even while exploring every bit of her.

The brother kings were different and Winter was painfully aware.

The Dark King's name, when she thought of it, sent shockwaves of lust rushing through her system. She doubled over, gripping the wall by the door harder, feeling her fingernails split with the pressure of it, and stared into that glittering shard until she could will her eyes to finally return to their correct color.

When she felt normal enough, Winter slid to the floor and cried in a terribly manic way. Everything she thought she knew about her life, herself, was coming apart at the seams.

Tor came quietly over to her, and she thought he would try to comfort her, even though she was the one abandoning him. Instead, he bent low and spoke to her.

"It's okay," he said slowly, "I know you don't love Bren. That much I do know about you. I will be waiting for you, Winter and I will do whatever it takes to get you back." He kissed her on the forehead, then calmly went back to the bed, sitting like a stoic Buddha on the only unscathed piece of furniture left.

Winter collected herself and brushed the splinters from the liquid silk of her gown, cleaning herself enough so that Gilroy would not think the worst of his future queen.

Tor might be right, maybe she did not love Bren, but she was terrified that she may love his brother instead. Winter didn't want to admit that though, not even to herself. What if it was just lust or his fame or his power that called to her?

No, Kieran would never be what I need, she told herself.

Winter left and shut the door on Tor forever.

Chapter Twenty-Seven

Kieran had made Dugan keep a watch at his half–sister, Ramona's, house every minute of the day, and he was glad for it too. She would come back for him eventually; he knew she would, especially when she thought of him so lovingly, like she had before. There needed to be someone there waiting for her, even if it could not be him.

Even now, he felt the way she silently spoke his name to herself reassuringly, caressing the word like one lover caresses another. The Dark King loved the way she thought of him with a mixture of longing, fear and uncertainty. She may not yet know how to properly summon him, but it would happen in due time.

And because of that, Kieran was very glad that he was in his bed when she reveled in her darkness tonight. Her first time battling back the side that belonged to him and to the Dark Court was the closest he thought he would ever come to heaven. Kieran would never have imagined that he would be able to feel her like that. Their connection must very strong indeed, for her to affect him that way.

Kieran was glad to be safely behind locked doors too. It felt like too intimate a moment for him to have experienced anywhere else but alone, wrapped in the sheets she slept on during her time on Ashe Street. He let her intense feelings of uncertainty pin him there, and he was a slave to them, incapable of freeing himself, until she shut them down without warning.

When they ended, the Dark King lay wasted, totally consumed and bled dry in their wake. If she could make him feel that way, drain him of so much power, without even being in the room, he was afraid he might burst into a million sparks of light, burning out hot and fast, when he could finally touch her the way he very much wanted to.

Kieran knew they could be happy together, but more, he knew he wanted--more than anything--to see her happy too.

And, of course, away from Bren wouldn't hurt either.

Amazingly, without even being told how, Winter had tapped into him and into the darkness of their Court and used it for her own selfish needs. He had felt the trueness of it. Winter drew from him, strengthening herself.

She was perfect.

There was no denying that there would be a time when she would sit beside him as his queen--no matter what Brendan tried. Bren wasn't smart enough, or brave enough, to come up with a way to prevent them from being together. Kieran knew that while his brother may love the Undecided Queen, she did not love him back.

Not nearly enough for it to matter in the long run.

The prophecy said that she must choose a king.
That was all.

Winter's indecision was all her own to deal with, but her life, devoid of the knowledge of Faerie, was his brother's fault. As far as the Dark King was concerned, Bren had tricked her into loving him, trusting him, depending on him.

Thankfully, she did not love Brendan the way she loved the Dark King. That was something he knew for certain.

Kieran rolled over to press his face into the generic green comforter, rough and cheaply made, that was on her bed in Ramona's house. It was strangely out of place in this well-appointed room, filled with dark colors and rich fabrics. One day soon Kieran hoped he would turn over to see her there, stretched out in this bed beside him.

He reached out longingly to stroke the hair of a woman who was not there.

***

Bren was glad he stayed behind, letting Winter handle things the way she saw fit. The White King knew he would have to start letting her have more freedom. She was no longer the child he had known. She was a fledgling queen, his future queen. He didn't want to rule her; he wanted to rule with her.

Bren spent some time wandering absentmindedly through her chamber with the heavy ring in his pocket, seeing the room with new eyes now that she actually set foot in it and then he optimistically opened the door that joined their two rooms. He debated the wisdom in leaving them open, lest she should feel obligated or pressured to love him too soon.

C. B. Cole

Bren couldn't imagine that she would want to share his bed yet, but he hoped that knowing he was close by would remind her of home.

Her room here was designed to his every whim, yet subtly echoed her own bedroom topside. The warm whites and glittering gold that ran throughout all the White Court rooms were evident here, but punctuated by luxurious light blue fabrics he thought would complement her eyes. Of course, there was a dressing table too, with a mirror, and the bureau with the finest clothes he could find. The couch, well, that was so strangely out of place, with its coarse, synthetic fibers and dull colors, but he thought he had done well by including it. Winter had noticed it happily and that was all the confirmation he needed of a job well done.

And the bed.

He was not sure what to presume about it, whether he should go big with the hopes of sharing it or small so that she wouldn't feel that he was pushing her for intimacy. In the end, though, he had chosen one fit for a queen, small enough that two occupants would lie close, or one person could sleep with room to sprawl. Bren was proud of himself for the effort he spent on every detail, and not just the furniture.

Crawling across every surface were ivies and flowering vines that also dripped from the porch on Ashe Street. Their writhing life made the room seem lush and wild, bursting forth at the very sight of her. There was nothing cold about this place and of that, he was very pleased. Everything was alive and needed tending and care, just like his Winter.

Bren liked the way the living greens snaked easily through the door he just opened, already weaving their way toward Bren's room, joining the two of them in that one small way at least.

The king of the White Court followed the slithering canopy into his own chamber and found it, for the first time, lacking. The furniture, of course, was utilitarian and functional, he did not require much more than that. Nothing lacked a purpose. Bren patted the smooth top of his desk, an oak masterpiece his own father had worked from throughout his rule, and pulled out a small felt-lined drawer. He removed the weighty ruby ring from his pocket and dropped it inside for safe keeping. Bren did not want her to find it before he was ready.

Bren flopped down into a nearby chair and surveyed the rest of the room trying to figure out what was wrong.

No, the furniture is fine.

He looked at the white and gold covers on the bed and decided that they were fine too. Still, it wasn't enough for her. Bren needed it to be different, to reflect the way he was different now too, because of Winter.

Everything in his room was still the same, while he was so painfully altered. She affected him, yet his world remained unchanged, unaware.

Instantly, he knew what he wanted, what would be a meaningful addition in honor of his queen. Pushing himself to his feet using the arms of the chair, Bren stood in the middle of the room and he remembered. He imagined the dappled golden light of the forest where they shared their first kiss. Closing his eyes, he recalled every tiny detail he could about the woods today.

The White King heard the twitter of the titmice in the trees overhead and the tapping of the nuthatches perched higher in the branches. He heard the soft scratching of the squirrels as they foraged in the leaf mold below them all. But mostly, Bren remembered the way the many colored leaves drifted silently down, kissing Winter on the cheeks as they drew ever closer to the ground.

When he reopened his eyes, his room had bloomed into the gilded forest he imagined. Periodically, golden and flame colored leaves drifted from branches that wound tight and close to the ceiling, floating gently to the ground only to disappear into the floor. He could hear the same infinite chattering of the birds that bore witness to their first kiss echoing in the bowery above.

Bren was pleased with the changes, and he thought Winter would like it as well. He surveyed his new domain carefully, making small tweaks in the new decor until a gentle knock on his door brought him back to the present.

"Enter," he said distractedly. He found himself slipping back into his familiar role of king, rather than Earthbound guardian.

Bren did not turn to face his visitor, but bent down instead to pick up a particularly beautiful leaf that landed on his bare foot. He was glad he never had to wear human clothes again.

Neither did Winter.

He blushed uncontrollably when he thought of seeing Winter in the gown he had given her to go see the boy. Though he enjoyed seeing Winter in his cast off clothes, it did not seem right that the future queen should be forced to walk around her new home in his used flannel shirt, no matter how much he may like the sight of her in it. Remarkably, she looked very comfortable in the attire of the Court and he was glad that she changed.

Gilroy cleared his throat behind him reminding him of his presence.

"My King, the Lady Winter is finished with the boy. Should I bring her back here to you, sir?" Gilroy didn't move. Bren held up the delicate leaf and turned thoughtfully toward him, but his valet didn't meet his eyes.

"Please, no. That is not necessary; see the future queen to her own quarters. She is to do as she wishes here." The king raised his hand up to release the flame kissed leaf and it floated back up toward the high ceiling.

Bren thought the delicate thing was too eager to embrace the fall, and the colors of it just now were so lovely that it should get a second chance. He wished it green again.

It was always something he hated, to lose anything to the cold.

Gilroy turned and left without another word. Bren stood for a long time and watched the endless cycle of leaves dropping down to the ground. The ones he liked, that he could save in time, he returned to the limbs above.

He heard the faint *click* of Winter's own door as it opened and then closed again. The White King released one last fragile leaf, watching it drop to the ground and disappear completely, then he went to stand in their adjoining doorway.

"How are you, My Dear?" he asked, very curious to see how it went for her.

***

His question was simple enough, but the answer was more complicated than she could handle. Winter wanted to crumble in despair. Or rather, she wanted to *want* to crumble in despair, but she didn't. She didn't feel anything at the moment besides the supportive press of the sturdy door behind her.

Winter thought back on her moment of temporary insanity in Tor's room. It was strange though, that being back here in the room Bren had given her, that she now seemed miles away from her madness. Here with him, she couldn't imagine that she ever felt that twisted, devious way at all. She was ashamed and wished she hadn't been so cruel.

It was not her way at all.

The boy generously absorbed her craziness, dismissed it, and offered forgiveness, all without judging her. She was wrong to have said goodbye like that, she knew, but she had no choice.

Bren stood there in the frame of a door she hadn't noticed before, leaning calmly against its wooden jamb, silently waiting for her to answer him. He looked so different to her now, yet nothing had changed about him, other than her knowledge of who he was. He was a gorgeous, lean, tan Adonis who

271

strangely, wanted nothing more than to please her, and that was odd to a girl who ever only had one boyfriend before now.

The one I just dumped, oh yeah.

While staring at him stupidly, admiring the look of him, she recalled that Kieran had changed somehow for her that night on the bus. Winter had sensed it, seen it, and known that Kieran showed some other secret part of himself. She still didn't remember much of that night, but she did remember that.

Now, after the fact, Winter wondered if he had shown her the way he looked in Faerie? Bren seemed nothing like his brother in personality, but surely, they held some common traits. She wondered if he could do the same thing or if it was a particular trickery of the Dark Court.

She tried to sound casual.

"Do you always look that way?" she asked. Bren looked surprised and a little affronted, then she realized her delivery may have come out more rude than intended. "I mean, do you change at all down here? You said I would look different after I chose, so I just..."

Bren shrugged cryptically, still keeping his distance. Winter thought that maybe he was trying to give her space. Of course Bren would know that she was hurting and respect that. That was a noble gesture of him, considering how passionately enthralled they had been earlier that evening.

Winter then realized he was probably just dying to know what had happened with Tor, wanting to know whether she had given Tor a parting kiss, or more. He waited expectantly, but she never said a word. Still, through all his curiosity, he was giving her room.

What an admirable thing!

Winter was suddenly grateful that Bren knew that much about her; her moods and quiet ways. He had always known what she needed and found a way to give it to her.

Bren waited a few more minutes, in which she supposed he was giving her sufficient time to supply him with the details of her encounter with Tor, but she didn't relent. Finally, he moved toward her with a sigh.

"I can show you, if it would please you." His words were stiff, more formal than usual, she noticed. Whether or not his physical appearance had yet changed, she could certainly tell his mannerisms were different in this place. Winter chided herself for thinking like that.

This place was her new home.

Nodding encouragingly, Winter crossed the room, leaving the comforting support of the door behind. She sat down on the edge of the bed that would now be hers, noticing the covering was the most beautiful shade of blue she had ever seen. Fleetingly, she wondered if she was supposed to share it with Bren right away.

She wasn't sure if she could just yet. It just didn't seem right.

He was coming toward her, smiling like the sun. As nonchalantly as she could manage, she leaned to the left a bit so that she could see into the room that he came from. There was a bed in there as well. Thankful for small victories, a relieved sigh escaped her lips, and Bren gave her a questioning look. Winter smiled back at him and patted the covers beside her.

"Come, show me,"

She smoothed the opulent, sky blue bedding beneath her. Something that looked a lot like desire flashed in his eyes at the sight of her on the bed, but she chose to ignore it momentarily. Bren crossed the distance between them in an easy lope and sat close to her on the edge of the bed. He had the grace and the looks of a runway model.

That much hasn't changed about him. Winter doubted it ever would.

"Promise you won't be frightened, Winter," he cautioned. There was look of concern in his eyes that he wasn't even trying to hide.

She shook her head emphatically to prove she was ready, then leaned back a little, not knowing what to expect of his transformation.

***

Bren had never dropped his glamour for Winter before. He hoped she wouldn't fear him when he did. But still, he thrilled at the chance to be his true self with her. Years passed where he had been forced to conceal himself just to be with her. She had never seen him as he should be seen. It was one of the biggest tests of trust she could have asked him to perform and he was a little scared. He took her hand and held it gently in his lap and then looked away.

He took in a few deep breaths and focused on light.

Bren let the dullness of his human glamour slide off him and fade into the air completely. While he

274

did this, he imagined the blooming of the first flowers of spring and the coolness of a mountain stream running high after the first thaw. He thought about the doe and her new fawn in the woods that day with Winter. It always felt like he found the shine of the sun on morning dew, and kept it, pushing the light out through his skin. He drew on the power of the White Court to fill him, raise him to his regal status. The feel of its warmth was reassuring and the raw electricity of its power zinged through him.

Bren wondered if Winter felt it too, the extra energy between them, where their hands touched. As a future monarch, he supposed his change would affect her in some manner, though he failed to see how his presence in his true form would not get anyone's attention in the first place.

Ramona always told him he was *shiny*, shiny like sun on glass. Bren smiled to himself over the thought, then resumed his focusing. It took less than a minute and when he was fully changed, he looked back at Winter.

She gasped when his eyes met hers.

***

Winter waited patiently while Bren changed for her. He grew...brighter, before her eyes. She couldn't yet see his face, he still turned it away from her, but she felt the intangible changes surrounding him. It felt like there was a warm light emanating from inside him, soothing her skin and swirling all around her. The room smelled intensely of pine and cool earth. Winter watched his hair lighten and brighten until it looked like each strand was made of silver, bronze and gold.

275

Bren was a god, cast in precious metal. Even his skin glistened with the dull shine of pearls.

She held his hand, feeling it warm in her own until he turned back to face her, then she was forced to drop it when she tried, and failed, to cover her mouth in time to conceal a gasp of wonder.

He was glorious.

His eyes were a piercing blue, the darkest part of a cloudless sky reflected in the Caribbean Sea. He was ethereal, regal, and *gorgeous*.

"Bren? This is you?" she asked tentatively. "You are so...beautiful." He laughed a little, surprised at her pronouncement but otherwise said nothing.

Winter couldn't stop herself from touching the delicate skin on his throat. He trembled. The pulse under her fingertips jumped nervously.

"Will I look like you?"

"I don't know what you will look like," he said honestly. "But whatever you become, I am certain you will be lovelier than any other creature in Faerie."

Winter smiled appreciatively at him. How could she not smile at the sight of him? She couldn't even take her eyes off of Bren. There was no more of the familiarity of her childhood on his face. This was a new man altogether. He was handsome, but *more*. His whole presence, not just his body, was alluring, attractive to her. He called to her in a strange new way. She felt like he was the tuning fork that pulled her discordant soul to its true notes and now, she vibrated with joy and anticipation before him.

But it wasn't lust she felt.

It was like she found the other half of herself, the part that reveled in the emotions of love and safety and friendship.

Winter watched him watching her. She knew he was wondering if she was afraid. After a moment, he finally spoke.

"Could you still want me, Winter, when I look like this? It's not very human," he sounded sad. Not bothering with words, she kissed his lips, soft as the brush of moth's wings.

And Winter thought that maybe she could want him. She was willing to try. Her body wanted him, that was evident. Her heart trusted him.

Was that enough?

She scooted further back on the bed, moving up to the head of it and then laid her weary head down on the pillow. She didn't invite him to join her, but merely stared at the bowery of vines above her and noticed that the white marble of the ceiling had changed to a new velvet midnight full of stars.

Winter was suddenly very tired.

"Bren," she said softly, trying to force the overwhelming tiredness from her voice, "Will you stay with me until I fall asleep?" She turned her face so that her cheek pressed against the cool pillow, facing the direction in which he would have to lay, and briefly closed her eyes. When she opened them again she fixed her gaze on the wall beyond the bed. Winter couldn't see his reaction, but she felt the warmth of him draw closer, announcing his presence as he moved up the bed to lie beside her.

"For you, My Queen, I would do anything," he said softly and not without some disappointment. He settled in beside her and wrapped her tightly in his arms. He didn't change back into the Bren she had always known, but stayed there as himself, hugging her tightly against his warm chest.

He didn't kiss her, or make a move on her, but held her like she was the most precious thing he could be trusted with. She was safe with Bren. He would keep her safe if she was to sleep, and she desperately wanted sleep, for it had been a very long day. Winter let the heat of his skin, and the smell of him surround her, cover her, comfort her until she could not keep her eyes open another minute.

"Thank you, Bren, for showing me the real you." she mumbled feebly, and then added, "Don't go back."

Just before she fell asleep, she was sure that the temperature in the room rose another several degrees.

Chapter Twenty-Eight

Tor stayed in that room where she had broken his heart, even after Winter was gone, not because he wanted to, but because no one would let him leave.

He had thought, there at the end, when Winter had that mini-breakdown, maybe she wasn't going to leave him after all.

But, of course, she did.

When she crumpled on the floor, he knew, without a doubt, that it wasn't her choice to do this to him. That helped a little.

Tor knew what was wrong. He certainly had had plenty of time to think about it. This was all Bren's fault. That bastard waited and waited until she was weak, then swept in to take her away from Tor. Bren wanted her all along. Tor had always seen it. He could see it in the way he looked at her, as if she was the only girl in the world.

But why did he want *her*? Why couldn't he let Tor have the one thing he wanted above all else?

Bren was rich and had been everywhere, of course. He always had beautiful women visiting him, and beautiful men too, whenever he was in town. Tor just assumed there was an endless parade of people who could keep him happy. Why did Bren want to steal the one constant ray of light in Tor's otherwise boring existence?

Tor tightened his hands into fists. Bren would pay for this somehow, Tor would make him. And when Bren broke Winter and left her behind, she would come back to him. Tor hoped that he would find her undamaged from her time here with his rival and when she was safely back in his arms, he would take his revenge on Bren.

The door opened loudly in on his reverie, and Tor jumped up, half expecting it to be Winter coming back to him. But it was only the thin blond who had been with Aunt Ramona. She briefly looked around the room, but made no comment.

Fiona is her name, he thought.

"What do *you* want?" Tor growled. He was not particularly in the mood for visitors. As far as he was concerned, she was just as guilty as Bren and Aunt Ramona.

"You can come with me," she said plainly. She didn't say it like it was a choice though. Fiona turned and walked out, clearly expecting him to follow her without making a scene.

Making a scene would be immensely satisfying, he thought, but he doubted that Winter would come out of her hiding place even if he did, so he followed Fiona without a word.

"He has her now, doesn't he?" Tor asked. He didn't offer any other information or clarify who he was speaking about. He knew Fiona would know exactly what he meant.

"Not yet, Boy. He doesn't have all of her yet. She still has to choose, you know."

Wow, he thought. *That was incredibly vague.*

280

"No. Actually, I have no idea what you are talking about," Tor said, a little too cuttingly. She gave him a pitying look over her shoulder, but they kept on walking.

The willowy and wild woman with the long, blond hair that looked like it could curl itself into dreadlocks at any moment, led him through the cavernous expanse of the marble hallways, navigating them easily. He couldn't help but notice that she prowled the halls, more than walked and found himself thinking it was a little sexy.

Which, of course, I shouldn't do since I still love Winter, right? Tor decided Fiona was the most dangerous creature he had ever seen.

And these halls themselves. They were not what he would have chosen for a secret passage attached to a closet, but who was he to say? Deep down, though, Tor knew he wasn't in some safe place Bren made under the house in Ashe Street, but somewhere else entirely. And it gave him the creeps.

Tor would have guessed that it would be cold and clinical feeling here with all that stone, but it wasn't. The crazy curling vines and improbable life springing out from all around, reassured him that things could thrive here. It was calming and safe.

No, he shook his head to clear it of the idea. Nowhere Bren was would be safe for him or Winter. He needed to focus on Winter.

"So, do I have any chance of getting her back?" he said sarcastically. She would probably never help him, but it never hurt to ask.

"No, Boy, not with her. Not anymore." Fiona answered cryptically as she marched him away with the precision of a soldier. Suddenly, she stopped in front of the only brown door in the white hall. It looked like a closet.

Bren's closet.

Tor was through with the crazy, vague answers and weird hidden vault they were in. He was through being nice and didn't care if he hurt her feelings. Fiona wasn't doing him any favors. Still, it surprised him that he had the bravery to even ask her.

"So, did he choose her over you too, then? Is that what your deal is? 'Cause honestly, you aren't winning any hospitality awards."

He knew it was none of his business, but Fiona didn't exactly seem to be thrilled to talking about the woman he loved.

"No, not him, Boy. Someone else chose her over me, though," she shrugged sadly, then remembering that perhaps she shouldn't be talking to him, eyed him speculatively, shut her mouth and straightened her back.

Well, any friendly moment that was going to pass between us is over.

"Goodbye, Boy," she told him decidedly and kissed him lightly on the forehead. Then everything went dark.

Chapter Twenty-Nine

Tor woke in his own bed. The sun was shining hotly on his face in a way that told him early morning had long since come and gone. He checked his cell.

Wow, it's Monday!

He couldn't believe he slept that long. Sure, he had expected to be a little late after the concert, but still. Work had already started, so today was going to be a pass. It felt like he had been dreaming forever. Strange couldn't begin to cover the things that he had seen in his sleep.

Tor rolled over, holding his phone away from the intense glare of the sun to check it for any messages. That concert was intense. He hoped that he hadn't done anything stupid. Or if he had, he'd gotten good pictures at least.

There was one text in his inbox.

I LOVE YOU.

It was from a phone number he didn't recognize, so he snapped it shut. It must have been sent to him by mistake. He didn't bother responding to it, but rolled back over in the bed in his little house that was all his own and wondered if the girl he met last night would see him again. She was pretty.

Backstage, man, that was great! The band members were all so cool. Shade, he had been the coolest of them all, he thought gleefully. And that girl, the blond, he wanted to take her out. He had been alone too long. There had been a girl once, but it had been years since she was his. He could hardly remember the curve of her face anymore. Besides, he was so lonely since Sean had gone.

Tor felt around in the pocket of his jeans he was still wearing until he found the wadded up paper the girl had written her name and number on. He unfurled the crumpled scrap. It said:

If you ever want your chance again, call me. Fiona.

Tor thought he would definitely call her.

***

Kieran was angry.

Normally, that wouldn't matter to anyone around here. It would probably be a welcome change in the quiet funk that always persisted when his tour was over. The largely ungrateful Dark Court would probably whither without the extra evil and malice his music provided for them, except for their fortunate strengthening in the longer days of fall and winter.

Normally, they would revel in his anger with him, gleefully raising glasses of wine to the cause of his irritation and cursing the agitator right along with him. Songs would be sung and general mayhem persisted if there was enough of a cause for the Dark King to be angry. His Court rejoiced whenever he raged. It was an occasion, a cause for celebration when the Dark King turned the full force of his foul temper on the denizens of the oft neglected Court. They looked to him to lead, and in this matter, he usually excelled.

Normally, he would take his frustrations out on the stage if it were summer, choosing only the most explosive songs to whip the crowd into a sinful frenzy that would certainly lead to more despicable acts once the music was gone. That was always one of Kieran's greatest sources of pride, knowing that humans would bend to his will so easily when his wishes were put to music. Tens of thousands of them, every evening he took the stage, took his suggestions to heart. The violence and crime that followed in their wake was legendary.

Normally, after the show, he would find some hollow hearted and overly willing woman to share his bed for the night, rejoicing in the carnal sins of the human flesh. He would leave them broken in mind and spirit after a long night with him, and laugh off their misery when he left them behind, crying on the asphalt as his tour bus drove away. Tales of his lothario ways ranged far and wide, and of them, he was very proud.

But the tour was over, so those things were not an option. He supposed he could still find a warm body to share his bed, but there was really only one he wanted.

And if Brendan wasn't so damn equal to him, rendering his powers almost useless, he could at least strike out at the White Court to relieve his tension. But the balance necessary right now because of Winter, rendered him practically impotent. He wouldn't risk any action that might turn her against him.

As it was, the Great Hall was currently devoid of all noise. Even his normally vociferous crows, now a ghostly white, retreated to roost quietly, high above in the massive bone chandelier that lit the musty room. His anger seethed and filled the room like low hanging smoke and for once, the celebrations were forgotten in favor of fear and uncertainty.

The Nucklelavee huddled together in the corner, drinking salt water from massive urns and filling the room with a stink of ages. Far away from their festering odor, the goblins that frequented the Hall, preferring the dark and dank atmosphere that permeated more and more as of late, sat quietly at the pocked wooden banquet tables, eating their plates of raw flesh in a silent funk, waiting for something to give. If any creature was to so much as stumble or step out of line, they would pounce unmercifully, they were so willing for some weakness to be shown anywhere. Nothing was happening.

The tension was palpable, a living thing that circled the Court menacingly, coiling tighter around the already wary subjects. They were all waiting, Kieran most of all, for something to change. The silence swallowed him, choking him down until he couldn't stand being caught in its maw any longer.

"Dugan!" he finally called to his most trusted lieutenant and friend. Dugan looked at him from where he had taken up position, thoughtfully staring in to space while leaning against a damp, stone wall, patiently reflective in the morbid atmosphere. Why he was content to just stand there, was beyond the king.

Dugan had always been stranger than the rest, though Daemons generally were, but that was part of what made them so interesting. His iridescent skin was a sickly green under the poor light and his subtle scaling played off the mossy stone, making him look more ancient than he was and decidedly deadly in a most disturbing way. Notoriously fickle as Daemons were, Dugan had been his constant, never once wavering from his side.

"Pull on something more appropriate. We go to cause trouble, my friend!" If Bren wanted to make it an unfair fight by keeping him away from the Undecided Queen, not giving him a true chance at persuading her, then he could be unfair too. Kieran suddenly felt alive with purpose. He would not be content to sit by and wait.

Dugan, sensing his intent already started toward the massive stone arch that signaled the entrance to the king's wing of the *bruig*. He changed his glamour from the favored attire of the Court into a pair of black jeans, donned a leather jacket and was doing his best impression of a Hell's Angel. It really wasn't that much of a stretch.

Kieran rose too, already wearing a full human glamour that he preferred in the presence of others, not wanting to remind them of his White beginnings, and followed Dugan out of the main room down the black and dripping hall. He heard the relieved sounds of the others that remained behind him, beginning to move or speak, already relaxing now that he had gone.

"You are an ugly, mean looking bastard, Dugan," Kieran congratulated. Dugan's black ponytail swung back and forth in front of him and Kieran thought he actually liked this look for his friend.

"Thank you, sir. What will we do today, My King?" Dugan asked. His even tempered voice never was an accurate indication of how he was feeling, but Kieran thought he almost seemed excited to cause some mischief.

"We will make ourselves at home with the humans, staying near my sister's house until the queen needs us," he said matter-of-factly. "And she *will* need us."

Kieran wondered if he made a mistake not telling her how to use his name properly. If only she would call for him, he could come retrieve her.

If that is indeed what she truly wants?

"She wants it, My King," Dugan replied quietly. The Dark King was taken aback, though he shouldn't have been surprised he would be listening. Still, his insecurities had no place being discussed out loud.

"Get out of my head, Dugan," Kieran growled. He pushed him forward roughly to keep him moving.

Of course, Dugan would know what he was thinking. They both shared that unusual talent. They could feel things, see things that would happen. Dugan was the only other one he ever met who could do that, so thankfully, he didn't think anyone else would know about his fears for the queen.

It was the gift, or curse maybe, of their mothers, two of the three White Ladies who were the pride of the Light Court. Together, even as children, they had known that they did not fit in with the dandies in his brother's Court. It was a blessed relief when they made the switch from Light to Dark.

I am glad you came with me, friend, Kieran thought to him.

288

"My lord," Dugan said and nodded slightly in acknowledgement.

Kieran clapped his hand on Dugan's shoulder and jogged to catch up.

Chapter Thirty

Winter woke with a start. Panting hard, she strained to see in the half light. As if by magic, the room lightened, as if it realized that she was awake. She tried to get up, but something was stopping her, holding her down. Fighting the urge to panic, she struggled to recall the events of the evening.

The gradual return of her memory of the night before finally restored her calm. Winter looked down to see Bren's arm still draped across her chest, just as it was when she fell asleep.

He kept his word, and now, he too, slept, fully clothed beside her. She lifted his arm gently away from her, not wanting to wake him, and slid quietly off of the bed.

The silent rooms seemed cavernous and cold without his constant movement and commanding presence. It was like they too slept without him to fill them with his energy. Winter trotted to a large oval looking glass hanging near a small dressing table. Frightened to even know what she looked like, she peered at her reflection in the mirror and almost burst into tears. Her face was puffy and dirty, and her pale skin was filthy from her fall and subsequent dash through the woods. She shook her head sadly when she looked back to the bed and saw the dirt that had shaken loose from her hair and marred the beautiful bedding where she laid her head. Upon further inspection, her fingers found grit and twigs still in her locks, knotted into thick clumps. She was afraid to take down the remains of her elaborate hairstyle, lest the entire contents of the forest drop to the ground at her feet.

Desperate to maintain some semblance of normalcy, she smoothed the wrinkles from the thin, golden gown Bren had given her, appreciating the way the fabric felt like liquid beneath her fingers. The touch of it on her skin made her think of Asrai, dancing fluidly in the clean water of the fountain and suddenly, she wished that she was clean too. Winter looked around for a bathroom she could duck into.

Nothing.

There were no other doors--anywhere--that she could see, other than the ones she used the night before to visit Tor. There was the one that led out to the hall and one into Bren's room.

That was it.

Winter wondered how she would be able to find a way to wash the nastiness from her body if the fae so obviously didn't believe in plumbing. She felt so dirty, so wrong here. Once again, Winter felt as if she stumbled into yet another place that she did not belong. Winter knew if she could clean up her appearance, it would be a step toward feeling better. Strangely, though, she noticed since she set foot here, she never once needed to use the bathroom.

Maybe one of the benefits of being Fae, is that you never have to pee, she thought hopefully. So far, there had not been many immediate upsides in her being here, but Winter decided she would take what she could get.

She was still standing in the middle of the room, looking like a lost child and staring down at her new clothes when Bren said, "What *are* you doing, Win?"

He had sat up on the bed, stretching his arms over his head slowly, looking more handsome and perfect than anyone had a right to. Well anyone human anyway, so she guessed maybe he did have a right after all. It made her happy that he called her by the name he always called her by when they were just friends, not partners in this new strange dance. She needed some familiarity.

"Just trying to decide how much of me is still here, and how much is gone." Winter smiled sadly at him, glad to see he didn't resent her for making him sleep on top of the covers. "And I was slightly amazed that I didn't have to use the bathroom this morning, not that it would have mattered because, I don't see one anywhere. We don't have to use chamber pots do we?" she asked, suddenly mortified at the thought.

"No, no chamber pots, Winter," he laughed at her. "That human function is one that I am sure you will be glad to leave behind. Maybe you are changing a little already." he said hopefully.

She didn't agree with him on that though. Winter thought it was a little sad, and a little too soon for her to say goodbye to her humanity.

"What brought all this discussion of body function on anyway?" Bren asked.

Holding her hands out in front of her in explanation she said, "I was just looking at my beautiful new clothes, and dirty hair and face, thinking that rocking the dirty-pauper-dressed-as-a-princess style may not fit in here," she laughed a bit, "And I can't seem to find a shower anywhere. Do I have to give those up as well?" Her voice rose a little with panic when she thought about never being clean again. She sat down in a huff on the cool marble floor, refusing to sully any other part of this paradise he had made her. Her gown puffed out all around her and then drifted slowly to the ground in the most beautiful way.

"Well, no, we don't have showers, unfortunately," he said apologetically. Winter thought she saw him blush, "But we have something you may like just as well." Bren got out of bed in one feline movement and, in three light steps, was back at the fountain that Asrai danced in. He gave her a mischievous smile.

"Come here. Watch how I do this," he told her softly, "So you can do it too. It's easy enough."

He put his hands purposefully on the lip of the fountain and slowly made a gentle parting gesture with them. The golden edges stayed beneath his palms, stretching and growing thin, like the heat in him melted, reshaped and cooled the metal all in one motion. He pulled slowly and gently until the basin was three feet in diameter and easily as deep. The lip of the fountain grew thinner and thinner beneath his touch.

He was making her a bath.

"Help me with this, would you? How big would you like it?" He reached out for her hand and put it on the cool metal beside his own.

"Bren, You. Are. Reshaping. Metal, before my eyes! I can't do that! I am not like you. You are a king, some sort of supernatural creature. I don't have that kind of power, I am just a girl." Winter backed away just a few steps shaking her head apologetically, but he held onto her small hand firmly. He returned it to the thin gold edge, then placed his own large, tan hand over top of hers. She balked again and was about to continue her refusal but he cut her words off.

"Of course you are, Win, and of course you can. You are no more a girl than I am just a boy. You are going to be a queen, remember? Just try. Like this." He pulled her in front of him so she couldn't flee, putting his strong arms on either side of hers and placed her hands beneath his own on the golden bowl.

He put his lips close to her ear and whispered, "Just imagine what you want it to look like and then find something good, like our walk in the woods, to draw on. It's the Light that makes you able to do it. You can do anything here." He kissed her just below her ear, on the soft skin on her neck above her necklace. "Then, when you have that good feeling," another kiss on the skin where her neck met her shoulder, "Push that feeling out from you, through your hands, and then pull back on the edge." He placed one last kiss on the nape of her neck. "Easy."

She thought she would be the one to melt this time, but before she could puddle into him, he moved away from her ear and still standing behind her, this time placing his hands on the rim of the fountain beside hers.

C. B. Cole

"And one, two, three..." and they slowly pulled, stepping away from each other in a strange dance of navigation. The basin stretched and grew even more, widening and deepening at their will. Winter ducked under his arms to make more room, reshaping the fountain until it was a tub that would hold her shape, and easily his as well.

She thought the edge of the tub looked impossibly thin and fragile, like a skin stretched tight and the slightest contact would crack it and its contents would spill out onto the floor below. Water toppled freely into the basin from a marble spigot on the wall and splashed into the pool below in the most melodic way. Dipping her fingers into the clear, deep water, Winter thought it was the perfect temperature for a bath, though the water was surprisingly cool when they began remaking the fountain. She wondered if the heat that poured out from her and Bren had warmed the water, or if it was just a product of the overall change.

Finally satisfied it would be enough to get her clean; she brushed her hands together and gave a triumphant smile to Bren.

"I did it," she crowed.

"You did it. I knew you could." He kissed her cheek proudly. "Now, are you ready for bath time? I can leave."

Without a word, Winter started shedding her clothes right where she stood. She was down to her underwear when she noticed that Bren was flabbergasted, conspicuously staring at anything else in the room but her.

295

And she knew it was wicked of her to do it, because he was so good to her, but she wanted to tempt him, to draw some emotion from him other than unadulterated love. He had to suffer the want of a woman just as any other male might, whether or not he was the king of all things good and pure.

"Bren?" she whispered, then dropped the rest of her clothes. When he turned back to answer her and saw her naked form, she was pleased at his reaction. The White King did lust after all.

"Join me?"

***

Bren could not believe what he was hearing. He spent minutes that all told, probably added up to years imagining this. Not necessarily imagining her naked, though he could hardly deny that it happened. Instead, he spent so long wishing that she would want him, that now that it was actually happening he was frozen in time. Hoping that one day, when she was ready, she would see him not as a friend, but as a man, or even as a lover.

And now it seemed that it was all possible.

He dared not to take his eyes from her own for fear that he would not be able to stop admiring her naked flesh, which he knew would be exquisite. And her eyes, they seemed darker and Bren swore he saw them shimmer and flash a dark blue that was so navy, it was almost black.

That was strange.

Offering her his hand while he thought, he helped her into the warm water. She stepped in lightly and sunk gratefully into the bath, the water covering her all the way to her thin, graceful shoulders. She gave him a look that silently echoed her previous request.

I shouldn't be doing this. But his decision was made.

Bren started to slowly peel off the clothes that he put on in Ramona's house the day before, sliding out of the white cotton tee and blue jeans, letting the clothes puddle at his feet. When there was nothing left for him to remove, and no reason to linger on the cool marble floor, he hopped the side and bravely lowered himself into the water with her, sliding in behind her and pulling her close so that she could lean against his chest. He may be king, but he was still a male and it was too new between them for him to be brave enough to look at her nakedness openly. That he was here in this position at all, was mind boggling.

Maybe the fae in her was coming closer to the surface all the time now?

"May I wash your hair for you, since it bothers you so?" he asked her. She did not answer him, but slipped under the water briefly to wet her hair. When she broke the surface again, she twisted back to give him a slow kiss over her shoulder, which he took to be her answer.

Bren reached back to the small table that was thankfully close enough he didn't have to get out again to fetch the things he needed. He selected the bottle that contained the soap that the elves made with the jasmine and clover that covered their hills, thinking it would complement her natural, sweet smell. He poured a little into his hands and began to massage her scalp.

297

Bren could not keep himself from every so often, placing a kiss on her ear, neck, shoulder or collarbone in between picking out twigs and, every now and then, an errant leaf. She shivered every time his lips touched her and it filled him with such desire, but so more than that.

He was hopeful; hopeful that Winter meant what she said when she told him she meant to choose him. Being here like this with her made him believe that she actually did mean it.

When he thought he had gotten all of the sticks and dirt from her hair and it was sufficiently clean, he turned her slowly in his arms, leaned her back, lowering her gently to rinse the suds from her hair. He had to turn her to the side, just so, to do it and he noticed that though her eyes were closed, she wore the most rapturous expression on her face.

"Winter?" he said gently, not wanting to disturb her if she was lost in some pleasant reverie. She opened her eyes and he swore they were the loveliest dark blue he had ever seen, then she smiled.

"Bren," she answered him, barely audible over the sound of the water that still poured into the tub. She came closer, turning to fully face him, wrapped her arms around his neck, and her legs around his waist so that she could sit in his lap. She kissed him deeply. It was the most passionate kiss they ever shared. Bren was drowning in her, dying slowly as she poured herself over him.

She nestled against him and pressed herself so close that he thought he would ignite with the heat of her. He couldn't help but be aroused by the closeness

298

of their skin. The water was a willing conductor of their passion, each tiny ripple they made, came crashing into him like a tidal wave. Bren was sure she could feel it too, the way he was pressing back against her.

"I am so scared, Bren," she said suddenly. She bit into his shoulder lightly and he shuddered in response. He lifted her slightly, and just before they went all the way, she whispered in his ear, "I am scared of the dark."

***

She *was* scared of the dark, but not the way he probably thought. She was scared of the darkness that lived inside her. It was growing stronger, begging to have a voice and be heard.

Winter sat there chest to chest with him, her face hidden by his shoulder as he slowly eased her onto him. She wanted him to drive it out of her, force that part of her away from the inside out. It never even occurred to her to stop him; that perhaps they should wait. She wanted this.

She just wasn't sure she was only thinking of Bren.

Winter always thought it would be a painful thing, to be with a man. She also thought, up until two days ago, that her first time would be with Tor. And then shockingly, she had been so close, wanted so badly to be with Kieran. That was unexpected; almost as unexpected as what she was doing now. But Bren would never hurt her, he told her so.

Bren was moving her gently, being so careful with her. His fingers barely grazed her skin, but where

299

they did, she was certain she glowed beneath his touch. Her cheek pressed hard against his own and his shaggy hair, blond no more, but golden, tickled her nose while his face, always just barely hinted with stubble, ground roughly into her skin. She wondered if Kieran had been her first, if he would have been as gentle with her.

He told her the day before that he hoped that when she did decide to have sex with someone, it would be out of love. Belatedly, it occurred to her he would take this as an admission of her love, though she never told him that. He would think that if she loved him enough to be with him and to be his queen, that her choice was truly made. She hoped that was what she was agreeing to. Winter already told him she wanted to belong to his Court, and she supposed that much remained unchanged. The only thing that was changing, rapidly at this moment, was her relationship with Bren. They never again could be classified as just friends.

And she did love him, it was just...complicated. But he felt so good. She never thought being with someone could feel like this.

Winter could tell he was trying to go slowly, but he was losing that battle with himself. Committed to the act she had begun, she pulled him closer to her, her teeth grazing his shoulder again and concentrated on loving him as hard as she could. She held her affection for him in a safe place inside herself and felt it grow, feeding on the warmth they shared between them and the years of trust and friendship, until it became a hot thing, that burned her from within. She realized she liked the way he felt, the slide of his skin on her skin, his lips on her lips. He could be passionate, Winter thought.

But not like Kieran.

She sucked in a shocked gasp, not because of the newness of Bren on her flesh, but at the unbidden thought of *his* name. The letters of it, knifelike and pointed, cut her straight to the quick. Bren moved against her faster, grasping at her thighs, thinking it a sign of her pleasure. And like a floodgate that had been opened, Kieran invaded her mind, waging war and fighting back her feelings for Bren with his raw memory. Winter thought of Kieran's fevered kisses, his unspoken promises, his fierce desire to see her become his queen and she lost control completely. Bren, unaware of her internal battle, came to her, his light, no longer trapped inside, blinded her.

But in her mind she was kissing her Dark King, lost in *him*, their limbs tangled into an unsolvable knot. Her hands were in his hair and her fingers were in his mouth. Kieran was the one loving her.

Winter shattered into a million pieces of glimmering need, breaking herself against Bren. Somewhere in the back of her mind she heard someone say *I'm coming for you*. Maybe it was Bren who said it, but she wished instead that Kieran would come for her too.

"I love you," Bren breathed heavily into her ear as they finished their new dance. The room around them shimmered with waves of heat and steam rose from the tub they shared. He kissed her face and hair, any part of her he could touch. He was so happy.

Kieran. She ached to hear him say those words to her.

I love you. She heard the Dark King's voice in her mind clearly, but he wasn't there.

"I love you too," she sighed, unsure who she was saying it to.

At her words another flash of light burst from Bren's skin. She felt her own flesh absorb the glow in the same instant and again she said it, "I love you, too."

Chapter Thirty-One

Kieran was riding with Dugan across this worthless city for hours, looking for ways to entertain themselves, but aside from the punks they scared half to death and sent running home to their mommies, not much had happened. Sure, they terrorized some drunken college kids, and mocked their girlfriends. And Dugan excelled at starting some fights on the street corners. Mostly, though, there was not much to do. This painful balance of the Courts, the fine line he and Brendan walked along, kept things boring. The simpering White Court fae simply refused to come anywhere near the city and that was annoying.

Dugan was driving them by the house on Ashe Street for the tenth time since Winter had gone, but still there was no change. The lights continued to blaze for no one, even though the new day was well underway. No one came to clean away the remains of the Oakman, so it was clear that Bren and Ramona would not be coming back. Kieran guessed it would eventually be the city that would bury that ancient creature. Figured.

They were just about to make the turn onto the next street, the one that would take them away again from her overwhelming memory, when Kieran saw Fiona standing on the corner, beckoning for them to slow. She smiled wickedly at the approaching car and

Kieran thought that whatever was making her so happy was probably going to piss him off.

"Let her in, Dugan," he said in an irritated voice and the car rolled to a stop just in time. He opened the door and Fiona got in, making a big show out of climbing over him so that he would be forced to touch her. She finally sat down with a huff and put her hand on his knee familiarly.

"Hello, my lover," she chirped happily. Kieran pushed her hand off disgustedly and she put it in her own lap unfazed by his refusal. In fact, she was practically vibrating with excitement about whatever news she was going to deliver.

"Don't call me that," he said testily. She merely winked and settled into the leather seat happily, rubbing her palms on the soft upholstery. Dugan began to drive again.

Kieran twisted to face her, slightly annoyed by her glee, resting his back against the door. She did the same, echoing his movements. He opened his mouth to speak, but at that moment, a strange feeling washed over him, stealing his words. It felt like a sucking, a pulling of the darkest part of him. It was being drug out of him and twisted painfully in the hands of another. The Dark King opened, then closed his mouth several times before he could get the words out. Fiona eyed him curiously.

"What is it, Fiona?" His words came out thickly, and Kieran swallowed compulsively to clear the lumps in his throat. He felt something inside him go loose and wobbly, breaking free and floating

C. B. Cole

around, viciously bumping into his heart and lungs, stealing his breath away.

"My king entertains the queen in her chamber, dear," she crowed triumphantly. "How do you feel now? Do you still feel like the victor?"

Kieran eyed her disapprovingly, but he was surprised she came to taunt him. He pretended to process the information that she was delivering, buying himself some time while concentrating on that part inside of him that just broke off and was floating free. He knew what she was insinuating, that his brother was having his way with the queen. The thought of it was so painful, so debilitating that he had a terrible time forcing out his next words.

"Is that so? Well, good for him," he said archly, trying to pretend it did not matter, but he already knew it was true and it was killing him.

He knew it was true because Winter was telling him so. She was pulling him toward her, drawing on him for strength. Kieran traced an indefinite shape with his finger on the leather seat to fill the silence. Hoping he looked like it didn't bother him, he made a dismissive gesture, but Fiona looked smug. The Dark King shouldn't be crumbling at the thought of Winter being with someone else, even if she could be his queen. He closed his eyes, ignoring his companion. Kieran did not want Fiona to see that he was falling apart.

"She asked him to *join her*. We all heard, not even moments ago," she continued, her voice low and evil. Kieran thought she was trying her best to wound him, but she couldn't hurt him any more than the queen just had.

He was about to raise his hand against her, to quiet her taunts with his violence, when something changed. Instead, he reached past her and pulled the handle of the door she leaned against so that her own weight pushed it open. Fiona let out a yelp as she tumbled into the street, but Dugan didn't stop the car. Instead, without having to be told, he turned back toward Ramona's house.

Kieran was glad that Dugan knew what to do, because he was in no position to give orders as he lay slumped across the back seat, twisted weakly, yet joyously in the splendid throes of passion she was sharing with him. His queen may be sharing herself with Bren, but she was making love to *him*.

She wanted him.

"I'm coming for you," he whispered to her, knowing she couldn't hear him, but wanting her to know just the same. He would go to her, now that she finally found a way to let him know she desired his presence. But it would be a hard road there. Winter was sucking his strength away from him unmercifully.

Dugan kept his eyes on the road and raised the tinted glass between them, pretending not to know the intense experience his king was going through. Kieran lay there until the end, panting and breathless, as Winter invaded his mind and covered his body with a thousand kisses.

She wanted him.

She wanted *him*.

"I love you," he said.

306

I love you too. He heard her voice, clear as a silver bell, her pronouncement ringing true inside him.

He could forgive her; he already had, for what she had done, if it was the only way that she could have found to be with him. Surprisingly, Kieran knew he could forgive her for anything, as long as she loved him.

The Dark King felt the car slam to a halt and knew they were back in front of the white clapboard house. Thankfully, Dugan, in tune with him as always, was aware of the speed with which they now needed to travel. Kieran accepted Dugan's help getting out of the car, grateful that he didn't comment on his weakened state, and together, they entered the house. The Dark King hoped his friend couldn't tell just how much of his power she needed to show him that. Weakness, for any reason, was not a desirable trait in a monarch of any kind.

"Should we go armed to the White Court, Sire?" Dugan asked warily. Kieran just eyed him silently, trying to gather his composure. He glanced around, hoping Dugan would not push him to answer.

It was a tomb in Winter's former home. A grave holding all the memories and lies that formed her life before, the life she lived without him. They stood in the foyer, orienting themselves with the unfamiliar location. It was obvious no one had been in the house since yesterday.

"You should be armed right now," a female voice behind them growled in warning.

Fiona filled the doorway. She was bruised and battered from her roll down the street. Blood crusted thickly on her shattered cheekbone, making her wild eyes seem even more feral. Her already serpentine hair curled around her head angrily. She eyed the Dark King maliciously, her murderous intent written on her face and her predatory eyes flashing in the porch light. Kieran felt the daggers she was thinking at him. Penalty of death be damned. She was going to try to kill him.

"Go, friend, take back the queen. She needs you." Dugan pushed the king hard down the hall, toward where the pull of Faerie was strongest, then stepped between the threat Fiona posed and his only exit. Dugan drew his knife with a deadly *snick* of his silver blade against leather. It was the same one he always carried concealed in his belt and he brandished it threateningly toward Fiona. She had also drawn a dagger from somewhere deep inside her tall boot and was tossing it from hand to hand, crouched low, coiled and ready to spring.

"You will be greatly rewarded, my friend," Kieran told him and fumbled down the hall.

He heard the clang and scrape of weapons behind him as he fumbled down the hall. The stink of Brendan was overwhelming this far inside the house. He found where he presumed his brother slept while caring for the queen all these years, and ducked into the room, leaving no time to spend being disgusted over his brother's deception.

There was a shimmer of gold, and a humming hint of vibration in the corner coming from the closet, and Kieran saw the faint glow of the gateway to Bren's

Court. He had not been to the White Court since he was a young man many centuries ago.

Not since he and Bren were both friends.

Not since he decided that he would not watch his brother be the only king in his family.

If Winter didn't really want him, if he had been wrong and she didn't desire him with her, then he would never be able to set foot in Brendan's Court. But Fiona's presence here made him believe that Winter did, very much, want him. Winter had told him so herself, just moments ago.

The Dark King closed his eyes and stepped into the void.

***

Bren held her against him afterward, afraid that if he let her go, he would rise up and float away to the ceiling with the incredible lightness he felt inside him.

She loved him.

She loved him.

She loved him.

His heart beat out those words over and over. Then she started to move, to awkwardly disentangle herself from his embrace. For once, he did not know what to do next. She pushed herself across from him, making ripples in the still water and leaned back against the far side of the bath, watching him silently with wide blue eyes.

He moved too, drawn to her, closing the distance she created to kneel right in front of her and kissed her very gently on the mouth, then he turned away and got out without saying anything. It was probably wrong to say nothing.

It was time.

He didn't bother to wrap a towel around himself, but dripped all the way through her room and into his own, where he shut the doors behind him, letting her soak on her own.

***

She heard the faint click of his door as he pulled it shut behind him, but she was looking up, instead of watching him walk away. The ceiling that was earlier the deep blue of midnight cast with stars was now the most amazing pinks and oranges of a desert sunset. It was the perfect echo of the cooling heat of the moment. And it was certainly cooling rapidly.

Winter wondered what she had done wrong, why Bren had just left her alone. She told him she loved him, had shared everything with him. She told him she had made her choice, yet he was unhappy.

What more does he want from me?

Maybe the better question was, what did she want from him? And what did she think that Kieran could possibly offer her? She quickly pushed him from her mind, knowing she needed to focus only on her happiness and Bren's.

She splashed unnecessarily as she got out, slopping water over the edge of the basin, but unlike Bren, she found a towel. Dried and clean, she padded to the bureau and opened it to reveal a staggering collection of gowns, gowns of every color and fabric, styles of which she had never worn. Winter selected a floor-length, gauzy, emerald green beauty that felt like silk and looked as though it was woven to match the color of the soft moss in the wood she and Bren loved. The color was perfect. The dress was light and airy, and dripped off her frame perfectly, not at all like the Greek gown that hung close at the chest, but floated all around her like mist.

Nearby, she found a small stool that was placed in front of the low mirror with brushes and combs and an assortment of things to adorn her hair with. Sitting, she brushed her black strands until they were perfectly soft, then twisted them up and secured them with two thin, silver rods that lay on the table, tipped with onyx and rubies. Somehow, Winter knew that the jewels were not costume jewelry, but the real thing.

She admired her reflection thinking Bren would be pleased. Being in his presence had darkened her fair skin just a little, kissed it with the heat and passion of summer. She looked even healthier than she had before and it looked like her skin glowed from behind, the way Bren's did. Winter couldn't imagine what other parts of themselves they may have just shared.

Satisfied she stood and...

Now what?

Wanting to know what she did wrong, she went to the door that joined their rooms and paused before knocking. She wanted to confront him, apologize for however she let him down, but had no clue how to start. She stood, thinking over the scenario in her head. The long, slender vines that covered her room writhed to be close to her and that made her feel better. A delicate blossom stretched out to be touched by her. She stroked it affectionately, then raised her hand to knock on Bren's door. Her knuckles did not even graze the wood before it opened away from her. Bren stood in front of her, and when he saw her, dropped to his knees, offering up a large ruby ring.

"My Queen," he said.

***

He certainly hadn't expected her to be standing on the other side of the door. Bren thought he would have time, that he would be able to talk to her, reassure her of his worth before presenting her with his mother's ring. But she looked so lovely when he opened the door and he saw her standing there that the king of the White Court was determined to do it then, without preface. His heart could not be contained inside his chest.

It was time.

He was still kneeling, looking at her toes. She had yet to speak, but he could see the exquisite fabric of her dress quiver as she trembled in front of him. Bren caught himself thinking that the green of the dress she had chosen suited her perfectly, and was just about to tell her so when he saw the first tear slap the stone at her feet. He cleared his throat, then looked up at her. Silent tears he couldn't interpret, rolled down her beautiful cheeks.

"My Queen?" he said again and this time, she sighed, and pulled him up off his knees so that he stood before her. Maybe her tears were because of him.

"Bren, it's me. I'm just Winter. Don't call me that, please," she pleaded through her sobs.

"Oh," he said softly, "Of course."

He was just about to continue his speech, when he recalled that what they had shared, what they had

312

done, was her first time just now, and he hadn't even thought to see if she was all right. He was so focused on her being his that he forgot to see if she had been hurt in any way. Bren cleared his throat uncomfortably and pulled her close. She silently cried into his shoulder and hot tears soaked through his shirt.

I am such a jerk.

"It was foolish of me not to ask if I hurt you, Win. Are you all right, My Love?" He took her face in both of his hands and turned it gently from side to side, looking for any sign of injury. She swallowed and shook her head.

"No, Bren. I'm fine, really. I just...what did I do?"

She thought I was mad at her, that she let me down? He kissed her and kissed her so that she would know she was perfect, then let his hands rest softly on the sides of her face.

"Winter, there is nothing you could do that would ever cause me to be disappointed in you. You have given me so much joy today. Every day."

Winter reached up with shaking hands and removed his palms from her face. Her eyes were so big and innocent, that he had to remind himself what his original purpose was, lest he get lost in them forever. Digging into his pocket of the linen pants he donned, Bren produced the Queen's Ring again.

He held the gem delicately, his hands resting low between them so that she would have to look down at it, not at him while he spoke, and concentrated hard on the words that were going to follow. He had to get them just right for it to matter.

"I love you, Winter. You are everything to me. You have given me the greatest gift in the world, and with that, the greatest happiness. We were made to be together." He took a deep breath before saying the most important part, "There is nothing I have that is not yours. I want to share your life and be your king, would you be my queen, my love, and accept this royal ring?" His voice strengthened on the last few words. The vows were some of the most ancient words his race used.

She remained quiet, but eventually held out a still trembling hand, so that he could slide the massive ruby onto it. He took her small, pale hand in his own and finding the right finger, slid the heavy ring onto her finger.

It fit.

She was his. Just like that.

Bren looked at it adoringly, loving the way it perched neatly on her finger. Then, he swept her up in a triumphant embrace. He kissed her lovingly, then hungrily, then softly until neither of them had any more breath left. They broke apart gasping and still she said nothing.

Bren looked at her expectantly, waiting for it. Waiting for her to change into the faerie queen she was, but...nothing happened. He decided that maybe it would take a while. Besides, he wanted to tell her what the ring meant.

"Winter..." he started, but never got the chance to finish. There was a tremendous thump, then a crash, and out in the hall, people were screaming. Quickly retreating footsteps echoed down the corridor outside their rooms. Bren pushed her behind him, wanting to protect her from harm. There was a sickly scent of evil wafting in from outside. The Dark Court was here.

How was it that Kieran's Court was strong enough to launch an attack here? Now?

Suddenly, the door to the queen's room burst inward, blown off its hinges by a tremendous force. The Dark King stood in the shattered doorway, shoulders grazing the wood on either side. He focused on Winter, seeing nothing else, his eyes filled with a ferocity Bren had never seen in him.

He held out his hand to her and said, "Well, come on then. We don't have much time."

Bren whirled back on her and saw the sadness and regret written on her face. But worse than that, she was happy to see him. Winter had betrayed him without saying a word.

"Winter, what have you done?"

Chapter Thirty-Two

It was hard for her to meet Bren's accusing glare. She hardly had any idea of what she caused, but she was still glad to see Kieran in the doorway, no matter how he came to be there. The White King wore the pained look of a wounded animal. He just stared at her, waiting for a response she could not give, and for a moment, she thought that he had forgotten his brother was there at all. Kieran, who had not forgotten about Bren, started across the room toward her, and that flurry of motion jerked the White King back into action.

He shoved her back behind him again and turned accusingly on his brother.

"How can you be here?" he asked incredulously. As an afterthought, he shouted for the guards. Winter thought that surely they must already be on their way if they were at all good at their jobs. Kieran's entrance had not been subtle.

The Dark King stopped just out of Bren's reach and once again held out his hand.

"We really don't have much time, My Dear."

Bren's eyes nearly popped out of his head at the words. Still positioning himself between her and his adversary, Bren's words came in an angry and high volume rush.

"Are you insane, Brother? She will never go with you. She loves me. She has *been* with me. She has chosen already!" Bren grabbed her left hand in a show of unity, carefully protecting the ring he gave her, and pulled her close. Winter shuffled awkwardly toward him. Kieran took a step toward her; practically daring Bren to strike out at him, then took her other free hand delicately, kissed it, and squeezed it gently.

"Nice necklace, Love. Did he tell you the story about it?" He spoke the words so casually, so conversationally, that if it hadn't been for the shattered doorway, someone overhearing them would have thought they were all old friends. Winter realized that indeed, he and Bren were old friends, much older than she knew. She nodded slowly in response, wanting to cover her neck from his blistering glare. His mouth was set in a thin, disapproving line.

"Let's go, Winter," he said again, more firmly, not letting go of her. His thumb gently rubbed over the back of her hand, tracing hot circles into her skin. "His guards will be here soon and I won't get another chance to get you out of here."

She didn't move, and his face settled into a resigned grimace.

"Wait," she begged and both men looked at her, Kieran, surprised at the sound of her voice, so strained with tension it didn't sound anything like her. Bren merely looked surprised that she needed time to think about her answer. Then, in a smaller voice that echoed her pain and indecision, she added, "I don't know what I'm doing anymore."

Kieran let her hand drop and nodded once, a silent signal that he would wait for her decision.

Before Bren could say a word, she turned her face to him and smiled.

Winter put her other hand, the one Kieran had kissed, on Bren's forearm and stroked it gently. It would be madness to leave with the Dark King, that much she believed. She barely knew him. They had had less than a day together all told, and that was spent either panting all over each other, or in a strange verbal dance of desire. He knew nothing about her, and she knew only bad things about him.

She had known Bren her whole life. He had cared for her, protected her and given her a home away from all of this insanity. He held her hand when she cried, and danced with her when she was happy. Most of all, he was good, a decent man and a decent companion, one she could depend on. She thought about the horror movie marathons they would have, curled up in tight balls on the couch. How he would read with her in the sitting room for hours on end, trading books back and forth so that they would each read the same passages and then after their long hours of silence, talk about the way the words moved them. She thought about how Bren knew what she wanted, and what she needed. He was so good to her and now he wanted to marry her, and keep her safe forever. She had given him everything, *everything*, and she did not regret it at all.

His brother though, merely *wanted* her.

What if he would not bother himself with getting to know me, or caring about my wants and needs? she thought, desperately trying to kill her traitorous inclinations. Kieran was known for his

318

cruelty in Faerie and his wild, sexual escapades and raucous rock shows back in the human world. She knew she would be setting herself up for lifetimes of heartbreak if she left with him.

Winter looked at Kieran, still staring at her expectantly. His eyes shimmered black with desire and she knew he wanted nothing more than to conquer her.

Bren loves me, she told herself.

But Kieran loved her too.

She didn't know how she was certain he felt that way, but she knew it; knew that he would love her the right way, without end or limit.

She stepped closer, so that she was drawn even with Bren, standing shoulder to shoulder with the king and slipped her left arm in his; the sleeve of the green dress fell long over her hands and kept the ruby secret. Winter was glad, she remembered what Kieran told her about the value of gifts and she did not think he would like to see her wearing not one, but two gifts from Bren. He barely concealed his disdain for the necklace she wore and Winter did not think that the Queen's Ring, as Bren called it, would rest well with him either and she desperately did not want to hurt him. Her arm remained there, wrapped around Bren's, linking them and she turned to face him.

Winter kissed him searchingly, not caring that the Dark King was watching, hoping to find an answer to her questions, then slipped her free hand into his own. She brought his fingers, joined with her own up to her lips and felt him relax with the unity that gesture showed. She was glad she could give him that small gift of relief.

319

Bren was still glaring down Kieran and didn't look at her, even when she lowered his hand and stepped back to stand beside Kieran, moving like she was set in reverse. She felt like her life was like that, fast forward, reverse.

Now pause.

The Dark King only had eyes for her, not caring that her lips touched his rival's, not caring that she held his hand in her own. His eyes held her. They bored into her, and she felt the heat of his dark stare penetrate her thin skin and find its way straight to her heart.

Winter could feel that same cool breeze caress her, like it did the day he came to her house on Ashe Street. The slithering fingers of the light wind he commanded, brushed her bangs back from her face softly and dipped down the front of her gown to tingle in the space between her breasts. It swirled around her, playing with the lengths of her dress, pulling it away from her body like a teasing child might. The soft tendrils of hair that lay loose on her neck, free from its pins and twists, moved like they were brushed by the lightest touch of a lover and eventually, the serpentine rush of air found its way to her ears, to sing Kieran's words of love and desire that she knew only she heard.

I love you, it told her, softly so that no one else heard. The whispers told her how he needed her and wanted to see her happy. It sang love songs about the mountains the Dark King would move to protect her and how he would worship her body with his own. Then, the sinister breeze retreated and left her alone.

320

Winter dared to hold on to him a moment longer as she said, "I love you, Bren."

"I know," he told her brusquely.

All the while, she never took her eyed from Kieran, and took a single step forward.

"Winter?" Bren questioned.

The Dark King's smile grew and he reached out to her. Bren tightened his grip on her fingers so that the ring dug an uncomfortable groove into her knuckle.

Bren patted her arm possessively and said, "I love you too." He tried to pull her back from Kieran's outstretched hand when he noticed she was reaching for Kieran too.

"I am sorry," she told him, but didn't look back.

Winter dropped the hand that she was holding and disengaged her arm from his. She took another small step forward.

Kieran pulled her away into his arms, holding her tight against his chest, leaving Bren staring, shocked, at them.

Then she took the Dark King's hand and ran away as fast as she could.

***

He would have liked very much to grab her and shove her up against the disgustingly pretty wall of his brother's winding hall, but he thought it would be rude. Normally, he wouldn't care about that either, but he planned on taking his time with the Queen and that was something they were unfortunately short on at the moment.

His thick leather soles pounded heavily down the bright hallway, the clicks of the copper nails imbedded in them, scratching the marble in a satisfying way, punctuated nicely by the slapping sounds her bare feet made on the stone. He heard her breathing grow ragged with the speed they were forced to keep up as they fled headlong away from Bren.

Kieran couldn't remember much about living here, much less the direction they needed to be heading, and he frantically tried doors as he came to them, but they all yielded little more than bedrooms or closets, nothing terribly useful to a man trying to escape with a kidnapped Queen. He wondered how long they would have before Brendan's guards rallied against him. He wished that Dugan could have been here.

It did please him though, to see the looks of terror and hear the screams of panic that the Court Fae made when they saw him coming. It gave him the strength he needed to go on. And that was a good thing; Winter had left him so weak, it took everything he had left to burst in her own door. He wondered if she knew what she was doing, when she let him hold her hand for so long back there, knew that it helped him regain enough strength to get her out of there.

But I finally won her, didn't I?

She was with him.

The memory of her telling Bren she loved him before she left him, slammed into the Dark King with a delayed fury. This time he did stop running and pushed her hard against the wall, forcing his mouth upon hers, claiming back what was his. He felt the electricity

C. B. Cole

bouncing wildly between them and he pulled her tight up against him so she could feel just how much he wanted her.

"You do love me?" she asked.

He laughed, thinking it was too late for her to be worried about that *after* she had already begun her flight from the White Court, but he was still high on his victory so the words he normally would never say just flowed out of him.

"Winter, I love you more than anything. You are my world. Without you, I would cease to breathe. Nothing would matter. All that I hold dear lies inside of you." It was a very un-Dark thing for him to say, and he knew it, but he was not ready to address the changes she caused in him. He kissed her again, just a peck over the wide smile she wore and then said, "But we should talk more about that later, because I hear Brendan coming."

It was true; Bren was further down the hall, looking for them in rooms and shouting orders to his guards. Kieran could not yet see him, but he could definitely tell that his brother was not alone.

"Shall we, My Dear?" he smiled, gallantly offering her his hand and then they were off again. They careened down the seemingly endless hallway until they were brought up short by a massive pair of double doors, blocking further progress. They were huge, floor to ceiling and filling the width of the corridor.

There was a carving on the door. On one side was a stag, leaping through a gilded wood, on the other, a great cat, stalking the deer from a steep, jeweled mountain face. Kieran remembered these doors from his childhood. He wondered if she would recognize the symbols from her necklace.

There was a great deal of festive noise coming from the other side of the wide white doors. Kieran doubted the rest of the Court would be so lighthearted if they already knew he was here. Thankfully, he would have the element of surprise on his side. Behind him, he heard Bren and the guards coming closer.

He snaked one arm firmly around Winter's waist and the other he buried in her hair and pulled her to him. He did not kiss her, though he wanted to.

"Do you trust me, My Love?" he asked her.

"I shouldn't," she said seriously and he laughed.

"No, you shouldn't," he agreed then twirled her in front of him and with a great kick, flung open the doors to the frightened screams of the denizens of the White Court.

***

"Hello, everyone! Did you idiots miss me?" he shouted as the doors banged loudly against the walls. There was a collective gasp as the Court recognized him. His presence seemed to suck the light out of the room. Creatures started to flee to avoid him and Winter felt a sinking feeling deep in the pit of her stomach. For the first time, she was faced with the effect the Dark King and his Court on Bren's people, the beings of Faerie she just made a promise to Bren to one day rule as their queen, and she felt very sad. Something inside screamed with the wrongness of her situation. She was letting them down.

324

C. B. Cole

The citizens of the White Court stumbled and fell over themselves to get as far away as possible from Kieran. Some of the stranger looking beasts actually managed to climb the walls using sticky feet and hands. The women were screaming loudly in protest while the smaller fae shoved past knobby knees of larger creatures to find a safe place. The frightened Court pressed flat against the walls, the mob spread wide and thin with fear. Some of the fae with wings were fluttering up against the ceiling, bouncing dangerously against each other and circling like excited moths.

Winter thought that the scene reminded her of when her high school was evacuated for a bomb threat last year and the students fled in terror out into the street without any teachers to guide them. She wanted to tell them it was all okay, but she thought Kieran wouldn't like that. It was rather contrary to his plan.

Winter supposed that he was quite an imposing figure on his own, notwithstanding his royalty, in a place that was predominantly goodness and light. He practically dripped darkness, from his dark hair, to his dark eyes all the way down to his big, black boots. His skin was dark in a way that Bren's was not. Kieran's was more pale olive rather than sun kissed like Bren's. He was sinister from head to toe. There was even a different smell about him, like licorice and spice, and it was even more noticeable here in this space, the heart of the Court.

She was just beginning to consider other ways that he contrasted from his brother when he roughly whirled her in front of him and held her hostage style against his chest. His hand that was wound in her hair, cupped the back of her skull and they began walking toward the crowd.

"Remember you trust me," he whispered. She shuddered at his warning and started to protest, but he cut her words off. He deftly grabbed one of the silver rods, dagger shaped and deadly, from her hair. Most of the rest of it came loose too, tumbling heavily down around her shoulders in a thick, dark mass. He thrust the sharp end of the makeshift weapon just under her jawbone, pressing it lightly into her skin.

"NO ONE LEAVES UNTIL WE FIND A WAY OUT. IF THE GUARDS GET HERE BEFORE I FIND AN EXIT, THE QUEEN DIES." He yelled in a voice that rattled the rafters.

His booming threat echoed from the high ceilings and stone walls, rolling like thunder. The collective gasp of comprehension from the Court's residents made Winter quite sure they believed his intent. She grabbed his hand at her neck dramatically, scratching at him with the hand that bore the ruby Bren gave her. Kieran, not even noticing her protests, grabbed the second thin hair pin free from her black and tangled hair and thrust it out for the assembly to see.

"I will hurt her, and while I will like it, I doubt very much that your king will." He told them all as he made slow steps toward them. There was nowhere left to go but forward and the crowd began to part, believing his promise.

She watched a thousand pairs of eyes grow wide at sight of the ring on her finger and wondered just what it meant for them to see it. Would they know the promise she made to Bren? To them? From the look of the crowd at the sight of her wearing it, Winter thought that yes, they probably did know just what it meant. *Damn.*

Then their expressions of awe were replaced quickly with fear as the Dark King pressed the pin deeper into her neck, just enough to draw blood. Winter screamed helplessly, mostly out of instinct and reaction to the pain even though she knew he wouldn't hurt her. She felt the trickle of blood run down her neck and it still scared her a little. The collective look of the Court told her they thought he meant business. There was a commotion at the far end of the hall and some smaller winged faeries and stronger beasts with the broad heads of cattle, pulled and pushed some of the bystanders away to reveal a shimmering light that radiated from behind a thin screen.

It must be a doorway!

She wished she had been given more time to learn about this place before fleeing from it. The citizens of Faerie were beautiful, interesting. Maybe she could find some way to come back someday and visit? Winter felt such a strange pang at leaving them this way.

Eventually, the rest of the men and women and creatures of the White Court comprehended their intent and moved silently, clearing a wide path. Some of the cattle-type fae dragged an ornamental screen away from a darkened corner of the Great Hall revealing a door that clearly didn't belong.

Winter immediately saw that it was different from the other doors she had seen in the hallway. It wasn't white like the others, but a dirty brown and industrial type, ugly wooden thing; it looked burned out and dilapidated. The entry had a slight shimmer about it, like the air around the door was golden and electric. Kieran was half pulling her, half dragging her toward it. The skin on the bottoms of her feet burned with the friction from fighting for purchase as he pulled her along.

When they were close enough, he dropped his spikes and they fell, tinkling like bells, to the ground. He grabbed her hand tightly and together they ran. They ran past the shocked and confused courtesans, past the flittering wings and the clicking cloven hooves of the strange creatures Winter wished she could examine closer. Together, they dove at the last minute into the gateway. They last thing she heard before she was sucked into the glittering void was Bren.

"Don't take her! Winter. I love you!"

I love you, too Bren, she thought, *but not enough.*

Chapter Thirty-Three

He watched them vanish through the gateway. His heart felt like it had been ripped out and followed her, leaving his empty shell behind. Winter didn't even turn back when he called out to her.

They disappeared into the exit that led into the city, just down the block from her high school. Bren knew he would be the only one who could follow them. There was far too much iron in the city for the others to come through safely and that was his fault. Iron was deadly to the lesser fae, only very strong fae, such as himself, Winter, and, unfortunately, Kieran, and maybe a few others, could walk in the iron jungles the humans made. Fiona could have gone with him as added protection, should he require it, but she was conspicuously absent from the evenings events.

Just as well, he thought. This was not something he wanted any of them to see, for his queen's sake as well as his own. He shouldn't have even called out after her as he did, lest any members of the Court correctly interpret the situation, but he doubted they would.

Bren glared at their escape route and silently cursed his own stupidity for insisting on the door's creation in the first place. He barely even used it, but merely insisted on its construction when Winter got Mono one year and passed out in her class. It scared him to death and he wanted to do something for her, but felt powerless to help in any real way. The gateway's construction made him feel useful, but now, it was just a problem. Now his brother had used something he created in her best interest, against him. For the first time, Bren thought maybe the King of Light could be capable of hate.

"Why did you let them go!" he shouted to the silent congregation of shocked and frightened members of the Court, witnesses to the Queen's guilty escape. Then immediately regretted it. He turned his face away shamefully, and tried to calm himself. Of course, no one answered his angered query. Who would dare?

There was a quiet movement of bodies and the crowd parted to let a small female fae through. One of his advisors, Maeve, the last White Lady, just as his own mother had been, one who lived three times as many lifetimes as he. She stepped forward slowly and faced him, not fearing the rage of a king. Bren knew she had seen many like him come and fall over the millennia and he was no different than any other. Maeve was not afraid of him, but rather looked like she pitied him in this moment. Being able to see into the future and supposedly even able to read the thoughts of others - though he had never seen any proof of it, she would understand what just happened here, not seeing it as it appeared, but as it truly was.

Maeve put her arm around him in a motherly fashion and led him away from the terrified mob, to a quiet corner. Bren angrily manifested two chairs so that they could sit and talk. When Maeve was finally

330

perched delicately in an ivory colored wingback, she leaned forward and put her hand on his knee.

"What has transpired?" he asked her.

"He had your queen, my lord," she told him softly. "He drew her blood, here in the White Hall, he told us she would die if we did not let them pass. How were they to know, to doubt? Surely, you can understand their fear." Bren nodded slowly. Kieran, of course, would have tricked them. The Court was right to let them go. His brother was indeed the type to kill, and they were not to be blamed for assuming he would also injure their newly crowned queen. Bren pursed his lips and let out a resigned sigh.

"Thank you, Maeve, your guidance is very much appreciated," he told her sincerely.

He meant it too, because she was still going to have to maintain order when he left, and the White King had yet to see Fiona throughout all of this disaster. The beautiful old woman, still seated regally, gracefully radiant in her advanced age, bent low to whisper something to him.

"What else can you tell me?" he asked.

"She wore the ring, my lord," She said it carefully and Bren didn't miss the implied question in her words. "The Court swelled proudly at the sight of it. I felt it," she added, visibly pleased. "But there is one man I do not think has noticed she wears it, Sire." It was neither a statement nor a judgment, but merely a well-placed reminder. He patted her hand appreciatively. Anything the White Lady said was valuable.

Bren knew what she was trying to tell him and she was, as always, right. The White Court knew he claimed the queen and they would rally behind him, giving him the strength he would need to bring her back. Bren could tell that the Court was getting stronger already, even in her absence. What happened now, would be of the utmost importance to them all.

"She hasn't changed, Maeve," he said sadly. "The prophecy said..."

"It's all in the words, My Child. The reader of the prophecy takes away from it what they want. If you believe that the person that she chooses and the person that she loves are the same, then you truly have a hopeful heart, Brendan. She is a grave danger for the Brother Kings. A king's rule will come to an end over this child. Go with care, my lord, and on the side of right."

Bren stood purposefully and put his hand on the ancient creature's small shoulders. He kissed her benevolently on the forehead.

"Thank you, Maeve. Take care to calm the others. I will fetch our Queen and return to set this right." Bren turned back to the guards, gesturing calmly, letting them know he would go alone and, with his head up, strode toward the gateway, determined to bring Winter home.

***

She and Kieran came through with a *pop* into an abandoned building somewhere near downtown. Winter knew they were deep in the city because she heard the familiar noises of traffic and people that were so different from where she lived in the quiet suburbs with her Aunt Ramona. She shook her head, not *Aunt* Ramona anymore. Helping Kieran to his feet, she kissed him lightly on the lips.

"We did it," she said incredulously.

"That was a very brave thing you did, My Love," he told her, then bent down to lick clean the blood from her neck. She giggled like an idiot when he touched her and even he had to laugh. She felt very much like the girl she had forgotten she used to be.

"How was I brave? I was a hostage! I will blame you for everything," she said diabolically. She wrapped her arms around him and planted a big, wet smack on his lips.

Kieran, for his part, looked completely mortified at her irreverent display of affection. Winter supposed that he had never had anyone love him just because he was worth loving. Maybe up until this moment, there had been nothing about him worthy of loving. To everyone else, he would have been a rock god, rich man or king.

"I think I love you more than I should," she said told him seriously "You are only going to end up hurting me in the end." It had taken her less time to profess her love for him than it had at all of Bren's prompting. Kieran stood there, his perfect mouth opening and closing like a fish. She could tell his mind was offering up too many witty possibilities for responses and that he was having a hard time trying to figure out just what to say next.

"You could tell me you love me, too," she prompted. With that suggestion, he regained a modicum of control and she saw the familiar, confident Kieran she knew returning.

"I do so love you," he told her, then with a devious smile, added, "I love you so much that I would break into a place that represents everything I despise to pull you from the clutches of my brother, who wishes to make you his bride. Oh wait. I did do that for you. See, it must be love." She laughed with him as they stood there happily in the filthy basement of the building surrounded by dust and soot.

Winter liked this side of him; if possible, more than the other more intense side he had shown her before. He was nothing but echoes of the stern Dark King she imagined, of what Bren described. While she loved the determined way he wanted her so badly and pursued her unswervingly it was a welcome change to see that he was not the frightening creature everyone else believed him to be. There was more to him than anyone else knew. Winter remembered asking him, *"What do you want me to know that you do not share with anyone else?"* and she secretly wondered if this hidden part of him was one of those things?

He had been so focused on winning me, on proving himself to me, she told herself, *and now that I am his, things will be different than they say.* She hardly formed the thought when his eyes went cold, hard and sparked like black diamonds. He pulled her close, roughly handling her by her upper arms and shoved her against a metal pole that ran through the center of the room, pushing her so hard her teeth clacked audibly in her head.

"You shared your body with my brother," he accused ferociously. He shook her briefly to make his point; she heard her teeth rattling again. Her head cracked hard against them metal and she saw stars. "If you had been one of my human lovers and I found that you betrayed me, I would have drugged you and passed you around to all of the members of my road crew, and then left you on the side of the road in whatever city we were in." He licked her cheek like an animal.

"If you had been one of my fae lovers, Winter, I would have taken my knife and peeled the skin from your bones and fed it, still bleeding to my hounds." She shivered violently in his arms; terrified as hot tears pushed their way out and ran silently down her face. She tried to turn her face away from him, but he held her firmly in place. For the first time since she had been with him, Winter was afraid. Afraid of him, but also afraid of the decision she made to leave the safety of Bren and his Court for a life with the Dark King.

What if I chose wrong?

He licked the other side of her face, capturing an errant tear and laughed a cruel, crackling laugh.

Then, without warning or cause, the fear melted away, releasing its tight coil around her heart, letting it beat again. His threats stirred something inside of her, woke a part of her that had lain sleeping like a great beast. Winter felt the deep well in her open up and let his cruel darkness flow into her, calming her, pulsing into her from his cool palms on her arms. It felt surprisingly good.

Bravely, bolstered by his nearness, she pushed forward against him, crowding him, putting her face inches from his. The voice that came out of her was not the voice she was accustomed to. It was feline, feral, and angry.

"I may have shared my body with him, Kieran and if you wish to be cruel about it, so be it, but you were the one I saw and I know you felt it too, or you wouldn't be here now. He may have taken that part of me," she gave him a sensual, full bodied kiss and then added, "But you have my heart and I think you always have. I have chosen you. Do you expect me to believe that you are innocent of sins of the flesh, dutifully saving yourself for me and this very moment?" She eyed him fiercely and he blinked in astonishment.

Then, she crushed her mouth on his and kissed him defiantly. He tried to resist her, withhold his love from her, but she felt him give in and finally, he kissed her back. His grip loosened on her and she felt the bloom of bruises well up under her pale skin where his hands secured her. When she thought she proved her point admirably, she pulled away. He looked at her indulgently, like she was a child who deserved a scolding he could not bring himself to give, and sighed.

"I would never harm you, Winter," he told her sincerely, "I love you."

Winter believed that. His blatant honesty about it moved her in powerful ways and she wanted him very badly. She thought her lust for him would consume her right there on the spot and leave her nothing more than a pile of ash at his feet.

Heartened by his confession, she grappled to put her hands on all the places she had yet to explore on his body. They pushed and tore and grabbed each other violently, like fierce animals battling for their lives, then tumbled hard to the ground. Winter kissed him over and over, blissfully unconcerned about injuring either of them on the trash and rubble strewn floor.

After minutes of nothing but mouths on flesh, she pulled away from him, fighting for air. She lay flat on her back, panting, and let him rest his sweaty cheek on the ripped bodice of her green gown, the gauze long since lost in their battle. She struggled to explain herself, though she wasn't sure if he wanted to hear it.

"I gave myself to Bren because I love him, Kieran." Her voice was thin and wavering, but she had to tell him the truth, and face the consequences of her mistake. He stiffened slightly at her words, bracing himself for the rest of it, her open declaration of her feelings for the White King. "But it was all wrong, I should have waited, Kieran. I was stupid and impulsive and I thought it was right, but it wasn't. I was trying to forget you, or maybe I was trying to find you, but I won't give myself away again until it is right." Winter tried distracting herself by straightening his shirt, fighting to keep tears at bay, only to find that the black fabric was torn instead of merely wrinkled after all.

"I can wait for you, Winter," he whispered. "Do you have any idea how long I have waited for you already? Maybe not celibately," he added with a small chuckle, "But waited for you just the same." The tough, hardened and cruel Kieran had vanished and left behind a forgiving, caring, loving man who would do anything to keep her happy. Winter smiled, secretly congratulating herself for believing in him enough to try to have a life together. He twisted to look at her.

"I have taken everything I have ever wanted all my life. I will not take you, or your love, by force." He shifted uncomfortably in the rubble, pulling them into a sitting position. Until he moved, she had been mostly unaware of the refuse and broken glass that littered the floor around them. "I want you to be my queen, my wife, my everything, Winter." He leaned in as if to steal a kiss, but instead, he rested his forehead against hers. "And if I cannot have all of you, then I will be happy with the pieces that you can give me." Then he kissed the tip of her nose.

"I want very much to be your queen," she said happily, feeling stronger now that she truly believed in the choice she was making. She nudged him with her own nose, and then nuzzled along his jaw bone. "I do so want to be yours." Kieran kissed her again, and Winter thought that her heart would burst with the love she suddenly felt filling it. It was different from the love she had for Bren, and the love she had for Tor.

It was a love all on its own that had no equal.

This was where she belonged. She loved the Dark King.

God help her.

The world around her started to spin and Winter blinked her eyes furiously. She tried to focus on anything, but nothing would hold still. She tried to find Kieran's hand, her own hand shaking so violently, but she could not grasp anything at all.

"Kieran, something is wrong," she told him, her voice quivering strangely, musically. He leapt up, prepared for action, peering into the shadows for any danger. "No, something is wrong with *me*." She tugged on his pant leg to get his attention. He knelt beside her and put his hand on her forehead. It felt like her skin would melt under his touch. She was on fire, and not in a good way.

"You are burning up. What happened?" She tried to answer but everything seemed to hum and go blurry about the edges.

"She is changing." Winter could barely see anymore, but she knew that soft voice. It wasn't Kieran.

She fought to stand, wobbling like a fawn and the Dark King helped her carefully. She closed her eyes, willing them to focus on the man she knew was there.

Then there was a scrape and a crash in the shadowy recess of an abandoned staircase and Bren stepped out into the light. Winter knew it was him, though the lines of his familiar face were blurred, he still emitted an ethereal light that was too familiar. She raised a hand to shield her damaged eyes from the glare.

"You shouldn't be here Bren," Kieran ground out menacingly. "She made her choice. She called me on her own and left you the same way. She is my queen now." There was a warning rumble from the Dark King's chest and Winter thought there was more than just an implied caution in his words. Kieran meant business.

Bren merely shook his head pityingly, like the warning meant nothing. "It can't be that way, brother. She loves me, you know. Did she tell you that?"

"I love him, too Bren!" she shouted angrily, wanting no one confused about the state of affairs, "I'm sorry, I want to stay here. I was wrong. Forgive me." Winter stumbled blindly toward Kieran, falling into him for support. He caught her and held her close. She could not see much, but she did notice Bren's skin flashed defiantly. Even half blinded, Winter could see the shimmer roll through him.

"Winter, what you are saying is madness. It's not possible anyway. You already made your choice," he reminded her, scolding her like the child she would always be to him. Then, in a more concerned tone, he added, "You are changing; you need your rest, Win. Come home."

Bren was moving, stepping out into the dirty light, suddenly brightening the room with his presence. His eyes were fixed intently on the way she had wrapped herself around Kieran and his skin continued to flash and shimmer with his anger? Hurt? Betrayal? Winter wasn't sure which of those emotions he felt more intensely at this moment, but there was something there, boiling just below the surface.

She twined her fingers protectively through Kieran's dark, spiky hair, using her rough grip on him as an anchor to keep him close, and buried her face in his chest. Everything was coming apart.

"No, Bren. You're not right this time. I am not a little girl anymore! I may be changing, but I am not crazy and my choice is to be with him," her words came out a muffled jumble from the folds of the ripped fabric of Kieran's shirt and she wasn't sure if Bren heard her.

Backing up her sentiments she heard, "You have lost her, brother. You took what she had, and then lost her in the end. You cannot do for her what I will. She is always going to be just a thing to you." Kieran's voice had an edge of mockery to it. Bren moved toward them menacingly, his fists raised in anger, and Winter jumped blindly to block him, but her disoriented mind caused her to stumble to the floor. There she sat there in a miserable heap, defenseless and unable to defend.

Winter had never seen Bren this angry before.

But when the king of the White Court realized that she was trying to protect Kieran from him, his rage dissolved. He stopped, barely a foot away and looked at her questioningly.

"Did you think I would harm him, Win?" he asked her sadly. He took a step back, wounded. "I should, you know. I want to. But I won't. It is not what I believe in. You don't believe in it either, Win, if you ask yourself."

He crouched down like an umpire, looking as weary and tired as she had ever seen him.

"You love him for what he is, I see that. His lust and his power call to you, as they are meant to do. The darkness in you is responding to him, but you aren't dark. He won't love you this way forever, Win. He isn't made that way. There isn't one thing in his life that he hasn't left bleeding, broken and crying on the floor." Bren eyed Kieran narrowly, then added softly, almost to himself, "Or dead."

Kieran didn't respond, but another low growl rumbled deep in his chest, so quiet that Winter was sure she the only one who heard it.

"Shut. Up. Bren," the Dark King warned.

"Come back to me, Winter. Let's go home. You can rest and I can teach you about your new life. The things you need to know, you do not want to learn from *him*."

The air was so thick between them, dripping with words unsaid and emotions not fully explored. Bren dropped his head lower, balancing on the balls of his feet and reached out just one finger toward her, like someone would do to a strange dog so that it would know no harm was meant. She raised her own hand, touching just the tip of her index finger to his. When they touched, the flames that had sprung up between them returned, igniting her skin and it rippled brilliantly beneath with his touch.

"I love you, Win, come home," he whispered. His eyes welled up with tears and she knew he could feel that she still loved him too, without her having to say it. She didn't answer but he nodded slightly, acknowledging what was between them.

Kieran wisely stayed back, letting Winter have her moment with Bren. She knew he was watching them, but didn't care.

It's too much, she thought, *Leaving home, finding out I'm fae and that I have to be a queen.* The thought reverberated within her. Queen. Could she find a way to be an eighteen year old ruler?

"I didn't want to be a queen. No one asked me!" she screamed suddenly and the floor rocked below them. Bren wavered from his carefully balanced stance but then righted himself, choosing to ignore the earthquake she made.

"No one asked me either, Win. I did not choose this," Bren attempted to scoot closer but the look on her face stopped him. "The only person who chose this life was Kieran." He nodded toward his brother. She whipped her head back to face him. Kieran wore a look that was apologetic and yet defiant at the same time.

"I won't apologize for the road that led me here," the Dark King said haughtily.

Winter had heard enough. She dropped her finger from Bren's, rose silently and walked away from both of them. For the first time, the brothers looked painfully alike, wearing the same surprised and concerned expression. She stumbled until she came to a wall that she could rest against and watched, seeing the bright light of Bren wavering before her and the dark smudge, the absence of light around Kieran.

No more arguments. No more bickering. She was ready to go home.

Winter knew this all had to stop. She reached out her hand, offering it freely.

Kieran started toward her just as Bren did.

It was into Kieran's arms she went, burying her face into him. He swept her up protectively and said, "Go Bren."

Bren's calm crumbled. He knelt before her and now he truly did weep.

"Don't touch him. God, Winter, please just don't touch him. Just come away and we can fix this," he pleaded, so desperate. "He can't love you the right way. It doesn't matter anyway. It's already done. I can't undo it, even if I would. You can't choose this, no matter how much you want it." Her heart broke to see him cry. She almost ran to him the pull to comfort him intense, but instead, Winter merely cried with him.

Kieran though, just laughed.

"What is done that can't be undone, Bren?" He held her close, in an open declaration of ownership. "She has already begun the change. It is over now. Go back to your rules."

Winter watched Bren kneeling at her feet, begging. Not so long ago, it had been she and Bren this way, locked in an embrace. They had been twisted as lovers. She remembered how he had called to her, and part of her sang with want for him still. She had lost some piece of herself in the White King that he would always keep safe in the warmth and purity of his touch.

But she would feel Bren's touch no more.

Things were different.

Every good thing Winter felt with the White King was dissolved by the Dark. Winter knew she should want to rule on the side of right, should want to be with the High Court. She felt an odd loyalty to them that she hadn't expected. Even now, she felt the most profound sense of betrayal by choosing to leave them. But Winter wanted the night and lust and temptation that came with her love for the Dark King. She thought she could be with him, and suffer the indignities that went with being the Dark Queen. She would always have time to remember her humanity and Bren, and mourn the loss of her goodness when the lights were out and she was alone with her choices. She just needed to find the words to claim her love so that the White King would understand.

Bren was creeping closer, trying to reach out to her again.

"Bren, don't do that," she cautioned. He froze and glared at her.

"You can't do that Winter," he said cautiously as if he knew what she was thinking. "The time for choices has passed."

Kieran, still holding her, grabbed her by the chin and forced her to look at him. His eyes held a fire for her that she thought she would never be able to fully explore. The time for contemplation was over. A choice had to be made.

Then Kieran said in a low dismissive voice, "If you wanted to go with him, I would not stop you. I would still live without you." His stinging words were loud enough so that Bren had a momentary flash of hope light across his face. The White King began to step toward her, always with his hand outstretched like a life line to lift her to safety from the evil she was drowning in.

Winter looked at his outstretched hand, and then back to Kieran, confused.

"Why are you doing this?" Had the Dark King changed his mind about her already?

No sooner than she asked it, could she feel little fingers of darkness caressing her, silently reassuring her. It was the same darkness the breeze had carried, whispering their treason on the dank, musty air. Then Kieran viciously pulled her to him, and breathed in her ear words spoken so softy even she barely heard them. He spoke quickly, trying to get them out before Bren could pull her free.

"I *would* still live, but my heart is dead unless you are with me," he told her. "Let him take you from me if you must, but you are mine." Winter died by inches at his words. She felt tears coming anew.

"But..."

She felt Bren's hands on her, pulling her gently, tugging her free and then wrenching on her, trying to pry her from his brother's grasp, trying to disentangle her legs from him, so that he could claim his prize.

She was not a prize to be claimed.

Winter had made her choice.

"I choose you Kieran, son of the Dark Court. I want to bring you love, share your throne and be your queen." She turned her back on Bren and looked expectantly to the Dark King, wondering what came next. It felt right to say those words aloud. She meant them. They felt true.

All the commotion surrounding her stopped. There was no sound at all in the room, everything sucked into the vacuum of her final words. Bren just stared at her dumbly, wounded, never truly believing she could love his brother over himself. Kieran stared at her too, his eyes full of wonder and...something else.

Love?

Surprise?

No one moved a muscle. Bren went into a full catatonic state of shock over her pronouncement. He slowly shook himself out of it and came back to the present. He quietly, almost privately, addressed her in a way that she remembered her teachers did when they wanted to spare a student embarrassment.

"Winter, you can't choose him," Bren said sadly. "It won't work that way."

"Stop saying that! I can choose! I have a choice!" She stomped her feet angrily and the doors rattled with her anger. Bren opened his mouth to speak and words may have come out, but Winter barely heard him. The hum that began to fill the air before Bren's arrival returned, but with greater intensity. The boxes and trash bounced across the room while the windows rattled angrily in their frames. A fierce earthquake, centered directly under her, rumbled the building from the ground up.

Winter felt herself changing. Frantic ghostly whispers from the night around them, and evil, hate and fear flowed into her, filling her, but not affecting her. If anything, they made her feel strong.

The Dark King moved, scrambling to stand back from her, awestruck by her transformation. He looked a little afraid. Bren just stared angrily past her, his jaw set, toward the shadows of the dark basement from whence he came, looking very much like he would like to leave her to her choices. The same choices he didn't have the heart to take from her in the first place.

She thought she heard him say, "It was not supposed to be this way."

Winter tried to ignore him. She reveled in the differences she could already feel. She could feel everything, not just the darkness that was filling her, but the scratching of the rats in the grates overhead, or the roaches in the trash on the street. She heard the scrape of the claws of the bats as they clung to their roosts in the attic far above. It felt like she was coming to life. The new, powerful Winter looked at the brother kings, their faces both an unreadable mask.

"Winter," Bren started again, now that the rattles and bangs the vibration caused, had ceased, "It can't be this way, no matter how bad you want it." He spoke to her in the same authoritative voice he always used on her when he was scolding her.

"Shut up, Bren. She has made her choice! Leave now, before I have to kill you." Kieran started toward Bren, but the White King dodged around him, grabbed Winter's hand, and shoved it in his face. The ruby ring, the Queen's Ring, peeked shyly out from the long silk sleeve. He looked right at her.

"You can't choose Kieran because you are my wife, Winter. You may love him, and he may have been the one that set you free from your bonds, but you wear the ring of the queen of the White Court. You have to come home with me. There is nothing that any of us can do to change it now. Stop this foolishness and come home. You are right, you did have a choice, and you made it."

Winter stared at him, dumbstruck.

Had he tricked her?

But no, Bren had been honest about every issue. This hand was forced all on her own.

348

Kieran, without saying another word, his face hard as stone, immediately turned away from her and walked into the shadows until she could no longer see him. There was a loud scrape and a bang and violent cursing from behind her. Sparks flew out of the darkness like fireworks and the wind he commanded howled all around them all. Lightning periodically illuminated the small, dark space, and she thought that in the flashes of hot, white light she saw him kneeling on the cold floor, his forehead down on the hard concrete.

Winter wanted to go back to him and tell him Bren was lying, but that wasn't possible. She knew by his reaction, as well as her own sinking feeling, twisting in her gut, that what Bren said must be true. Bren was staring at her apologetically.

"I wanted you to love me, Winter," he said quietly. His words cut her with their painful honesty.

"I do, Bren."

"But not the way that you love him," he gestured toward his brother, still in the process of melting down in the corner. As if in response, the wind intensified, whipping trash and paper through the room dangerously.

There was an unholy wailing, a sound she never heard, coming from the Dark King. It sounded like every scream and sob the world had ever created was pouring out of him into the air all around, liquefied terror drenching them. Again, Winter wanted to go to him, tell him it would be all right, but she couldn't do it. Even if she could convince him it was a lie, it would not help him.

"No, it is not the same," she agreed, her voice wavering. "You are not the same people, Bren." Winter couldn't help herself and she started to cry again. Bren came toward her, but then stopped, thinking better of it, and left her alone. He knew his wife well enough to know she didn't want his comfort.

Kieran came back after a long moment, looking like he imploded. His face was taut with pain and suffering and his eyes, once so dark and vibrant, were as dull as burned out shells of cars. He eyed his brother unmercifully, the hate in him so close to the surface, and then dropped to his knees again to wrap his arms around a sobbing Winter. She leaned toward him and together, they mourned the life they never got to share.

Finally, Kieran looked up and said, "You win. Give me a moment, Bren," he pleaded "If you have ever been my brother, let me say goodbye." His tone was nothing like the Kieran she had ever known. He seemed defeated, deflated, crushed. His words were no longer confident, but flat and lifeless.

Bren, being the good person he always was, not knowing how to be anything but honorable, nodded solemnly and stepped into the shadows, giving them space. The Dark King held the White Queen silently until her tears subsided.

"I am not going to tell you it will be all right," Kieran said finally, his chin resting on the top of her head.

Winter shook her head in agreement, not wanting to bluster through tears and choked out apologies, and touched his face warmly. She didn't want him to. She knew it wouldn't be. He kissed her

350

gently, then smiled at her wistfully. It was the first time Winter ever saw him look regretful.

"You aren't so evil, you know?" she whispered to him. "I think you are perfect."

"Well, you aren't so good, either." He gave her a half hearted smile. "You will be the wickedest White Queen ever. Even now, look how cruel you are. You just had the Dark King crumpled at your feet." He kissed her gently.

"Would it be better if I had never tried to be with you?" she asked."Would it hurt less for you?" She didn't ask if it would have been better for her, she knew she could have never made another choice than the man in front of her.

"No, and then again, yes." In a very un-Kieran like gesture, he looked down at his shoes, not meeting her eyes.

She dropped her hand from his face, stung by his admission. Winter struggled to get to her feet, but his strong hands flew around her waist and slid up her back, keeping her on down with him.

Instantly, Kieran's face drained of all color and he choked out an "Oh." His hands explored her back gingerly. She felt him patting the cloth and she felt like his hands were sending volts of electricity through her new sensitive skin. When they reached the point between her shoulders he sucked in a quick breath.

"Winter." He whispered. "You *are*...free."

"What?" She slapped around awkwardly, trying to see what he had found that was wrong with her body. She heard a slight tearing, the sound of fabric ripping and she was filled with a sudden rush of panic.

Bits of what was left of her thin gown drifted down to the ground behind her like dead leaves falling back to the earth. Then, her hands discovered what he had felt.

Nothing was wrong with her. She smiled sheepishly at him and choked out a hysterical laugh.

"You have wings," he croaked incredulously.

Winter twisted and craned her neck back to see lovely, black, translucent wings, sheer as a dragonfly, black as the night and flecked with silver, had sprouted from her pale skin. They unfurled slowly, wet and not yet shapely. She turned to face him and smiled again, this time proudly.

Winter felt, stronger, better and it was all because of him.

Then she remembered that he told her he wished she never loved him at all.

Bastard, she thought.

She slapped him hard across the face, drawing blood and then grabbed his handsome face in her new, powerful hands, and kissed him punishingly on the lips. He kissed her back, defiant and willing. When she finally pulled away, she had the taste of his blood in her mouth from where she had split his lip. Winter licked her lips clean in front of him, daring him to retaliate, to hurt her for her attack. She desperately wanted to feel *something*. She could taste the slither of the dark shadows in his blood and they swam gleefully through her now, owning her, making her his, making her his equal and connecting them in some small, tangible way.

"I change my answer then," he said finally with new pride. "I love you *this* way, bruised and conquered." Kieran leaned in close and bit her shoulder affectionately and spoke softly so that Bren, wherever he was perched waiting for his bride, could not hear, "And you will be the White Queen in love with the Darkness. We will find a way, Winter." He straightened and put a little distance between them. A strange curtain dropped behind his eyes and his face went cold. "Go with your husband," he spat wearing a scornful expression that Winter was sure was only a mask to cover how he really felt about dismissing her into the care of his brother.

The Dark King turned on his heel and started to leave her, picking through the crusty remains of whatever had been stored in that vile basement. She followed him, step for step, without thinking, and grabbed his hand. Lightning zinged between them.

"You said I was yours." She spun him hard to face her and told him in a conspiratorial whisper, "You said if you could not have all of me, that you would take whatever pieces I could give you." She kissed him one last time, maybe for forever and grabbed his hand and pressed it over her chest. "Then you can have my heart. If yours is truly dead without me, then mine will beat for both of us until we can be together."

She was glad Bren could not hear her confession. A single glittering tear betrayed Kieran and he nodded silently.

She made her choice, no matter how uninformed or impetuous. The deed was done and she could not fix it, but they would find a way.

Winter tried to crumple to the ground in misery, but could not. Her newly-functional wings would not let her fall. They fluttered supportively, lifting her whenever she stumbled. They saved her from slicing up her still bare feet as she drifted silently away from the retreating Dark King. Winter watched him leave her; counting the steps he took away from her until she reached 112 and could hear them no more. Finally, when Kieran was gone, she called out to Bren. She knew he was still there. Waiting.

"He is gone, Bren."

The king of the White Court appeared at her side in less time than she would have thought possible and he took her hand gingerly. Winter could have snatched it back angrily, but didn't see the point. She turned to him with all intention of smiling at him, but she never did. He looked away.

"Winter, I am sorry I am not the one you want. God knows I tried to be. I know I will be a hard man for you to love," he told her solemnly, "I only ever wanted you to be happy. His Court, his people, they would break you."

Bren started to walk forward, still holding her hand, but something stopped him. Finally he turned to her, not daring to meet his new bride's eyes.

"We are in this together and if I cannot be the man you want, then I hope that one day I can at least be the man you need."

Bren still did not look at her and Winter wondered if he would ever be able to bear the sight of her again.

Regardless of their feelings, twisted and confused in a knot in their bellies, Winter could feel their combined power swelling out from them, pulsing like a vein between their two bodies, connecting them. They were strong together, much stronger than she was even when she shared her darkness with Kieran and she felt the rightness of the White Court inside her. She squeezed the White King's hand and stroked it lightly, wishing for all the world he was someone else.

Bren held her hand tightly, then he stopped suddenly and dropped it.

"I love you, Winter, I know I shouldn't, but I do," he told her honestly.

"I know Bren. I don't want to, I don't deserve you, but I love you too. Just..." She did not bother finishing. He knew what she was going to say. She let her hand slide free of his own.

Winter thought she saw a myriad of expression play out on his face, anger, desperation, sadness and a tiny flicker of hope. Then just as suddenly as he had looked weak in the seconds before, he looked resolved and grabbed her hand once more.

"I hope I can find a way to be worthy of you, My Queen."

"Take me home then, My King." she said wearily. "And because I have always loved you, we will find a way to make it work somehow."

"As you wish, My Queen."

Epilogue

Kieran never truly left her alone. Of course, he wouldn't. He stayed, hiding in the shadows, watching Winter leave with his brother. She looked destroyed and he wished for all the world he could save her, but he couldn't. She had done this.

He waited quietly, and then, when they were gone through the portal, picked his way through the nasty basement, kicking aside broken things and peering into the darkness until he found what he was looking for. He bent down and retrieved a tiny, green scrap of her gown that had come free when her wings unfurled. He held it gently, like a wounded thing in his hand.

"I choose you Kieran, son of the Dark Court, to bring you love, share your throne and be your queen."

Well, he had been right after all.

Winter would choose him in the end, but unfortunately, her choice would come too late. She had said the words once, and he was sure, if he could find a way to get to her, she would choose him again. He only fooled himself into thinking he could have her. She found a way, despite all of his Darkness, to love him. All the evil in his life had predetermined his fate. His faults left him unworthy of her. Kieran told her he would find a way to be with her again, but how, he had no idea. Bren would keep her there at Court forever now.

"You said I was yours. You said if you could not have all of me, that you would take whatever pieces I could give you. Then you have my heart. If yours is dead without me, then mine will beat for both of us until we can be together."

She could keep his heart, he would let her. It would hide inside her own and she could keep it safe until she was able to give it back to him again.

Kieran would let them go for now. Bren would find out soon enough that he could make her his queen, but he couldn't make her love him the same way she cared for the Dark King.

Kieran would find a way to be with her again.

And then, he would reclaim his heart.

C. B. Cole lives in Western North Carolina with her family. Growing up in a petri dish of a small town, filled with the children of academics, she was exposed to a staggering variety of cultural and educational opportunities from an early age.

For her high school years, she attended a posh boarding school. Her experience there and a fantastic English department has fostered not only a love for writing, but also gave her plenty of writing material for which to draw upon.

C.B. Cole did not realize that she wanted to write paranormal books until she met her husband, whose sincere affection for the horror genre fascinated her. She also is incredibly interested in myths, fairy tales and other fantastical stories, and not only a paranormal junkie, but also a die-hard Star Wars fan.

To learn more about C.B Cole, visit her at her website at **www.cbcole.com**.

Be sure to check out C. B. Cole's newest book, *Deadly,* coming in 2012 to Amazon and other retailers:

Lighting flashed in response, striking nearer than I would have expected. Thunder chased after it in warning. Asher glanced up at the sky.

"You're starting to lose it, Rainey," he chided. "Maybe you should just calm down. Better yet, maybe you should run on home to Mommy and see if she can make you feel better, because I'm not going to keep kissing your ass and covering your mistakes!"

"I think you need to leave my family out of this!" Another lightning strike, this one even closer, illuminated the gentle curves of the mountains in the night. Asher turned his face up to the sky for a moment, judging the nearness of the storm. Then, he whirled on me and fired back at me.

"Your family is already in this whether you want them to be or not! If you would spend half as much time doing your job as you do wondering whether or not Daddy made your favorite dinner, you would be twice the fighter you are!" His eyes glinted hard with anger and I clenched my hands into tight fists, wanting to strike him. *How dare he?* Another flash of lighting, less than a mile away and a loud clap and boom followed. I marched right back up to him and stuck my finger in his chest.

"You're just jealous because you never had a family. You never had anyone give a shit about you the way my family loves me and you can't stand that I don't give you every bit of my attention! If anything, *you* are the spoiled little brat, Asher." I poked him one more time, hard in the sternum, and he drew in a deep, ragged breath. I turned on my heel and marched off.

But he caught me in a second, grabbed my upper arms and shook me. "You don't deserve to do this job, you aren't good enough! You don't fit anywhere, Rainey, no matter where you go, you will always just be a freak."

My teeth clacked in my head, and I struggled to fix my eyes to any stationary object after he stopped. I raged at him, for daring to lay a hand on me.

"Asher!" A singular streak of lightning lit the sky, striking somewhere very close by and the answering thunder crashed loudly, shaking the ground beneath our feet with the rumbling growl that sounded simultaneously.

Asher gave me a look filled with disgust, "See, you can't even control your Gift." Then he dropped my arms and walked past me.

I stayed there, my mouth hanging open, stung by his words. Freak, I could deal with. I'd heard it all my life, but to have someone who understood you tell you that you would never be good enough, hurt. I whirled after him. This was beyond our worst fight.

"Asher! W...wait, where are you going? I'm not done here!" I called as I ran after him. His long legs carried him down the slope faster than mine and I had to run double time to keep him in my sight.

"I'm going back to the Organization, Rainey," he called over his shoulder with no emotion in his voice. "I can't do this anymore."

"No, wait! This is stupid. Wait!" Then he stopped dead in his tracks, watching something further down the path. I caught up quickly. I placed myself in his way and grabbed both of his hands in my own. He seemed too tall when I stood downhill from him, so I raised myself on tiptoe to meet his eyes.

"Oh come on, Asher, you can't be *that* mad. You didn't mean what you said," I pleaded, squeezing his hands. "Neither did I. I'm sorry! We were out of control."

Asher didn't move. He just kept staring, looking past me down the hill toward the house with his jaw hanging open.

"Dammit, I said I'm sorry! Aren't you listening?" I got up in his face, trying to force him to look at me. His eyes were unblinking, focused on something far away. I watched his face transform slowly from anger to horror, melting like wax.

With the cold dawn of realization, I turned to see what he saw, wondering whether it was as bad as I feared, or even worse. I moved in slow motion, the world swimming by through Jello as I turned to face the flames of hell that were slowly growing, reflected in Asher's eyes.

Oh God.

I leapt forward, tried to run toward the flames, but Asher caught me and tackled me. Together we dropped onto the ground, knees first. Then I was flat on my belly pulling myself forward. He threw himself over me, keeping me down no matter how much I struggled to free myself from his grip. He held me tight against his chest. I tasted the cool, red Carolina clay, stinging my lungs with every breath when I tried to turn away from him.

"No, Rainey." He said it over, and over, and over.

I kicked and slapped him, bit and cursed him, but his strong arms held me firm and kept me safe though I didn't deserve it. His arms encircled me and his weight kept me down. Asher kept me from running straight into the flames that consumed the house where my parents lay sleeping. I lay there, pinned to the dirt watching in horror until the final timber fell in on itself, and nothing but ashes and hot cinders remained.

And then I screamed.

I screamed until my whole world went black.